KNIFED IN NICE

KNIFED IN NICE

TRAVEL P.I. BOOK ONE

ZARA KEANE

BEAVERSTONE PRESS

Published by Beaverstone Press GmbH (LLC)

eBook ISBN: 978-3-03938-005-3
Paperback ISBN: 978-3-03938-006-0
Hardcover ISBN: 978-3-03938-007-7
Large Print Paperback ISBN: 978-3-03938-008-4
Large Print Hardcover ISBN: 978-3-03938-009-1
Audiobook ISBN: 978-3-03938-010-7

My transformation from Goth chick to pregnant Barbie wasn't voluntary. Had I been able to choose my disguise, I'd have opted for one with more panache. Think gold-painted street performer, wimple-clad nun, or whip-wielding dominatrix.

On this occasion, I was forced to keep my costume ambitions in check. The pink wig, fake baby belly, and maternity jumpsuit represented the sum total of my costume options. I had less than forty minutes until the train to Paris left London, and a public bathroom in which to perform my makeshift makeover. And unless I wanted to get flagged by security, I had to look like the woman whose passport and suitcase I'd stolen. I hadn't planned on a trip to Paris, but then I hadn't planned on shooting a London crime lord in the arse.

Ignoring the line of women vibrating with

impatience to use the sinks, I whipped the passport out of my pocket and scrutinized Monique Beaufour's photo. Dark, defiant eyes framed by powder-pink hair. Lips stained the hottest pink. Slightly pointed chin, held high. Even in a stern passport pose, this woman exuded sex appeal. Could *I*, Angel Doyle, pass for *her*?

Now that the initial adrenaline rush had subsided, panic gripped me by the throat, making it hard to breathe. The reason for my need to skip the country loomed large in my memory, a mental film reel of last night's events playing on a never-ending loop. I forced oxygen into my lungs. I had to pass for Monique Beaufour. I had to get past security. I had to board the train to Paris. If I stayed in London, I was as good as dead.

Pushing past my fear, I examined my handiwork in the cracked mirror. A pink-haired stranger stared back at me, unfamiliar except for pale blue eyes that were red-rimmed from crying. I'd ditched my faded jeans and tatty hoodie in favor of the ballet-pink maternity jumpsuit and matching platform heels I'd found in her suitcase. The maternity jumpsuit fit fine, but the shoes were a size too small.

The fake pregnancy was a blessing in disguise—literally. I was roughly the same height as the real Monique but several kilos heavier. Growing a mini human gave me an excuse for having a fuller face than the one in the passport photo. And who was Monique Beaufour, exactly? Why did she have a wig, a fake pregnant belly, and a sizeable wad of cash in her suitcase? She'd been flat-stomached when I'd spotted her on the Tube. However, I wasn't in a position to have a retroactive uneasiness about the woman I'd chosen to rob. After all, this wasn't my first foray into the world of theft.

I finished my new look with a slick of the fuchsia lipstick I'd found in Monique's makeup kit and adjusted my pink wig. Then I checked my new watch, pickpocketed from a woman who'd been studying the departures board near the bathroom. I'd gotten rid of my smartwatch last night—too easy to track. The one I'd nicked was analog, but the message on the dials was crystal clear: time to get moving.

Check-in for the Eurostar closed thirty minutes before departure. I had just five minutes before the cutoff point. My metamorphosis wasn't perfect, but it'd have to do. I had a train to catch and a gangster to evade.

Sliding on Monique's diamond-blinged heart-shaped sunglasses to hide my blue eyes, I wheeled her suitcase out of the bathroom and into the whirl of activity that was St. Pancras International train station. Was everyone in London heading to Paris this weekend? It sure seemed that way. As long as Monty Carlyle and his muscled minions weren't planning on joining us, I was okay with a crowded train.

Exuding a calm I didn't feel, I maneuvered my way through the throng to check-in and security control, keeping an eye out for Monty and his thugs. Even if they were here, they'd never expect me to have turned from a black-clad Goth into a pregnant, pink-haired fashion victim.

I kept my head down and my feet moving. To my intense relief, checking in and passing through security was a breeze. My only luggage was the small suitcase, and I could keep that with me on the train. The heavyset lady operating the scanner barely glanced at me, and I was soon on the move again, this time toward passport control. I checked out the crowd. No sign of Monty's gang.

So far, so good, so scary-easy.

So easy that a hiccup had to happen. It was practically predestined. And I didn't have long to wait.

I spotted the security team checking IDs, and my stomach performed a flip worthy of an acrobat. I gripped the suitcase handle tighter. I'd planned to use the ePassport gates and had my story ready if the scanner flagged me as not matching the details on Monique's biometric passport. The fake pregnancy would help to account for my fuller face. Unfortunately, today was a manual spot check day. I'd have to trot out my cover story. Was I prepared?

Stinking Blarney Stone. I sucked in a breath, held it, and exhaled slowly, slowly, slowly. Now was not the time to lose my cool.

Mental pep talk or not, sweat slicked my upper lip. Could I walk through without getting caught? Stealing an identity qualified as a serious crime. If I did get busted, I'd wind up in police custody. Monty Carlyle had cops on his payroll. Getting caged would make me a sitting duck.

I slipped a hand into the pocket of my jumpsuit and squeezed my boss's lucky pen, a Saint Patrick's Day present from a regular drinker at The Lucky Charm. My eyes filled with tears. The leprechaun-emblazoned pen hadn't brought Frank any luck during last night's raid on the pub.

Forcing my leaden feet into motion, I shuffled into the queue of people waiting to show their IDs. The passport control team was fast and efficient, yet each waiting moment added extra weight to my shoulders. My pulse pounding, I checked out my fellow passengers.

And then I spotted him, standing opposite the queue, scanning the line for me. My heart punched against my rib cage. It was Boris, one of Monty's main muscle men and a colossal pain in the behind. And if it wasn't Boris, it was his twin brother, Ivan. I couldn't tell their shaven heads or bulldog faces apart. I'd weathered the Terrible Twins' sexist comments on several occasions during my ill-fated sojourn as a barmaid at The Lucky Charm, and it'd taken all of my self-control not to knee them in the nuts. Shame I hadn't indulged the impulse. Perhaps I'd get another chance today.

I kept my gaze pinned on the man in front of me,

my sight blurring from staring too hard at his pin-striped shirt. I didn't dare glance in Boris's direction. And I didn't have to. I knew the instant his reptilian gaze settled on me. The hairs on the nape of my neck stood on end with prickling awareness, and my limbs turned to cement blocks. His perusal seemed to take an eternity but could've only lasted a few seconds.

Finally, the tension in my body slackened. From the corner of my eye, I checked the twin's position. He'd shifted down to the end of the queue and examined the new additions one by one. My lungs released air like a busted balloon. One hurdle down. Now for the next.

When it was my turn to hand over my passport for inspection, a large man with a florid complexion took it from me with a grunt of acknowledgment. He cast a cursory glance at Monique's photo and then turned his attention on me. An icy prickle crept down my spine. How long was he going to keep staring at my boobs? The seconds ticked by. The man ended his unsubtle once-over at my bump and then recoiled.

Behind my shades, I rolled my eyes. *Seriously, men.* I should fake a pregnancy more often. His reaction jerked me out of my state of panic and gave me a much-needed confidence boost. I could pull this off. Buoyed by my newfound positivity, I curved my lips into a coquettish smile. "Is there a problem, *Monsieur?*" I inquired in my best French-accented English.

I sounded convincing. Not surprising. Courtesy of my feckless French mother, I was bilingual.

Convinced of my authenticity, the man handed back the passport and gestured for me to join the group of people waiting to board the Eurostar.

I strolled through the gate, dragging my case in my wake. Through the safety of my shades, I checked out the crowd, searching for faces I didn't want to see. This time, there were no unwelcome surprises, but it'd be naive to think Monty wouldn't have his entire gang scouring London in search of me. I just had to hope Boris and his cronies didn't have train tickets and stayed on the other side of the boarding gate.

The train doors slid open, and the queue pushed forward to board the Eurostar. A surge of adrenaline quickened my step. Next stop, Paris. And then what? Courtesy of Monique Beaufour, I had enough money to survive for a couple of weeks. Longer if I left Paris and headed for a less expensive town. But where could I go? My mother owned a house near Montpellier, but knowing Maman, she was gallivanting around the globe. I might've called her to check—*if* I'd had her number.

Another option was to catch the ferry to Ireland and take refuge with my relatives on Whisper Island. I dismissed this idea in an instant. My aunt Noreen and my cousin Maggie would help me, no question, but at what price? My dad's connection to Whisper Island was widely known, and it'd be among the first places

Monty Carlyle would look for me. I couldn't put my family at risk.

I found my assigned seat and stashed my case on the overhead luggage rack, belatedly remembering I was supposed to be pregnant. Did pregnant ladies heave suitcases onto luggage racks? Probably, right? It wasn't as if we were living in an age of chivalry. How often had I given up my seat on the Tube for a pregnant woman after observing a carriage full of people ignoring her? Way too often.

I settled into my window seat, adjusted my watch to Paris time, and opened Monique's French edition of *Vogue*. I had zero interest in fashion, but I'd noticed that burying my nose in a book or magazine tended to ward off conversation. Given the steady stream of people boarding the train, I was unlikely not to have a neighbor.

Behind the safety of my sunglasses, I kept one eye on the magazine and the other on the passengers weaving down the aisle. My stomach twisted every time I clocked a guy with a build suitable for one of Monty's cut-rate cutthroats: meaty, muscular, menacing. Numb-fingered, I flipped the pages of the magazine. The train would start soon. Once we were on our way, I'd calm down. Maybe even sleep.

As if on cue, the train lurched into motion. Late-to-board passengers scrambled to find their seats, abandoning any pretense of politeness. I still had no neighbor, and I was happy to keep it that way. I buried my face in my magazine. If the train was on time, I'd reach Paris in just over two hours. Maybe I'd have a plan by the time we pulled into the Gare du Nord—a plan more concrete than "avoid vertically challenged psychopaths and their muscled minions."

I was staring at a photo of a hideous tartan ball gown when a tall, lanky guy flopped into the seat next to mine. I gave him a surreptitious once-over from the corner of my eye. He was around my age—mid-twenties—and looked as if he'd stepped out of the pages of my magazine. He wore a canary-yellow-and-black-checkered suit, black high-top Converse, and square black-rimmed glasses. He'd brushed his fair hair upward and forward, making him look like a crew member on a sci-fi TV series spaceship. The look should've screamed fashion disaster, but he managed to pull it off.

My new neighbor angled his long legs toward the aisle and flashed me a sunny smile. The smile elevated his lean face from average to striking—in an underfed, fashion-model kind of way. Well, we were headed to Paris.

He extended a long-fingered hand, revealing a watch with a five-pronged crown logo. A Rolex. That watch probably cost more than I made in a year. "Hi, there," he drawled in an accent that screamed nannies and posh schools. "I'm Sidney. Well, Peregrine, actually, but *everyone* calls me Sidney. Sidney's one of my middle names, along with Roland, thus making me

Peregrine Sidney Roland. You can understand why I'm not fond of Peregrine." Here he gave an exaggerated shudder. "People inevitably shorten it to *Perry*."

He stared at me with an expectant expression, waiting for a reaction to this speech. Receiving none, he retracted his hand and repeated his long-winded introduction in French.

His swift language switch served as a sharp reminder that I was impersonating a woman with a French passport. I cast a silent thank you to my feckless mother, wherever she might be, for insisting I learned to speak her native tongue.

"Hi, Sidney," I replied in French. "I'm An—" I stopped myself in the nick of time and course-corrected. "Monique."

"Anne-Monique?" My neighbor raised an eyebrow in question.

"Just Monique." Lies came quickly to me. I'd had plenty of practice. Slipping up on my new name was due to exhaustion. I needed to be more careful.

"Why were you in London?" Sidney asked. "Shopping? Museums? Visiting friends?"

Oh, boy. This guy was a talker. Unless I wanted to be quizzed on my fictional life, I had to cut him off now. I opened my mouth to deliver a cutting remark, but the words died on my tongue.

My attention was riveted on the dude who'd just ambled past our seats. Close-cropped brown hair, a build like a heavyweight boxer, and a snake tattoo on the back of his muscled neck. His strut, verging on bow-legged, conjured memories that hit me like a blow to the solar plexus.

Cam Carruthers, the man I'd helped put in prison, was on the train.

2

Black dots floated before my eyes. I was losing my mind. There was no way that guy could be Cam Carruthers. Yes, he had a similar tattoo to Cam's, plus a similar swagger and similar fists. But Cam was safely behind bars. And even if he was a mean son of a gun, he'd never been part of Monty Carlyle's gang.

My ragged breathing evened out. My imagination was running wild. I'd only seen the back of the man, yet here I was, conjuring images of every nasty blast from my past. Sleep deprivation and frayed nerves were a bitch of a combo.

"Are you okay, Monique? Do you need a doctor?"

My seat companion's voice penetrated the ringing in my ears. I stared at him blankly, his features gradually coming back into focus. He was staring at me with alarm-tinged concern.

"I'm fine, thanks. Just a touch of travel sickness."

Relief flooded over his face. "Whew. For a moment there, I thought you were going to pass out."

I forced a smile and repositioned my magazine for protection. "Nothing so dramatic."

"Is this your first time taking the Eurostar?" Sidney asked as we whizzed through London suburbs. "Or are you a seasoned pro?"

"Neither. I've taken it once before." I kept my eyes on my magazine and flipped the page, hoping he'd get the message, but no such luck. Sidney, it seemed, had a bad case of verbal diarrhea.

"It's my first time. I usually fly, but my new boss booked me on the Eurostar." Sidney leaned back in his seat, his fingers drumming a restless beat on his armrest. "I don't like the idea of traveling under the sea. All that water above us...don't you find it terrifying?"

I gave a noncommittal grunt. "It's no worse than hurtling through the air in a metal tube."

"I guess, but somehow, flying bothers me less."

I pressed my nose into the magazine and applied myself to an article about the latest trend in ruffled skirts.

"Do you live in Paris?" Sidney asked, seemingly oblivious to my disinclination to converse. "Or are you catching a connecting train at the Gare du Nord?"

Good questions. Did Monique live in Paris? I had no idea. Did it matter? Probably not. As for catching a connecting train, I needed to figure out where I could go. I had an ex-boyfriend in Nantes, but he was an ex for a reason. I had cousins on my mother's side in Marseille whom I could barely remember, let alone contact out of the blue.

My failure to answer his last set of questions was no deterrent to Sidney. "I'm starting a new job on Monday," he said. "Can't say I'm thrilled about that, but it'll be fun to live in Paris. What do you do for a living?"

I turned a page with an exaggerated rustle. "This and that."

He chuckled. "I know all about 'this and that.' I'm an actor. Which means I've spent most of the last three years working for a temp agency."

From behind my magazine, I stifled a grin. I seriously doubted Sidney's temp agency jobs had included hacking a bank's security system, cracking a diamond smuggler's safe, or liberating funds from a drug dealer. Admittedly, my most recent job as a barmaid at The Lucky Charm had been legit—which was ironic, considering it'd gotten me into my current predicament.

"Are you moving to Paris for an acting job?" I asked, not really caring, but his mention of acting had triggered a memory. Jerry Gallo, one of my mother's ex-husbands, ran a theatrical costumier in Nice, slap-bang on the French Riviera. I'd spent a couple of glorious summers there during Jerry's brief marriage to my mother. Oddly, it was the second time I'd thought of him in the last few hours. Monique had mentioned Nice during her phone conversation on the Tube, and I'd immediately remembered my former stepfather.

Sidney's theatrical sigh dragged me back to the present. "My father finagled me a position at the British Embassy."

His funereal air made me smile despite my best efforts not to engage with my new companion. "Cushy. Doing what?"

"Pen-pushing and making tea for visiting diplomats." For a moment, a frown line rippled between his blond eyebrows, but he laughed off his momentary mood blip. "It's my fault for paying attention in French lessons. If I'd failed foreign languages at school, my father couldn't pressure me to follow him into the diplomatic service."

"You speak French very well." Not as well as I did, but then, I could pass for a native speaker. My absentee mother had made sure I spent many school holidays with her parents while they'd still been alive, and she'd paid for me to attend a French boarding school for two years during my teens. I'd loathed every minute of it, but it had done wonders for my French.

Sidney beamed at my compliment. "Thanks. I muddle along quite well during conversations, but my reading comprehension and written French leave a lot to be desired. I'm hoping to fit in French lessons around my job. If I get good enough, perhaps I can even audition for a play."

His tone turned wistful at his mention of acting. I didn't see Sidney's career in diplomacy lasting long. Not if he showed up for his first day at the British Embassy wearing his canary-yellow suit. "Good luck," I said. "Paris is filled with theaters, small and large. There are also options for English speakers. I'm sure you'll find opportunities."

Sidney's phone buzzed loudly, making us both jump. When he glanced at the screen, his face crumpled into a frown. "Sorry, Monique. I have to take this."

He hit connect and began a strained conversation in English with someone I suspected was his father. I tuned out his labored responses to his caller and forced my tired brain to focus. Now that the initial danger of being pounced upon by Monty's men had passed, I had to come up with a plan. Where could I spend the next few weeks?

Sidney's mention of acting brought me back to Jerry Gallo and Nice. Could I roll up on Jerry's doorstep and bag a bed for a week or three? He was a decent bloke and the only one of my former stepfathers to keep in touch, even if it was just the occasional Christmas card.

Sidney finished his call and slid his phone back into his pocket. "He couldn't even let me get as far as Folkestone without delivering a lecture," he muttered in English. His open smile had vanished, and tension was etched across his angular face.

"Is there a problem?" I asked, careful to speak in French. The last thing I wanted was to encourage my chatty travel companion. Still, he looked so forlorn that I couldn't help feeling sorry for him.

Sidney's smile returned, albeit somewhat forced. "Nothing either one of us can solve." He leaned back in his seat and dropped his voice to a conspiratorial whisper. "The parental unit was making sure I boarded the train."

"Family pressure can be intense."

I should know. My father—an enforcer for a Scottish loan shark—had been furious when I'd dumped Cam, his boss's son, and torpedoed Dad's plans for promotion. And he'd been livid when I'd helped the police gather evidence that put Cam behind bars last year. Any other parent would've rejoiced to see Cam Carruthers exit their daughter's life, but not Dad.

"Enough about me," Sidney said, jolting me back to the present. "You look exhausted."

I rubbed my eyes. "Yeah. I didn't get much sleep last night."

This was the understatement of the decade. I'd spent the night hopping from one bus to another, and then one Tube to another, trying to evade Monty Carlyle and his hired goons. Sleep was impossible when you expected a heavily armed thug to pounce on you at any moment.

"Take this." He pulled a neck pillow out of his

canvas bag and handed it to me. "You need to rest in your condition."

I stared at him blankly, my brain too sleep-deprived to keep pace. "What condition?"

Sidney raised an eyebrow. "You are pregnant, aren't you?"

"Oh." Heat spread across my cheeks. "Right."

"How far along are you?" He eyed my bump. "Six months?"

When was I due? I was clueless when it came to judging how far along a pregnant woman was. I snuck a glance down at my bump. Why hadn't I thought to check my side view in the bathroom mirror? The pregnancy was noticeable. Did that make me around six months? Or closer to eight?

"Seven months."

Sidney nodded, seemingly accepting my wild guess as fact. "Is that why you're not flying to Paris?"

I stared at him in confusion. "Ah, no. I just decided to take the train."

"Not that I know much about pregnancy, but my sister keeps having babies, and she tells me more than I ever wanted to know. That's why I wondered if you were too pregnant to be allowed to fly."

"I just find the train more comfortable." I hadn't a clue about airlines' cutoff dates for pregnant women. I ran my fingers over Sidney's velour neck pillow, anchoring my senses. If I was going to keep my fake backstory straight, I needed all my synapses firing. "I think I'll take you up on your suggestion of a nap. Will you wake me if I'm still asleep when we reach the Gare du Nord?"

Sidney grinned at me. "Certainly. Can I borrow your copy of *Vogue* while you snooze?"

"Sure." I handed him the magazine and snuggled into the pillow.

Within seconds of closing my eyes, I fell into a dreamless sleep, only waking when Sidney gave me a gentle shake.

"Sorry to wake you," he said, "but we've just pulled into the Gare du Nord."

It took me a moment to get my bearings. After I'd straightened my sunglasses, I disentangled myself from the neck pillow and handed it back to Sidney. "Thanks for letting me borrow this."

"No problem." He waited until the aisle was free before standing and retrieving his case from the overhead luggage rack. "Is this pink case yours?"

"Yeah." I suppressed a shudder. The case was a hideous faux animal print, but it fit with Monique's overall bling look.

He lifted the case down for me and set it on the floor. "Here you go."

"Thank you." I eased my way out of my seat and took the handle of my case from Sidney.

The Eurostar passengers shuffled up the aisle, chattering in a variety of languages. I observed my fellow passengers, searching for unwanted faces.

When I stepped off the train and onto the platform, I repeated my surveillance. There was no sign of Monty's men, but if they'd been checking out the Eurostar passengers in London, I couldn't rule out that they'd boarded the train. Thank goodness I'd had the sense to don a disguise and keep my sunglasses on the entire time. The idea of Boris and Ivan patrolling the aisles while I snoozed turned my blood to ice.

"Can I help you get your case to your next train?" Sidney stood beside me, leaning on the handle of his suitcase. "Or is Paris your final destination?"

"No, thanks. I can manage." Although I hadn't seen any sign of Monty Carlyle or his thugs, the less information I gave Sidney, the safer it'd be for both of us.

He hesitated, shifting his weight from one foot to the other. "Okay, then. If you're sure."

"I'm sure." I moved to the side of the platform, out of the way of the stream of passengers alighting from the train, and accidentally bumped into a lady with a yappy dog. "Sorry," I murmured. The woman glared at me, and her Shih Tzu strained against his leash, intent on attacking my ankles.

Dodging the dog, I scanned the departures board for a connection to Nice. Even if Jerry didn't let me stay with him, Nice was as good a place as any to hide out for the next few weeks. How long would I need to lie low? Monty Carlyle looked like a clown, but he was a clown who knew how to bear a grudge. And I was the waitress who'd witnessed him shoot a man dead. The whole situation was surreal. Overnight, my mundane but safe existence had been overturned by a dead pub landlord and a vertically challenged psychopath.

"I'm going to do a museum tour this weekend," Sidney said, cutting through my thoughts. "I want to kill time before my job starts on Monday. If you're staying in Paris, would you like to join me?" His gaze slid to my bump. "Assuming it wouldn't be too tiring for you. I don't know anyone in Paris, you see, and—"

"Sorry, no. I'll be busy all weekend. Family commitments." His reluctance to be alone was palpable, but I was running on zero emotional energy, and I had none left to spare.

"Oh, sure. No problem." He rocked back on his heels and launched into a detailed description of the potential museums he could visit.

I tuned him out and focused on the list of departures. There was a direct connection to Nice, departing at ten thirty-five. I checked my watch. If I hurried, I'd make it. I pivoted with my case, poised to move toward the main hall. "It was nice to meet you, Sidney. Good luck with your new job."

I started to walk past him. And froze. A few meters down the platform, two burly men in identical leather jackets, combat pants, and buzz cuts scanned the crowd. An icy tingling spread through my limbs. I ducked behind Sidney, breathing heavily.

He frowned down at me. "Is something wrong?"

"Don't move for a sec," I commanded, my attention riveted by the Terrible Twins. When I'd seen one of them at St. Pancras station, I'd figured the other couldn't be far away. Unfortunately, I'd been right. The twins wore matching expressions of dogged stupidity, but what they lacked in brains, they made up for in muscle. After a nod to one another, they split, each twin scouring a different side of the platform. As they stepped apart, a third man came into view.

Blind panic rolled over me in paralyzing waves. I tasted bile. Cam Carruthers, my ex-boyfriend and the reason I'd abandoned life in the gray zone for an honest, tax-paying job at The Lucky Charm. I hadn't imagined seeing him on the Eurostar. Since when did Cam work for Monty Carlyle?

At that moment, Cam looked my way. For a horrible moment, I felt his hazel gaze bore into me. I jerked my head to the side, shielding my face from his line of vision. Pure dread trickled down my spine. Had he recognized me? I didn't have time to waste finding out.

I pivoted my case, pushed past Sidney, and promptly tripped over the yapping Shih Tzu.

As the ground rushed to meet me, Sidney grabbed me, breaking my fall. "Are you okay, Monique?"

No, I was not okay. My sunglasses slid off and landed on the platform with a clatter, promptly followed by my wig. The dog, deciding he'd been attacked, strained at his leash, determined to nip my ankles. But an outraged Shih Tzu was the least of my worries. I was more concerned with an outraged man. I sucked in a breath and snuck a glance in Cam's direction.

Smug satisfaction had settled over his hard face. He'd recognized me, no question. He plowed through the crowd, closing the space between us at stomach-churning speed.

Adrenaline kicked me into action. I yanked my arm out of Sidney's steadying grasp. Abandoning my stuff, I leaped over the dog and fled.

3

Crazy crowded train station. So many people moving at a snail's pace. I shoved past passengers, luggage, and an endless number of small dogs. What was it about the French and their obsession with small dogs? The main exit was within sight. I just had to ignore my too-small shoes and keep running. I could reach the doors before Cam caught me. *Almost there.*

Cam grabbed my arm, bringing me to a stumbling halt.

Adrenaline zapped through my veins and pushed me straight into fight-or-flight mode. Common sense had never been my thing. I chose to fight. With my free arm, I nailed a right hook that would've made my boxing-obsessed brothers proud. It caught Cam on the jaw, sending jolts of pain down my wrist. The impact caused him to stagger, but he didn't let go of my arm.

"You bitch," he snarled. "You deserve everything Monty plans to do to you."

"Hooking up with you was one of my poorer life choices, but kicking you out was one of my best. Who did you bribe to get parole?"

His eyes narrowed to serpentine slits, and his expression went full rage. How had I ever loved this man? Anticipating a blow—physical or verbal—I kept talking. A distracted Cam was a Cam less likely to predict my next move.

"You *are* out on parole, right? You've never been the quickest of cats, but even you have to see that hanging with the Carlyle gang is a one-way ticket back to the slammer. What's Monty got on you that makes you goose-step on his command?"

A fiery flush spread across his cheeks. I almost expected sparks.

"Did I hit a nerve?" I made my tone perky-sweet, and then I ducked out of punching range and kneed him in the nuts.

Cam let go of my arm and crumpled to the floor, clutching his crotch. His pain-tinged roar rocketed through the station.

"I recommend frozen peas," I called over my shoulder, already on the move. "I'd offer to pick up a pack at the station shop, but I have places to go. So long, Cam. Tell Monty I hope his arse feels better soon."

One of the Terrible Twins, Boris—or was it Ivan?—

responded to Cam's roar. He shoved his way through the crowd, his flinty gaze pinned on me. I accelerated into a sprint, executed a perfect high jump over a luggage-laden cart, and crashed through the crowd.

I ignored the squawks of outrage and kept running. I was almost at the exit. *Just a little farther.*

I glanced over my shoulder. That blasted twin was hot on my heels. Fear kept my blood pumping fast and my feet pumping faster.

I burst out onto the pavement, and the Parisian summer morning hit me with all its might. Blasting horns, heavy heat, and heaving humanity. People, traffic, buildings, noise. London on steroids.

I would have enjoyed the atmosphere, the sights, the hurly-burly of this almost-new-to-me city. But with a massive muscle man in pursuit, the only thing I wanted from pretty Paris was a rapid exit.

A long line of people stood waiting for taxis. But even if ten taxis were waiting to whisk me away, I had no money to pay the fare. No suitcase, no passport, no cash. I uttered an oath but didn't break my stride.

"Hey, Monique. Wait up."

My step faltered. *Sidney.* The voice was too posh and too quintessentially English to be either Scottish Cam or the Russian twins.

Sidney appeared at my side, panting from running, pulling my case and his. He rolled my case up beside me. "You left this," he wheezed. "And these." He handed me my wig and sunglasses.

"Oh, thank you." At that moment, I could've kissed him. The case would slow me down, but I desperately needed the passport and cash. I glanced behind him and groaned. That lousy twin loomed at the door to the station, searching the area for me.

Shooting for nonchalance, I gave Sidney a sunny smile, put on my shades and the pink wig, and turned away, pulling Monique's case behind me. "Thanks again. See ya."

"Who was that bloke you took down in the station?" Sidney came up beside me, once again failing to get the message. "Are you in some sort of trouble?"

"If I say yes, will you go away and leave me alone?"

"Well..." He scrunched up his forehead and quirked up his mouth like a mime performing for a crowd. "I'm not the chap who has your back in a fight, but I won't walk away when a friend's in trouble."

"Sidney, we barely—"

A tall man in a three-piece suit stepped in front of me, startling me into silence. "Ms. Beaufour? I have your car ready." He gestured to a sleek black Mercedes parked in the no-parking zone.

Monique had a car waiting for her? Surely my getaway couldn't be this easy? Once again, a weight of unease settled on my shoulders, and I replayed our joint trip on the Tube.

Monique had prattled on her phone, speaking loudly in her native French to an unnamed friend. She'd talked of fashion shows and upcoming meetings in Montpellier and Nice. I'd pegged her as an easy mark—distracted and distractible.

Her mention of traveling on the early morning Eurostar had sealed her fate. A ticket to Paris was exactly what I needed. The opportunity to travel on a stranger's passport was an unexpected bonus. With a deft hand, I'd snagged her suitcase when we got off the Tube at King's Cross and made for the exit. For once, fate had been smiling down on me. But, as my Irish granny used to say, if it seemed too good to be true, it probably was. Her belongings indicated she was more than the fashion-obsessed ditz I'd taken her to be.

And here was providence working in my favor again, this time in the form of a ready-made getaway vehicle. Did I trust fickle fate? And did I want to add yet another crime to my growing list of felonies?

I glanced back at the train station door. Boris/Ivan loomed in the entrance, scouring the area for me. The moment he spotted me, my skin crawled.

Just then, a toddler on a trike zoomed down the pavement toward the twin, forcing her grandmother to break into a trot to keep pace. Boris/Ivan was so focused on me that he failed to notice the oncoming kid. The twin tripped over the trike and landed across the handlebars in an unwitting repeat of my fiasco with the Shih Tzu. Gravity took care of the rest.

His weight pushed down the front of the trike while the seat part shot up, ejecting the toddler. The force catapulted the child onto the twin's back.

Alarmed by the abrupt end to her imaginary car race, the little girl wailed. The twin struggled to regain solid ground, thus upending the child onto the pavement. At this stage, her grandmother had reached the scene of destruction. She raised her large leather handbag above her head and clobbered the fallen man, showering him with a torrent of French invective.

The scene had transfixed me, but I had to pull myself together and act fast. I had no more time to waste. I grabbed the key from the mystery man. "Thank you."

The stranger spoke just loud enough for me to hear. "You'll get the rest of your instructions in the car, as arranged."

First, the wig, the fake baby belly, and the cash. Now, a mysterious car. Who *was* Monique Beaufour? The man in the suit melted into the crowd before I had a chance to ask questions. Under other circumstances, I'd have chased after him and demanded to know what he'd meant. But any moment now, the twin would be on his feet and on the move. On autopilot, I hit the button to open the boot.

"Allow me." Sidney rushed to pick up my case. He stowed it in the boot, then hesitated. "I don't want to pry, Monique, but you're clearly in a spot of bother. Do you want to get out of here and talk about it? I've been told I'm a good listener."

"That's sweet of you, Sidney, but—" The words froze on my tongue. Cam staggered out of the train station entrance, stepping over the prone Terrible Twin and glaring right at me.

"Gotta move," I said to Sidney. I slammed the boot, ran to the driver's side, and opened the door. No wheel. *What the—?* Too late, I remembered that the French drove on the opposite side of the road.

"Thanks so much." Sidney took the door from me, interpreting my opening the passenger door as an agreement to take him with me. "Can I put my case in the boot with yours?"

"Huh?" My gaze was fixed on Cam. He was moving fast, pushing past the people waiting for taxis. I bolted across to the other side of the car and pulled open the door.

Too late. Cam reached Sidney and shoved him roughly to the side.

"Hang on, mate," Sidney protested. "You can't just—"

A flash of silver sliced through the air. Cam had drawn a blade.

"Sidney, watch out," I cried.

Sidney sidestepped Cam's first swipe with more luck than finesse.

From the corner of my eye, I registered the fallen twin. He'd extracted himself from the trike fiasco and was rushing down the pavement to Cam's aid. I swore in English and French, and used the few Irish swear words I'd picked up from my dad. Sidney stood no chance against Cam. Adding a Terrible Twin to the mix spelled disaster. I had to distract them somehow.

Oblivious to the interest we were garnering from the crowd, I tore open my jumpsuit, ripped off my fake baby bump, and hurled it at Cam's outstretched hand. The fake bump knocked the knife out of his fist. Startled, Cam watched his blade's descent to the pavement.

"Get in the car," I yelled to Sidney, belatedly realizing I'd addressed him in English and even more belatedly deciding I didn't care.

Sidney didn't need to be told twice. He leaped into the passenger seat. Just as Cam reached down for the knife, Sidney neatly kicked our nemesis in the backside. Cam toppled directly into the path of his idiot companion. Before the thugs hit the ground in a tangle of limbs, I gunned the engine and tore into the traffic.

4

My abrupt burst into traffic forced the car behind me to hit the brakes. I ignored the driver's enraged honking and kept my foot down.

"Close your door." I swerved to avoid a cyclist. "And do it fast."

Sidney shut the passenger door and wrestled with his seatbelt. "That bloke pulled a knife. Is he trying to *kill* you? Is he trying to kill *me*?"

"Looks like it." I darted a glance in my rearview mirror. There was no sign of Cam and the twins in pursuit, but it wouldn't take them long to commandeer a car.

"What's going on, Monique?" Sidney's tone rose an octave, more fear-tinged than angry. "Assuming that's even your real name. Your switch from French to English was lightning fast, and you have a touch of

Irish in your London accent. Where did you learn to speak French like a native?"

"If you'd prefer me to switch back to French, no problem." I nudged the Mercedes a couple of spaces forward. The traffic was moving, but not fast enough.

"French, English, whatever." Sidney shifted in his seat, gesturing with his hands. "Just tell me what you did to incite a knife-wielding lunatic."

A chill-inducing vision of a snarling Cam loomed large on my mental TV screen. "He's got anger-management issues, true, but he's more a sad bloke with a temper than psycho-killer crazy."

Not that this would stop Cam from hurting me. I'd helped to put him behind bars.

"He pulled a knife. On. Me." Sidney gave each word a slow emphasis. "And from where I was standing, the blade looked mighty sharp. How is that not psycho-killer crazy?"

"Fair point. I guess Cam's stint in prison exacerbated his violent tendencies." I dodged a moped and then swiped a fingertip over the dashboard computer. "I'm dropping you at the British Embassy. Can you input the directions? I gotta concentrate on driving on the right side of the road."

"No embassy." Sidney's tone rang ominously adamant. "I'm not setting foot in that place before eight a.m. on Monday."

The tension in my jaw reached vibration point. "I don't have time to hash out your life crisis, Sidney. I need to get out of Paris, and I don't need you tagging along."

"Seems to me you're in the middle of your own life crisis, *Monique*—or whatever your name is. I want answers before you ditch me and roar off into the sunset. Besides, you told me to get in the car, remember?"

"Only because Cam was about to knife you. I never intended to make this a joint road trip." A red Peugeot zoomed behind me, hovered on my tail. I studied my rearview mirror to get a good look at the driver. A woman—not Cam, not the twins. The coil of tension in my stomach eased. I shot a glance at my unwanted passenger. "You want answers? Fine. I'll give you answers. The people who are after me don't mess around. They won't hesitate to kill you to get to me. I'm screwed no matter what I do, but you? You have a winning trifecta. You're a British national, the son of a British diplomat, and the British Embassy's latest employee. The embassy staff will keep you safe."

"What about you? Who's going to keep *you* safe?"

The genuine concern in his voice floored me. How long had it been since anyone had tried to protect me? My cousin Maggie during our fateful weekend in Ireland last year? I swallowed past the lump in my throat and aimed for nonchalance. "Short answer: me, myself, and I. I'm used to looking after myself."

"No offense, but you're not exactly rocking at the job. If I hadn't hauled your suitcase and mine through the entire train station, you'd—" Sidney stopped mid-sentence and slapped his forehead. "Aw, no. My case. I forgot all about it when that crazy bloke attacked me."

I uttered a string of expletives that would've filled my Irish granny's swear jar. "Do you have your ID on you? Or did you leave it in your case?"

"Um...I think so?" Sidney patted down his suit jacket before pulling a wallet from his pocket. His expression flipped from concerned to relieved and then back again. "I've got cards and passport, but everything else is in the case. Everything apart from the stuff I sent over with my father last week. But my favorite clothes, my best shoes, my bespoke shaving foam...."

"Hang your bespoke shaving foam. I'll buy you a can of Gillette."

"But—"

"I'm sorry you lost your stuff, dude, but in case you haven't noticed, we're in a situation. Is your bag tagged? Is your name on it? Or in it?"

He blinked at me, owl-like. "Well, yes, of course. It has a label with my name and address, in case it gets lost."

I banged the wheel and swore again. "Not. Good. News." The last thing I needed was a person to babysit. I'd spent the past eighteen months keeping a low profile after helping the police secure a conviction against Cam, but this was my first time on the run. I could barely figure out a plan to protect myself, never mind someone else.

We neared a busy traffic junction, and our pace slowed to a crawl. Cars merged into various lanes in staccato bursts of movement. I dragged my mind away from Sidney's case to our more immediate problem. "Any clue which direction I need to take for the embassy?"

He snorted. "How about the 'Highway to Hell'?"

I flexed my tight jaw and struggled to keep my temper in check. "Jeez, Sidney. Are you deliberately obtuse? I'm trying to help you here."

"And *I'm* trying to help *you*. If you want to put distance between those thugs and us, there's a sign for the motorway up ahead."

I slowed to a cruise, checking the signs. I didn't want to hit the motorway until I was sure Sidney was safe in his embassy, but I hadn't a clue in which direction it lay. Messing with the dash computer while navigating busy Parisian traffic wasn't healthy.

The car behind me sat on his horn, pushing me to make a decision. "Keep your hair on, mate." I hung a right so tight I gave both Sidney and me whiplash.

He pressed back into his seat and gripped the armrest with white-knuckled strength. "I've never gone around a turn on two wheels before, at least not in a car. You left sparks."

"Forget my driving and focus. What about your watch? Is it a smartwatch disguised in vintage clothing?"

"Absolutely not." He sounded horrified. "This was

my grandfather's Rolex Submariner 1680, purchased in nineteen seventy-two. It's a collector's item."

"As long as it's not connected to the internet, I don't care." I pictured Sidney's suitcase in my mind, recalling every detail. "Your case has a built-in laptop bag, right?"

"Yeah."

"Is your laptop in it?"

"Well, yes, but why—"

"Because you need to get rid of your phone. Right now." I hit the button for his window. "Throw it out."

Sidney clutched the jacket pocket that contained his precious phone. "My whole life is on this device."

"If Cam catches us, your whole life will be over."

He slipped his hand into his pocket but didn't take out the phone. "Cam—he's the bloke with the knife?"

"Correct. Cam saw you take off with me. If he has access to your laptop, he'll track you down to find me. Which is why you're ditching your phone." I jerked a thumb toward the open window. "Now. Or I swear I'll kick you out into the traffic."

Sidney's eyebrows arched higher than the Arc de Triomphe. "Steady on. Give me a chance."

He fumbled in his pocket and pulled out his phone with the black and gold case I'd seen him use on the train. With a great show of reluctance, he dangled it out the window.

"Get rid of it. I'm not messing around."

"To misquote the Bard, farewell, my beloved.

Parting is such sweet sorrow." Sidney moaned, groaned, and dropped his stupid phone.

I closed the window. "Thank you."

"You didn't give me much choice."

His tone was so comically dour that I almost laughed. "I'm sorry, Sidney."

"For the phone? For faking a pregnancy? For my run-in with that knife-wielding thug?" He blew out his cheeks. "Seriously, Monique? What's going on?"

"What's going on is me looking for a way to get you to the British Embassy, even if that means hitting the motorway for a while and then doubling back. The less you know about the mess I'm in, the safer it is for you."

Incredulity gave his features a rubbery yet frozen quality. And then, out of nowhere, he burst out laughing. "Oh, you are so busted. That has to be the most clichéd line ever. No one outside of a script would say that. Ricardo put you up to this. That scoundrel."

I swerved around a corner without braking. "I don't know anyone called Ricardo."

"Sure you don't. This situation has all the hallmarks of one of Ricardo's pranks. What is it this time? A reality prank show?"

"This isn't a prank. We're in genuine danger."

"The lady doth protest too much, methinks. I should've guessed it was a prank when you whipped off that fake baby bump and hurled it at the bloke with the knife. The shock of seeing it put my brain in snooze mode. Now it all makes sense."

"You don't get it. They're—"

"So what's the deal? Is Ricardo meeting us somewhere, or are we sending him the footage?" He flipped down his visor and ran his fingers over the fabric. "Where's the hidden camera?"

Seriously, this guy? "No camera. No Ricardo. No prank."

He finished checking his visor and reached for mine. "Mm-hmm. Because blokes with blades routinely attack me for no reason."

I drew in a slow breath and tried to stem the maelstrom of anger rushing through my body. I had to make Sidney take me seriously.

We stopped at yet another set of traffic lights. While the engine purred, I turned my options over in my mind. I didn't buy the adage that honesty was always the best policy—life had too many shades of gray for that to ring true. But in this situation, blunt candor might blast Sidney out of his false belief that we were starring in a reality TV show.

"Sidney, this is real. The no ifs or buts kind of real. I'm on the run from a London gang, and they'll kill you to get to me."

"Uh-huh." His eyes twinkled. "What did you do to incite a gang to chase you across Europe?"

I drew in a slow breath before answering in a sharp

blurt. "I shot their boss in the arse with a ketamine dart."

Sidney's crack of laughter cut through the sound of the horns blasting behind us. I'd missed the light change. I hit the gas, and the car lurched forward. "That's brilliant," he said between bouts of laughter. "Straight out of an East End crime comedy."

"For heaven's sake, will you listen to me? This is no comedy." I took a deep breath and formed the words on my tongue, tasting their bitter truth. "Sidney, I witnessed a murder."

5

The biting nausea I'd experienced on and off since Frank's death hit me with its full force. I kept my eyes on the road, deliberately not meeting Sidney's gaze. I didn't need to see him to read his reaction to my news. His shock and disbelief hovered in the air like a mushroom cloud. My revelation had stunned him into silence—a rare state for chatty Sidney.

The seconds stretched to a minute. I could take it no longer. "Say something, Sidney. Your silence is freaking me out."

"Your news is freaking *me* out." He ran a hand through his hair, mussing his perfect styling. "I prefer the idea of participating in a reality prank show to starring in a true-crime documentary. Who got murdered? Who did the murdering? Is Cam the killer?"

My hands tensed around the wheel. The last thing I wanted to do was talk about last night, but there was no way of avoiding it now. "I'll take your questions in reverse order. No, Cam isn't the killer. As for the murderer's identity, I'd rather not say. The murder victim was my boss, a pub landlord called Frank O'Malley. Frank was attacked after the pub had closed for the night, and he and I were tidying up."

"Why did this unnamed killer knock off your boss? Did they get into a fight?"

"Frank double-crossed him." I twisted my mouth into a mockery of a smile. "The killer isn't a man who takes kindly to betrayals."

"So the killer burst into the pub—" Sidney began.

"The killer and his hefty henchmen," I added.

"And they started, what? Shooting?"

My throat convulsed, but no words came out. I jerked my head to confirm Sidney's assumption.

"How did the situation lead to you aiming a tranquilizer gun at No-Name's rear end?" he demanded. "Did he threaten to shoot you too?"

"Long story short, I crouched behind the bar counter when he and his dudes burst into the pub. The only thing I had to defend myself with was the pen I was using to check the accounts." I gave a bitter laugh. "That wouldn't have done me much good. I peeked over the counter to see if I could make a run for it, but there were five of them, and they'd blocked the exits."

"You poor thing. That must've been terrifying."

Sidney gave my arm a comforting squeeze. "What happened next?"

"The gang's leader put a bullet in Frank's leg. I ducked out of sight, and five more shots rang out. I have no recollection of making a noise, but I guess I must have cried out. At any rate, one of the guys looked over the bar counter, spotted me, and gave the alarm. I panicked, remembered Frank's tranquilizer gun under the cash register, and grabbed it."

"What in the world was a tranquilizer gun doing at a pub?" Sidney demanded, cutting through my flow of thoughts.

"The pub wasn't Frank's only source of revenue," I said. "He sold goods on the black market, mostly stolen cigarettes and booze. A few months ago, the crate his mates stole contained dart guns and tranquilizer darts instead of the cigarettes they'd expected to find. Frank kept one as a souvenir, complete with a single ketamine dart. He had a loaded revolver, too, but he always kept that on his person. He never regarded the dart gun as a serious means of protection."

"Unfortunately for you, that dart gun was your only means of self-defense when those thugs burst into the pub."

"Yeah. After the thug alerted his friends to my presence, I pointed the dart gun at the man guarding the back exit to get him to move. He did, but in my haste to get out of the pub, I tripped over a bar stool, and the dart gun went off. It was pure dumb luck that the dart hit one of the men and caused enough chaos for me to slip out the back of the pub before they could catch me. It was pure bad luck that the guy I hit is one of the most notorious gangsters in London." I took a ragged breath. "I'm telling you the truth, Sidney, not the plot of a bad B movie."

"I believe you," he said in a quiet voice. "But why didn't you head straight to the police? Why go on the run? You hadn't done anything wrong. You acted in self-defense. The cops would've protected you."

I slid a glance at his open, trusting face. Had I ever been that innocent? "The killer—the gang's boss—has paid informants everywhere, including the police. My bag was back in the pub, containing my phone, my purse, my life. My only chance was to get far away from London and his sphere of influence." My voice broke on this last sentence. "It seems I didn't get far enough."

I switched lanes, grateful for every meter I put between the train station and me. Right now, I'd do just about anything to forget the events of last night. I owed Sidney an explanation, however abridged, but talking about it was like pouring alcohol on an open wound.

"Did you flee to France because you speak French so well?" Sidney asked. "I'm not a native speaker, but your French is mighty good for an Irish person."

"I have dual nationality," I said after a moment's pause. "My dad is Irish, and my mother is French."

"So Monique *is* your real name?"

I hesitated for a moment, debating whether to maintain that particular lie. But what was the point? He knew too much already. "My name's Angel."

Sidney burst out laughing. "For real? That's a misnomer if ever I heard one."

I shot him a wry smile. "You're not the first person to voice that opinion. The name's short for Angélique."

"That's pretty. And very French."

I scrunched up my nose. "The kids in school told me it sounded like a porn star's name."

And seeing as my mother had been a bona fide porn star in her youth, I'd endured relentless teasing from my classmates and judgy comments from their parents. I decided not to share this particular tidbit with my unwanted passenger.

"Now that we're sharing, want to tell me who the guy with the knife was? The one you called Cam? I assume he works for your killer gangster."

I swallowed a sigh. "I assume so too. The Cam story is long and not one I'm in the mood to tell."

"If we're going on a road trip, you'll have plenty of time to tell me."

"We're not going on a road trip together, Sidney." I glanced at the sign indicating I was driving in the correct direction to reach the motorway. "I should turn around and head for the British Embassy. They should be able to keep their new employee safe."

"Officially, I'm not their new employee until

Monday," he pointed out. "Besides, if I'm on the radar of a crazed thug, I want more details."

I cast him a sidelong look. "It's more than one crazed thug you need to worry about. You're safer not knowing more details. I've shared too much as it is."

"Oh, bosh. That's the sort of thing my mother says when she doesn't want to discuss my father's latest affair." Sidney leaned forward in his seat. "What's the plan? I assume you have one. You got that man to drop off this car for you."

"Yeah, about that...he didn't exactly deliver this car for me. And now that Cam's seen the vehicle, I'll have to dump it and find an alternative method of transport."

"Wait, what do you mean the man didn't deliver the car for you? He handed you the key."

"He handed me the key because he thought I was Monique Beaufour. I accepted the car because I saw Cam and his cohorts and needed a getaway vehicle." I twisted my lips into a grim smile. "Talk about jumping from the frying pan into the fire. I have a bad feeling about Monique and this car, but I was desperate."

Sidney's eyes widened. "Monique *exists*? Like, there's a real Monique, and you've just nicked her car?"

"Yeah, there's a real Monique. And I nicked more than her car." I jerked my thumb in the direction of the boot. "The suitcase you lugged through Gare du Nord? Hers. That's where I found the pink wig and the fake baby belly, plus her passport, Eurostar ticket, and cash.

I have no idea who Monique Beaufour is or what she does for a living, but I doubt it's legit. For all I know, the passport's a fake, and she's sketchier than the people I'm on the run from."

Sidney let out a low whistle. "Impressive. I'm an accessory to how many crimes now?"

I winced. "I feel bad you got dragged into this mess."

"I feel bad I lost my favorite shaving foam," Sidney confided, "but I haven't had this much excitement since Bart Rutherford set his hair on fire during fourth form chemistry class."

"I'm thrilled you're having fun," I said dryly, "but we're in genuine danger. I wasn't joking about needing to get rid of this car. Monique's bound to show up in Paris eventually. If she's not dodgy, which I doubt, she'll report the car stolen, and then we'll have the French police on our tail. If she is involved in questionable activities, she'll come after us, or her associates will. And then there's the more immediate danger from Cam. I can guarantee you he'll have hijacked a car by now and be in pursuit."

"If this were a pilot for a TV show, it'd never get made," he said. "Way too many coincidences and crazy characters."

"In my experience, real life is often crazier than fiction. Can you program the address for the British Embassy into the navigation system? The sooner I drop you to safety, the better it'll be for the both of us."

"I'll plug in any address except the British Embassy," Sidney said cheerfully. "I have to show up there on Monday morning. Until then, I'm helping you evade whatever ruffians are on your tail."

This guy was killing me. "You know nothing about me, Sidney. And you know even less about the guys tailing me. I'm your crazy traveling companion who faked a pregnancy and got chased through the train station by thugs. Why would you help me?"

"Because you need help, and I sense the promise of an adventure. I'm about to start a dreary desk job next week. Why not let me accompany you to wherever you're going? If you think this Cam bloke will still be a problem on Monday, I'll call the embassy and get protection." He held up both palms. "Promise."

I jabbed at the dashboard computer, locating the navigation. "I'll drive you part of the way, but only because Cam now knows your name and address. He and his buddies will track you down, and they're not men you want to mess with. Until you agree to contact the embassy, you're safer sticking with me."

He beamed at me. "Awesome. You won't regret this, Angel."

I cast him a sidelong glance. "I'm already regretting it."

"Now that I'm your new sidekick—"

"Temporary sidekick," I corrected.

"—let me take over the navigation."

I shrugged. "Okay, but I'm still not telling you my end destination. Put in Aix-en-Provence for now."

"Excellent choice. I've always wanted to visit Provence." Sidney swiped the touch screen and inputted the city center of Aix-en-Provence. He hit the start button.

"Hello, Madame Beaufour."

Sidney and I both bolted upright but were pinned in place by our seatbelts.

"The navigation system is programmed to take you to the drop-off point," the deep voice continued in fluent but heavily accented French. "Don't deviate from the directions. In the glove compartment, you'll find a burner phone. When you park, take the phone with you for instructions on where to leave the briefcase. The number you'll need to call is saved on speed dial. Hit the number five to connect. The phone will cease to work once you've delivered the money. And Madame Beaufour? No funny business this time. And no contacting the police. Césaire's life depends on your full cooperation."

The recording ended, and the navigation switched to a synthetic female voice, which instructed me to take the next left.

"What in the blazes was that about?" Sidney looked from the dashboard screen to me. "Who's Césaire?"

I turned the car as instructed and filtered into the appropriate lane. I felt light-headed and had to force myself to focus on the road. What hot mess had I leaped into this time? "I have no idea. I've never heard of anyone called Césaire, and I have no idea why they're in danger."

"What's this Monique Beaufour involved in? What sort of person has burner phones, hacked satnavs, and fake baby bellies?" He peered at me. "Are you sure you don't know her? You seem to be acquainted with any number of villains."

"Oddly enough, I don't know every crook in Europe," I replied, deadpan. "And I don't know Monique. She's just the woman whose suitcase I stole. I picked her because she sat across from me on the Tube and annoyed me by constantly yapping on her phone. And because I can understand French, I couldn't tune her out."

"Do you usually rob people who annoy you?" Sidney asked, eyebrow raised.

"It's been known to happen. Look, I was Tube hopping and hoping I'd shake off the guys who were after me." I pulled a face. "Seems I didn't do a good job. As far as I was concerned, Monique was a stranger who was roughly my height and build and was stupid enough to mention she had a ticket for the early morning Eurostar to Paris. I had no idea what else the suitcase contained, and I definitely didn't know she was traveling to France to deliver the ransom money."

"When she was yapping on the phone, did she say anything connected with Césaire or a drop-off?"

I shook my head. "She kept going on about a fashion show she'd attended. Honestly, she struck me as a spoiled, vacuous, overgrown brat. I was happy to choose her as my mark. Now I have to assume it was an act, or all the fashion talk was a code. She was way too chill to have an emotional attachment to this Césaire person. Either that or she's a stellar actress."

"The fake baby bump in her case didn't alarm you?"

"Well, yeah, it gave me pause, but I didn't find that until after I'd taken the case. Besides, I was desperate, and here was a ready-made costume just waiting to be embellished. I intended to use Monique's passport and Eurostar ticket to get to Paris and then shed the persona."

"Only, you encountered Cam and ended up taking Monique's car," Sidney finished for me. "What a mess."

"A mess of epic proportions, even by my low standards. Soon, I'll have two sets of criminals on my tail and no way to acquire another false identity. Even if I'd wanted to keep using Monique's passport, she's bound to report the passport stolen. Now, I have no idea if the passport's a fake or the real deal. Either way, I can't risk using it again." I gestured to the glove compartment. "Can you check to see if Satnav Dude was telling the truth about a burner phone?"

Sidney opened the glove compartment and took out a mobile phone. "Seems he was." He examined the device with interest. "This looks like a phone from twenty years ago."

"It's a non-smartphone," I said. "It's good for calls, texts, and that's about it."

"No internet access?"

I smiled at his appalled expression. "In normal cases, there's limited internet access on dumb phones, but I'll bet it's blocked on that one. There's a reason Satnav Dude and whoever he works for opted for that particular model for the burner phone."

"I'll check the backseat for the briefcase he mentioned." My unplanned passenger leaned into the back and pulled a small black briefcase onto his lap. "Satnav Dude was as good as his word. Want to see what's in this thing?"

"You're assuming it's unlocked," I said.

"I am," Sidney replied, pressing two buttons. "And I'm right."

He eased up the lid, revealing the contents. Sidney swore, and I sucked in a breath. The briefcase contained stacks of tightly packed hundred-euro notes.

6

I held my breath so long my lungs ached. A car in the next lane sounded the horn. In my distraction, I'd veered into her lane. I breathed out, tore my gaze away from the cash, and concentrated on the road. "There's got to be a hundred thousand euros in there."

Sidney's head jerked up from his awed contemplation of the money. "You can tell how much it is at a glance?"

"The stacks look to be fifty notes thick, and each note is worth one-hundred euros. There are ten stacks visible, and the case is a depth to accommodate two layers, max. That's one hundred thousand." My voice was quiet, controlled—a far cry from my emotions. A hundred thousand euros could get me a long way away from Monty Carlyle.

Sidney whistled. "You must be a math whiz."

"I'm not bad."

This was an understatement. I was very good with numbers. However, my ability to calculate the amount of cash in the briefcase had more to do with my shady past than my mathematical prowess. I'd spent my childhood operating the money counter in the smoky back office of my dad's pub and arranging Cam's father's ill-gotten gains into neat stacks. Sandy Carruthers was most particular about keeping track of his cash.

"From what Satnav Dude said, this has to be a ransom payment." Sidney slumped back in his seat. "What have we gotten ourselves into?"

"Nothing good," I replied, my tone reaper-grim. "I had misgivings about Monique Beaufour the moment I opened her suitcase, but I had no idea she was involved in a ransom plot."

A ransom plot involving a real person—a person I couldn't abandon to their fate, however much that cash tempted me. I curse my moral compass to Hades.

"So, what's the plan?" Sidney asked. "You're clearly familiar with this crime malarkey. What are we going to do?"

"*We* are going to do nothing. Your getting dragged into this situation was pure chance. This is my hot mess, and it's up to me to sort it out. I insist on taking you to the British Embassy." I jabbed at the navigation buttons, but it refused to cooperate. I slapped the wheel in frustration.

"Satnav Dude said we wouldn't be able to override the directions," Sidney reminded me. "You'll have to use your phone to look up the directions."

"No phone," I muttered. "I left it in the pub, along with the rest of my belongings."

"You have no phone. I have no phone." He said the words in a singsong voice. "Looks like you're stuck with me."

A muscle flexed in my jaw. "Let's try the burner phone. Just in case it can access the Net."

Sidney obeyed and jabbed ineffectually at the screen.

I sighed. "Give it here."

"You're not supposed to use a phone while driving," he countered in mock disapproval.

"The last twenty-four hours have been full of things I'm not supposed to do. Adding one more item to the list won't make a difference."

He held the phone out of my reach. "No way. You can check when we stop."

I sighed. "It's more than likely a waste of time. The kidnappers will have made sure the internet doesn't work. I know I would have. If I had the time and the equipment, I could override their hack, but as I have neither, it's a moot point."

"Well, then." His smug smile irritated me.

"Why are you so keen to throw in your lot with me?" I demanded, exasperated. "It makes no sense. I'd give my left boob not to be in this situation."

"Angel, this is awesome. You have no idea how boring my life's been for, well, forever. And let's get real. I've accepted a full-time permanent position that's unlikely to leave me time to pursue acting. If I don't get to experience adventure on the stage, then at least let me have this one weekend."

"This one weekend could land you in a boatload of trouble," I pointed out. "Legal trouble. Do you want that?"

"I helped you escape from men who intended to harm you, and we're now on our way to rescue a kidnap victim. Who's going to object to that?"

"The police, for one. The British Embassy, for another." I shot him a sidelong glance. "I know you're not keen on working for them, but surely you don't want to lose the job before you've even started?"

He wrinkled his nose. "It'd be one way to get my father off my back, but no. Even I wouldn't go to such extremes to avoid a sensible job."

"At this stage, you should consider contacting the police and getting help. Just leave my name out of it."

"No way. Satnav Dude specifically told us not to contact the cops. What if he follows through on his threat to kill the guy they're holding hostage?"

"I was referring to you getting help from the police to reach the British Embassy. Also, Satnav Dude's instructions were addressed specifically to Monique Beaufour."

"Whose stuff and car you stole," Sidney said. "So you kind of owe her."

"Why do you think I haven't already dumped this car? If Monique was on her way to pay a guy's ransom, I must deliver the money. I've done plenty of bad things in my life—some well into illegal territory—but I can't let a man die because my actions prevented Monique from getting to Paris and collecting this car."

We fell silent as we neared the motorway. The navigation system instructed me to take the entry that headed south. Finally free of the heavy Parisian traffic, I hit the accelerator.

"Can you guess where the navigation is sending us?" Sidney fiddled with the dashboard computer. "I can't make it zoom out and show our end destination."

"It estimates our journey will take seven hours and thirty-six minutes, and we're heading south. If we continue dead south, that's maybe Toulouse or Montpellier or Marseille. If it's programmed to send us on a wild detour, then your guess is as good as mine."

"Either way, it's a long drive, and we can't make this car play music."

"If that's your unsubtle way of telling me we should talk the whole journey, forget it. I had enough of your verbal diarrhea on the train."

"Charming," he said, but without a trace of rancor. "I was thinking more that you'd do the talking. Like expanding on what happened to you last night in London. Who is the mysterious London killer-gangster you plugged with a ketamine dart? If we're now partners in crime, I deserve to know."

"We're not partners in anything, Sidney. We're temporary traveling companions."

"Temporary traveling companions in a stolen car and on our way to deliver ransom money."

"I'm glad one of us is finding the situation exciting." This guy was killing me. I'd never been Little Ms. Sociable, but it'd been a while since anyone had talked me to death. "The last time I was forced to communicate this much was during my disastrous stint as a hotel manager in Ireland."

"You? A hotel manager?" Sidney grinned. "How'd that work out?"

"Not well. One weekend, I was foolish enough to let my private investigator cousin and a bunch of cat contest attendees stay for the weekend. In addition to talking me to death, the attendees had an unfortunate tendency to wind up dead."

"Killed by you?" Sidney's eyes grew wide, but with wonder, not fear.

"No. Odd as it might seem, I'm not in the habit of tripping over dead bodies."

"Hey," he exclaimed in excitement. "Did you bring the tranquilizer gun with you?"

I rolled my eyes. "Hardly. I'd never have gotten it through security."

"That's a shame. We could do with a weapon if we're about to face off with a bunch of criminals."

"We're not facing off with anyone." The words were sharper than I'd intended. Sidney's unflappable cheeriness was getting on my nerves. "We'll drop the money at the appointed place, dump the car, and get out of there."

"Do you think the ransom is connected with your gangster and his buttocks?"

My lips twitched. I had to force my voice to sound cool. "I doubt it. He has his fingers in a lot of pies, but I've never heard of him involved with kidnapping. I think us stumbling into the kidnapping is a horrible coincidence."

"Seeing as we're going to be hanging out for the next while, and you don't want to tell me the name of the man you're on the run from, will you at least tell me about Cam?"

Of the two, talking about my sorry history with Cam was the least preferable. Should I confide in Sidney? At this stage, what difference would it make? Monty's men were after both of us now. He deserved to know who he was dealing with. "The man I shot with the ketamine dart...does the name Monty Carlyle mean anything to you?"

Sidney's mouth gaped wide enough to accommodate a ten-ton truck. "No way. The bloke who allegedly broke into the Victoria and Albert Museum and stole two paintings? The man the police suspect of multiple art thefts, but can't pin anything on?"

"That's the dude."

"Whoa. That's not good. The papers say Monty Carlyle has a reputation for brutality."

"For once, the papers are correct."

"Epic." Sidney was practically bouncing in his seat with excitement. "You took on a bona fide mob boss."

I cast him a look of reproach. "Not willingly."

"Yet here we are, on the run from one set of thugs and toward another."

"You needn't sound so happy, Sidney. The bona fide mob boss is bona fide dangerous. And the group we're delivering money to doesn't sound like a peace-loving bunch."

"Happy's the wrong word. Curious is closer to the mark. My interest is most definitely piqued."

"Remember that old saying about curiosity killing the cat?" I asked dryly.

"Which is why we need some sort of weapon." Sidney considered this for a moment, then added, "I don't know how to work any sort of gun."

"You point and shoot," I said. "Hitting a moving target is the hard part."

"I doubt I could hit any target, moving or still," Sidney confided. "I have terrible hand-eye coordination. Even toy foam blasters defeat me. And isn't there that safety catch thing to release? I wouldn't know where to find that."

I shook my head. "And you're the guy keen on throwing yourself into a dangerous adventure."

"I avoided getting knifed by your Cam."

"He's not *my* Cam." And I definitely wasn't his Angel. Not anymore. Not ever again. My stomach twisted at the memories. "Cam didn't hurt you because I hit him with the fake baby belly."

"Fair enough." Sidney leaned back in his seat, unperturbed by my disapproval. "I've never been on the run before. This is exciting."

"I can think of many adjectives to describe our situation. 'Exciting' isn't one of them." I treated him to a stern look. "I'm still of the opinion that you should take refuge at the British Embassy, pronto."

"I don't see the embassy as a place of refuge," Sidney said. "They'd likely present me with a stapler and tell me to get to work. Monday's time enough for me to embrace my inner pen-pusher."

"For heaven's sake, Sidney. You need to take this situation seriously. You're in danger."

"As are you. And may I remind you that your gangsters have my suitcase? A suitcase that contains enough clues about my identity that they can trace me to the British Embassy?"

"A fact that would've passed you by, had I not pointed it out to you. Look, I'm so sorry you got caught up in this. This is my problem, not yours. You were only trying to help me."

"Fiddlesticks," Sidney said. "This is fun. I can't think of a more interesting way to spend my last weekend of freedom. Now let's turn our attention to the kidnapping, seeing as our next task is a rescue mission. Have you heard of any rich blokes called Césaire? The sort worth holding to ransom?"

"No. Frankly, I don't want to know any more than I have to about this situation. I feel obliged to deliver the ransom money, as Monique presumably would've done so had I not stolen her stuff. Beyond that, I'm happy to remain in blissful ignorance."

"I wonder who's holding him hostage," he mused. "A criminal organization? A business rival? A jealous ex?"

I sighed. "Are you going to talk all the way to wherever we're going?"

"I suppose I could try napping," he said dubiously. "Although I'm not in the least tired. Why don't I sing a song to pass the time? Did I mention I have a penchant for musicals?"

I bit back a groan. This was going to be a very long journey.

Seven hours of singing, talking, and in-seat dancing later, Sidney fell asleep. His loud snores provided the backdrop of the final thirty minutes of the drive. I envied him his untroubled slumber. I'd been exhausted before I'd embarked on a seven-hour car journey. Now, I was running on empty. I took a swig from the takeout coffee we'd purchased at a motorway service station. It tasted gritty and gross, but I forced it down—anything to stop me from dozing at the wheel.

The satnav's synthetic voice instructed me to take the exit for Montpellier, one of the three potential destinations I'd estimated to be roughly a seven-and-a-half-hour drive south from Paris. Nice to know my knowledge of French geography was up to speed, even if the rest of my life was well into hot-mess territory.

I took the exit and joined the procession of cars

headed for downtown Montpellier. The traffic slowed to a crawl, making me squirm. I got antsy sitting in traffic. Always had. Both Dublin and London were traffic bottlenecks, especially at rush hour, and I made a point to avoid driving in either city.

This evening, I had no choice. The waiting gnawed at my already frayed nerves. I wanted to get the drop-off over and done and be on the move again. The sooner I parted ways with this car, the safer it'd be for both Sidney and me. Once we put the briefcase wherever the kidnappers wanted it, we'd dump the vehicle and sever all connections with the Mercedes and the number plate I had no doubt Cam memorized. And then I'd find a way to get Sidney back to Paris and the safety of the British Embassy.

Sidney was still snoring when the satnav directed me into a parking garage near the famous Place de la Comédie, a large square in the south of Montpellier. He woke the instant I killed the engine.

"Are we here?" His excitement was evident. "Where is here, by the way?"

"Montpellier." I failed to keep the smugness out of my tone. Hey, I'd had a crappy day. I deserved a little self-praise.

Sidney slapped me on the back with more strength than I'd credited him with. "Well done. You guessed correctly."

"It was one of three possibilities," I conceded,

flexing my sore shoulder blades. "If I knew the area better, I'd have named more."

I grabbed the briefcase from the back seat and got out of the car. I opened the boot and replenished my cash supply from Monique's stash. My fingers hovered over the passport, debating the wisdom of leaving it in the car while we made the drop-off. In the end, I pocketed it, along with all of the cash. If things worked out, we wouldn't return.

Sidney leaned against the beat-up Peugeot next to our Mercedes. "What do we do with the car key? Do you think we should hang on to it, just in case we need to get back into the car after the drop-off?"

I shook my head. "Let's leave the car unlocked, with the key and the parking receipt inside the glove compartment. Cam might manage to trace the number plate, but he'll have no other way of tracking our movements. And we know the kidnappers have at least one tracking device on the vehicle."

"The one you located while we were at the service station?"

"Yeah. It was the only one I could find, but that doesn't mean the rest of the car's clean. I don't want the kidnappers to be able to trace our movements after we drop off the money."

We ascended a stone staircase and emerged from the dark underground parking lot into the heat and sun of a July evening in the south of France. We'd barely taken a few steps when I started to sweat. I'd changed out of the hideous maternity jumpsuit and platform heels at the motorway service station and was back in my faded jeans, worn T-shirt, and biker boots. The air-conditioning in the car had made the outfit bearable, but jeans in the heat were no fun.

Sidney scanned the square with its cafés, bistros, and shops and gave a happy sigh. "This is gorgeous, Angel. I've never been to Montpellier. Do you think we'll have time to sightsee after we drop off the briefcase?"

I tugged at the neck of my T-shirt and fanned the material against my sweaty skin. "I'm not exactly in the mood to play tourist. All I want is to drop off this briefcase and leave. Besides, it's nearly six thirty. Places will be closing soon."

"In France in the summer?" Sidney laughed. "Not likely. The shops and museums might close, but the bars and cafés will stay open."

Unfortunately, he was right, but I didn't want to fuel his desire to hang out in Montpellier for one second more than we had to. He might find our mad mission entertaining, but my sense of adventure was all tapped out.

"We're here for one purpose only," I said firmly. "Once we part ways, you can do as you please. Until then, we stick to the plan."

He put his palms together and batted his impressively long eyelashes. "Pretty please, Angel?

Can we at least look around while we make our way to the meeting point?"

"You are exasperating. Don't you get that we're in danger? Now isn't the moment to take a city tour." I grabbed Sidney's arm and hauled him after me. Ignoring his objections, I marched us past an old-fashioned carousel, past cafés, shops, trams, and tourists. I didn't pause for breath until we reached the Three Graces Fountain at the center of the square. As instructed by Satnav Dude, I opened the burner phone and hit the five button. The dial tone set my heart thundering in my chest.

On the third ring, Satnav Dude answered. He didn't bother with social niceties, but then, I wasn't in the mood to make small talk. "Walk to the Place du Peyrou," he growled. His gravelly pronunciation of "Peyrou" lent it a bourbon-soaked twist.

"Hello to you too," I muttered. "Nice to know you're no friendlier live than recorded."

The man ignored my quip. "Leave the briefcase in the Château d'Eau and discard the phone. Then drive the Mercedes out of the city."

"I'd rather leave the car in Montpellier."

His low laugh was as reassuring as a roller coaster car without a safety belt. "You're not in a position to negotiate. You'll deliver the money to the appointed place and then get rid of this phone. After that, you'll take the car as arranged and dump it far away from Montpellier. Then we're done."

I shifted my weight from one foot to the other. I didn't like the way this conversation was going. "How do I know you'll release Césaire?"

"You don't. But my boss is a man of his word. You'll get Césaire back—if you obey my instructions. *All* my instructions."

I let out a breath. "Okay. I head for the Château d'Eau in the Place du Peyrou, leave the case, and then drive the car...where?"

"That's up to you." His low laugh turned my insides to liquid. "Don't worry. We'll be able to find it."

"I have no doubt you will." I didn't bother to hide my sarcasm. "But I don't—"

He disconnected.

"—want the stupid car," I finished, speaking over the tinny beep. "I'd rather take the train to Nice."

"Nice?" Sidney perked up. "So *that's* where you're heading."

I pushed a sweaty strand of hair out of my face and glared at him. "You weren't supposed to hear that."

"Then you shouldn't have thought it out loud." He whistled a show tune, his hands shoved in his pockets with an ease I envied. "I'd like to visit Nice. I don't suppose—"

"No way. As far as I'm concerned, *you* can keep the car. But I'm not taking you to Nice." I strode away from the fountain, heading in the direction of the Place du Peyrou.

Sidney jogged after me. "Shame you don't want me

tagging along to Nice. It looks gorgeous in photos. And I've always wanted to visit the Riviera."

"You want to visit everywhere, Sidney—everywhere that's not Paris."

His insouciant grin was unapologetic. "True. There's the small matter of money, though. My coffers are depressingly low until I get my first month's salary." His jaunty stride seemed an insult to my tired plod. This was an errand I was reluctant to run. "Where's this Place du Peyrou? You're walking with intent. Do you know where we're going, or are you just winging it?"

"I know where it is." I shot him a reluctant look. "I went to school outside Montpellier. I know the city well."

"Well enough to add in a trip to the beach on our way to Nice? Pretty please?"

"*Our* way? *My* way. Once we drop off the money, you'll contact the embassy, and they'll get you safely back to Paris."

"We can discuss that later," Sidney said breezily. "For now, I intend to enjoy Montpellier."

"While delivering ransom money to a bunch of anonymous crooks," I added wryly. "Not my idea of a fun day trip."

To be fair, it was hard not to like this small coastal city nestled on the edge of the Mediterranean Sea. The city center boasted gorgeous historical buildings, including the Opéra Comédie, the Gothic Cathedral

Saint-Pierre, and an Arc de Triomphe I found prettier than its Parisian counterpart. But today was not the day for me to take a trip down memory lane, or indulge Sidney's urge to explore.

"The Place du Peyrou is a ten- to fifteen-minute walk from here," I said. "If we hurry, we can make it in closer to ten."

I increased my pace, trying to ignore the rumbling in my stomach that was exacerbated by the glorious scents carried by the gentle evening breeze. The aroma of freshly ground coffee and sweet treats wafted from the square's numerous cafés, while the glorious smells of a hundred different meals met me each time we strode past a restaurant.

Sidney panted beside me. "Can we hurry a little slower? I'm not dressed for this heat."

I eyed his outfit. He'd shed the suit jacket but still wore a long-sleeved, canary-yellow shirt and yellow-and-black-checkered trousers. "Neither am I," I admitted. "If the shops are still open after we dump the briefcase, we can pick up a couple of suitable items."

He grinned. "You must be on the verge of heatstroke if you're willing to delay long enough to shop."

The corner of my mouth twitched. "As you said, it's hot."

We wove our way through the narrow streets of the old city center. I had to drag Sidney through the Arc de Triomphe, down the Promenade du Peyrou, and past the Peyrou Garden. The garden was in full bloom. Even though I insisted we not walk through the park—I didn't trust Sidney not to linger over every flower—the light sea breeze carried the glorious scents down the Promenade. I was terrible at naming plants and flowers, but I'd always had a phenomenal sense of smell. I picked up on individual scents, even if I couldn't connect them to a particular plant. Two I could identify were lavender and gardenia—favorites in my Granny Doyle's garden.

Sidney's glasses had fogged up by the time we neared the Château d'Eau. He whipped them off and cleaned them on his shirt. "For a short person, you sure know how to move."

"I know, right? Thank goodness I'm back in my sneakers. If I were wearing those stupid platform heels, we'd still be on the Place de la Comédie."

"I take it the pink maternity jumpsuit and platforms aren't your usual style?"

"Not even slightly. I wore what I found in Monique's suitcase." I stopped short of the flight of steps that curved up to the Château d'Eau. "We're here."

Sidney's forehead creased. "I thought you said it was a castle."

"It's a water tower." I laughed at his confused expression. "The French like to be fancy. And to be fair, it is fancy for a water tower." I pointed to the water pool that spread out from the side of the hexagonal building. "The Château d'Eau connects to the Aqueduc Saint-Clément and supplies all the fountains in Montpellier with water. After sunset, this whole area is illuminated." I caught his pleading look. "No, we're not sticking around until then. Let's get this over with."

I led the way up the winding stone steps and stopped at the entrance to the water tower. A gaggle of tourists clustered inside, posing for a selfie. I beat an impatient rhythm with my left foot until they left. The instant they descended the steps, we darted inside.

"Where should we leave the briefcase?" Sidney asked, looking around the room.

"Satnav Dude didn't get specific." I plopped the case down on the floor. "Seems like a crazy drop-off point. The whole place is crawling with tourists."

"Perhaps that's the point."

We stared down at the hordes of tourists exploring the garden and the Promenade.

"Any one of them could be the person assigned to collect the cash," I said, a sudden chill eclipsing the July heat. "We've done what Monique was supposed to do. Now let's get out of here. This situation gives me the creeps."

8

<hr>

I descended the steps from the Château d'Eau two at a time. The sooner I put distance between me and that briefcase, the better I'd feel.

The reality of dropping off a briefcase filled with ransom money had dimmed Sidney's enthusiasm for playing the tourist. We retraced our steps down the Promenade in a tension-laden silence, passing two police officers on patrol. The skin at the nape of my neck prickled. I increased my pace, not daring to breathe until we were far enough away from the police.

"What if they find the briefcase before the kidnappers get to it?" Sidney whispered, looking anxiously over his shoulder at the retreating backs of the officers. "An abandoned case will cause mayhem. They'll treat it as a potential bomb."

"Not our problem," I said, but increased my pace.

"The kidnappers chose this spot. I have to assume they picked it for a reason."

"It will be a problem if we were seen leaving the case and get arrested for disturbing the peace."

"Where's your annoying optimism, Sidney? We need it back, stat."

A flush stained his lightly tanned cheeks. "Not feeling it right now."

He stayed quiet the entire distance from the Arc de Triomphe back to the Place de la Comédie, and didn't even comment when I dropped the burner phone into a rubbish bin. I'd spent the day wishing I could gag the guy, but his brooding bothered me.

"Are you okay?" I asked when we reached one of the narrow streets that forked off the Place de la Comédie.

"What do we do now? Are you sticking to your plan to abandon me on your way to Nice? Wouldn't it be smarter to find a place to stay here for the night? And then decide where to go in the morning?"

"Maybe it would be smarter to stay in Montpellier, but I want to keep moving. Satnav told me to dump the car far away from Montpellier. I don't know what would happen to Césaire if I disobeyed. I plan to leave the Mercedes somewhere on the way to Nice. Then I'll find a place to sleep and continue my journey tomorrow."

"You haven't mentioned me in any of these plans.

What harm can it cause to let me tag along? In for a penny and all that?"

"Even if the kidnappers know nothing about you, Cam will be looking for both of us. It's smarter to split up. And it's extra smart for you to—"

"Go to the British Embassy," he finished for me, his cheeky grin back in place. "I've no intention of leaving you to fend for yourself. You drove the entire journey from Paris, and you were exhausted before you ever got in the car. Let me take over driving duties, at least for a while. Besides, we haven't seen any sign of Cam. Are you sure he can follow us? You took off in the Mercedes like a bat out of hell."

"I'm not making any assumptions. Cam's got an eidetic memory. Like a photographic memory," I added, seeing Sidney's confused expression. "He'll remember the car's license plate. If he can figure out how to track us, he will."

"Then let's ignore Satnav Dude's order to get the car out of Montpellier. If we're not in the Mercedes, neither Cam nor the kidnappers can follow us."

"I can't help feeling there's a reason for the order," I said. "What if it's connected with Césaire's safety?"

Sidney snorted. "And what if the reason is the car is due to blow up with us in it?"

I shook my head. "I already checked for obvious potential bombs when we were at the service station, and I'll do a more thorough check when we get back to the parking garage."

Sidney whistled. "I don't know what scares me more. The thugs on our tail or your past. How did you learn to check a car for bombs?"

My dad's mate, Jimmy the Rat, was an IRA bomb maker and my godfather. I'd never liked the dude, but I had to admit several of Jimmy's unorthodox life lessons had come in handy. "I don't think your innocent English ears need to hear that answer."

"My ears aren't all that innocent, and they're not even one hundred percent English. My grandmother is Russian."

I gave him a bow. "I stand corrected."

"If you're determined to obey Satnav Dude's orders to the bitter end, why don't I drive you to Nice—or close to Nice—and then dump the car?"

I opened my mouth to object, but he held up a finger to stop me.

"You're exhausted, Angel. The couple of hours of sleep you got on the Eurostar can't have made up for not sleeping the previous night. If I go with you, I can drive, and you can rest."

He had a point—and a valid one. I was dead on my feet. The drive from Montpellier to Nice was what? Three, four hours? And most of that would be in darkness.

I let out a long breath. "Okay, but only as far as Aix-en-Provence. I don't want anyone following me to Nice."

"It's a deal." A grin spread across his face. "See? Accepting help wasn't that hard, was it?"

I grunted. "I prefer to rely on myself."

"An admirable trait," he replied smoothly, a twinkle in his eye. "But there are moments when we all need the assistance of others."

"No need to rub it in. I said you could drive. We'll stick together until Aix-en-Provence, and then we'll part ways."

Sidney fingered his shirt collar. "Regardless of our travel plans, can we grab food on our way to the car? All I've had since this morning is an energy bar. And maybe hit up a couple of shops for lighter clothes?"

I ran a hand over my sweat-damp hair. "Okay, we can shop. And maybe eat. Do you have cash?"

He patted his trouser pocket. "A little. And I have my credit card."

I scrunched up my nose and tried to make my tired brain process this information and its implications. "You should make a cash withdrawal with the credit card. And make it substantial. It's harder to track cash payments, and anyone looking for us will trace us to Montpellier thanks to the car, so it makes no difference if you withdraw cash here. After Montpellier, though, you'll want to start covering your tracks."

"All right. I bow to your experience." He drew to a stop outside a bargain-price chain store. "This place looks like it won't cost the earth."

As we were opposite Galeries Lafayette, an

upmarket department store I felt sure was closer to Sidney's taste, I awarded him several nice-guy points. "Perfect. Meet me back at the entrance in ten?"

He blinked behind his black-rimmed glasses. "Ten? As in ten minutes? How can anyone shop in ten minutes?"

I heaved a sigh. "This isn't a shopping spree, Sidney. We need to grab the basics and get out. Besides, have you checked the time? They close in fifteen minutes."

"I'll sweet talk the shop assistants. Give me twenty minutes, and I won't whine about sightseeing. Pinky swear."

His pleading expression made me laugh. "Okay. Twenty minutes and not a second more."

I sped through the shop like a whirlwind, acquiring sandals, underwear, two pairs of shorts, three skirts, and five T-shirts in less than ten minutes. I peeled off my sweaty clothes in a changing cabin and pulled on a skirt and clean T-shirt. I shoved my boots into a shopping bag and wriggled into the sandals. I flexed my toes, enjoying the air on my bare skin. *Bliss.*

At the cash register, I went all out and actually paid for half of the items, neatly concealing the rest in an impromptu baby belly. When the alarm went off on my way out of the shop, I played the wide-eyed, helpless pregnant lady and showed the security guard my bag of purchases. His apologies were profuse, and I left with a smug smile on my face. The smile faltered when the implications of adding yet another misdemeanor to my fast-growing list dawned on me. I should be more careful, but old habits died hard.

Sidney emerged from the shop thirty minutes later, wearing shorts, a polo-neck, and snazzy sunglasses. He carried several shopping bags.

I tapped my watch. "Call this twenty minutes?"

"At least I paid for all my stuff." He eyed my baby belly with disapproval. "I saw you work your charms on the security guard. Naughty, naughty."

"Force of habit," I said breezily. "Besides, I don't even like the clothes I stole. I'll give them all to a charity shop when we get to Nice."

"You steal clothes and then give them to charity shops?"

"All the time. So many brands—from the cheap to the luxury—use sweatshops to make their clothes. Why shouldn't they be forced to do some good?"

He shook his head in bemusement. "You're a weird woman, Angel."

"I've been called worse." My stomach rumbled loudly, making us both laugh.

"Time for that snack?" Sidney nodded to a nearby food stand. "Those baguettes look delicious."

The smell was killing me. "I could eat. I want to pop into the grocery joint first and stock up on toiletries. They stay open until eight."

Sidney eyed the cramped shop and failed to hide a

shudder. "I doubt they stock any toiletries I'd let near my skin."

"Suit yourself. I'm buying the basics."

His expression wavered between distaste and resignation. Finally, he let out a dramatic sigh. "Fine. Seeing as I left my bespoke shaving foam with that thug, I need a few essentials."

In an unconscious repetition of the clothes shop, I sped through the aisles, acquiring the bare necessities in record time. Sidney dawdled over each item, taking an age to make up his mind. I'd paid for and bagged my purchases before he'd even joined the queue at the checkout. While waiting for him, I pilfered a bright red lipstick in a cheerful summer shade and slid it into my pocket.

Back on the street, Sidney regarded me with suspicion. "What did you nick this time?"

"I paid for all my toiletries," I said indignantly.

His eyes narrowed. "So, what *didn't* you pay for?"

I stared back at him, channeling innocence. "Didn't you mention food? Don't you want one of those divine baguettes from the stand across the street?"

"You're trying to change the subject." He wagged a finger at me. "No more nicking things, Angel. We're in enough trouble as it is."

"Trouble you could easily get out of if you'd call the place I'm not allowed to mention."

Ignoring me, Sidney strolled over to a food stand and ordered two enormous filled baguettes.

I joined him in the queue, earning a few stares when I shoved my hand under my T-shirt and removed my baby belly.

"What on earth?" An elderly lady gaped at me, her mouth open so wide I thought her dentures would fall out.

Shoving the stolen clothes into a bag, I smiled at my onlookers and executed a bow. "What can I say? I flew with Cheapskate Airlines. They tried to charge me a hundred euros to check a bag. This solution beat wearing my entire wardrobe on the plane."

Sidney tut-tutted. "You're shameless."

"Shameless but effective." I ordered a toasted brie and cranberry sandwich and a large mineral water. Despite my churning stomach, the smell alone triggered a ravenous hunger. I wolfed down the sandwich and ordered a second to eat on our way back to the car.

"Feeling better?" Sidney asked when I tossed the sandwich wrappers into a bin outside the parking garage's entrance.

"Yeah. I've been surviving on nerves and caffeine."

He opened the door to the parking garage and indicated I should enter first. We took the stone stairs down to our level and found the Mercedes.

Sidney retrieved the parking receipt from the glove

compartment. While he paid our parking fee, I stashed our new clothes neatly in the suitcase.

On impulse, I retrieved Frank's lucky pen from the pocket of the hideous maternity jumpsuit. The crazy leprechaun stared back at me from his perch on a pot of gold. A hard lump formed in my throat. Despite his illegal wheelings and dealings, Frank had been kind to me when I'd needed help. He hadn't deserved to die. My grip on the pen tightened. Once I figured out a way to contact the police without falling into Monty's clutches, I'd do all I could to see that Frank got justice.

I slipped the pen into my skirt pocket, along with a wad of Monique's cash and the red lipstick I'd stolen. Since we'd decided to keep the car for a while, I might as well stash the rest of the money in the suitcase, along with the passport.

After I'd shut the boot, I hunkered down to check under the Mercedes for incendiary devices and other signs of sabotage. To my relief, I found nothing suspicious.

"We're a bomb-free zone," I said to Sidney when he returned from paying our parking fee.

"That's good to know. We're on the run from at least two groups of thugs, but at least we won't blow up."

"Smart aleck." I tossed him the key and went to the passenger door. "Drive carefully. I don't want to leave any dents on the car."

"You're a most considerate car thief," he replied

poker-faced, "but if I'm driving, you'll need to sit on the other side."

"Oh," I said sheepishly, noticing my mistake. "Right."

Now that we'd fulfilled our mission, the dashboard computer had reverted to business as usual. Sidney input our destination before reversing out of our parking space. "It'll be nearly ten p.m. by the time we reach Aix-en-Provence, and then we have to reach Nice somehow. Do you have accommodation lined up?"

"Not exactly." I paused, debating how much to tell him. "I have someone I can probably stay with in Nice, but I don't know where he lives. I'll have to wait until he opens for business in the morning and swing by his shop."

"In that case, why don't we find a place to stay in Aix? We're bound to have more public transport options to Nice during the daytime."

I wasn't keen on the idea of lingering too near the car once we dumped it, but Sidney was right. Staying overnight in Aix made sense. "Okay. But we leave first thing in the morning."

"That's fine. If we want to stay in Aix, we'd be smart to call ahead and book a hotel."

"We don't have a phone," I reminded him. "I dumped the burner phone as instructed."

For a split second, an emotion I couldn't pinpoint flickered across his face. It was gone before my tired brain could connect the dots. Was he reacting to my mention of the burner phone? Or was my stress-tinged exhaustion making me paranoid?

"Right," he said, his expression curiously blank. "I forgot."

He was probably still resentful I'd insisted he ditch his beloved smartphone back in Paris. I bit back a snarky remark and leaned back in my seat.

Our progress out of the parking garage and through Montpellier took forever. Sidney's preferred driving speed hovered between a Sunday driver and a stationary bike. By the time we reached the motorway, I'd tested every radio station I could find and blasted us with one bad song after another.

"It's official." I stifled a yawn. "There isn't a single good song playing on the radio tonight."

"If I still had my suitcase, I'd loan you my neck pillow again," Sidney said.

"S'okay," I murmured, my eyelids drooping.

I guess I must've dozed off after that. I had no memory of the following couple of hours. I was even too tired to dream.

I was jolted awake by screeching tires and Sidney screaming. I sat upright in my seat, my senses on high alert. A black and yellow blur leaped from the dashboard and landed on my lap with a yowl. I recoiled, pushed back in my seat, and screamed.

My scream melded with Sidney's in a perfect cacophony. He hit the brakes, causing the car behind us to honk violently. In a panic, Sidney hit the accelerator, and we surged forward at breakneck speed.

"What is that thing?" Sidney demanded. "And how did it get in our car?"

Ignoring the menacing hiss emanating from our feline friend, I fingered the cat's silver name tag. "We misunderstood Satnav Dude. Sidney, meet Césaire."

9

"A cat?" Sidney's eyes bugged, and his lips had developed an elasticity that would've been comedic under any other circumstances. "Someone paid one hundred thousand euros for a *cat*?"

The blare of a horn made us all jump.

"Eyes on the road," I yelled, my heart thumping hard. "We're swerving into the next lane."

Sidney gripped the wheel tighter and corrected the car's sideways trajectory. The driver of the vehicle we'd almost run into sat on his horn again, picked up speed, and left us in the dust.

"Sorry." Sidney grimaced. "I got distracted. The sudden addition of a cat to this farce of a day came as a surprise. Frankly, if this were a choose-your-own-adventure story, I'd say we'd turned the wrong page."

"I turned the wrong page the moment I stole Monique Beaufour's suitcase. But how was I to know she wasn't the fashion-addicted airhead she was projecting on the Tube?"

"Well, quite," Sidney said in perfect sympathy. "It's easy to make assumptions. When I met you, I had no idea I was dealing with an experienced criminal who was on the run from a notorious gangster."

I slid him a look. "Concentrate on the road, Future Diplomat. What are we going to do about this cat?"

As if sensing we were talking about him, the cat glared up at me and dug his claws into my lap, piercing the fabric of my skirt and stabbing my thighs.

"Ouch. Not friendly." I tried to lift him off me, but he snarled in a menacing manner and dug his claws deeper into my skin. Wincing at the pain, I held my hand out to the cat. "Hey, Césaire. Cut that out. We mean you no harm. We're just surprised to find you in our car."

The cat treated me to a slit-eyed glare and took a cautious sniff of my hand. Progress—although he didn't relinquish his grip on my thighs. Actually, I wasn't sure if Césaire was a *he* or a *she*. Given the cat's prickly personality, I didn't dare check to be sure. Instead, I cooed to him, hoping to calm him down. After a painful few minutes, he retracted his claws and allowed me to stroke his soft fur. He kept his back arched and his gaze wary, but his low purrs reverberated against my hand. And then a warm, wet sensation spread over my lap, the liquid making my wounded thighs sting.

I squirmed in my seat. "I'm pretty sure the cat's peed on my skirt."

Sidney shuddered. "I'm willing to face down criminals, but I draw the line at cats, particularly one who's liable to pee on me."

"I'm not exactly thrilled by the situation. I'd hoped our association with Monique Beaufour and the kidnappers would end once we dumped this car. Now we're stuck with a cat whose owner just paid a small fortune for its safe return. And we have no idea who this owner is or where they live."

"Where did the animal spring from?" Sidney demanded. "I thought you checked the car thoroughly before we left Montpellier."

"I checked the places most likely to contain a concealed explosive. I didn't take the car apart." I peered into the back seat. "There's a cat cage on the floor. The kidnappers must've left it in the car after we delivered the money."

"How considerate of them," Sidney said, his tone parched as desert sand. "Especially the part where they forgot to close the cage door."

I examined the cat, noting the odd expression in his eyes. "I'm surprised the cat took this long to start his acrobatics routine. Do you think the kidnappers drugged him?"

"Drugged? Asleep? I don't know. Anyone who'd kidnap a cat is a terrible human being. I wouldn't put anything past them."

I shot him a grin. "All this from a man who claims to dislike cats. You're a big softie at heart."

He grunted, but the corners of his mouth quivered. "My grandmother had a marmalade beast when I was a child, and it delighted in using me as a scratching post. Ever since, I've been nervous around cats. And they don't like me."

"Well, yeah. Your anxiety triggers theirs." I dropped my gaze to the cat. "I bet if you got to know this little guy, you'd be the best of friends."

Césaire blinked up at me. Although he wasn't fully committed to the idea of sitting on my lap, he showed no signs of wanting to get off. He shifted restlessly, finally settling into a stiff sitting position. His movements rubbed the wet fabric of my skirt against my skin, and I wrinkled my nose at the pervading smell of cat pee. "I need to get cleaned and changed. Is there anywhere we can stop for a while?"

Sidney peered through the windscreen and pointed to signs overhead. "There's a rest area in three hundred meters, but it doesn't look like it has a shop or service station."

"Not ideal. Still, it'll have to do. I'm too tired to process my thoughts, and we need to come up with a plan for dealing with the cat. Maybe I'll be able to think more clearly if I splash water on my face."

"I'm so tired, only sleep will help me formulate a semi-coherent plan, but I'm willing to try your water trick. Anything that'll help us find a way to offload this cat."

I grinned at him. "Where's your sense of adventure? You were all for an exciting weekend a few hours ago."

"That was before our weekend involved battling with a feral feline."

"Life skills, Sidney. Think of it as a learning experience. Did you have pets when you were growing up?"

"Ours was a strictly no-pets household. Like me, my father was traumatized by my grandmother's succession of attack cats." He flipped on the indicator and filtered into the lane that led off the motorway to the rest stop. "Besides, I'm happy to remain a pet-free zone. I have enough trouble looking after myself."

"Pets aren't all that different from small kids. You told me on the train that your sister kept having babies. Surely you're an experienced babysitter by now?"

"Only for those who've reached the age of continence," he replied primly. "And these are the perfect progeny of my saintly sister and her barrister husband—a man so boring you could bottle him as a cure for insomnia."

I snorted with laughter. "You sure know how to sell your family to outsiders. Are any of them worth knowing?"

Sidney cocked his head to the side and appeared to give my question serious consideration. "My mother's a good egg. She's obsessed with gardening and local committees. And afflicted with selective sight and hearing. But she's a decent sort."

"Selective sight and hearing? I'm impressed. How does she manage that?"

"Hers is a skill honed by years of ignoring my father's affairs and my grandmother's caustic comments."

"Sounds like domestic bliss. Perhaps my parents' penchant for multiple marriages isn't such a bad idea after all."

Sidney wound the car down the spiraling road that led to the rest area. Several vehicles were parked when we arrived, and we found a free space next to the toilets.

When I climbed out of the car, the cat hissed and drew its claws across my cheek. "Hey, there. You're one antagonistic kitty cat. What did I do to deserve scratches this time?"

Césaire glared at me through narrowed eyes. Despite his aggression, he was a pretty animal. He had dark markings on fur so golden that it appeared yellow in the dim light.

I gave him a tentative stroke. He trembled under my touch. "Poor baby. You're terrified. What did those nasty brutes do to you?"

Sidney shook his head in bemusement. "Why are you cooing over him, Angel? He's just shredded your face."

"A mere scratch or two." I shoved Césaire at him. "Here you go. You're on cat-sitting duty while I get changed."

Panic froze his expression in a horrified grimace. He leaped back and collided with a tree trunk. "No way. That creature's insane. You saw how he leaped around the car. And look at your face and legs. You're bleeding."

"You'll be fine. If you don't want to hold Césaire, I'll put him on the grass next to the tree you've just assaulted. Just make sure he doesn't climb it. Because if he does, you're going up after him."

"I'll get his cage," Sidney muttered, running an unsteady hand through his fair hair. "And I'll make sure the door's closed this time."

"Don't forget to put water in his bowl," I called over my shoulder. "You can fill it with one of the bottles we picked up in Montpellier."

He hauled the cage out of the back and peered inside. "How did you know there were bowls in here?"

I rolled my eyes. "It's a travel carrier. Of course, it has a place for food and water."

"Forgive me for being blissfully ignorant in the ways of felines." Sidney cast a wary gaze over the cat. "I guess it's just you and me, Césaire. Angel is abandoning us."

"You'll cope." I put the cat on the grass and urged him into his cage. To my astonishment, he went in without protest. "See? He's a good cat. Aren't you, Césaire?"

The cat turned his back and dismissed me with a disdainful flick of his tail.

Leaving Sidney to deal with Césaire's water supply, I grabbed clean clothes and shower gel from the boot and headed to the toilets. They proved to be as grim and grotty as I'd anticipated. I wasted no time in cleaning the cat pee off my skin and washing my wounds. They stung like the devil. I'd underestimated the damage Césaire's claws had done to my cheek. I made a mental note to buy antiseptic cream when I had an opportunity.

Once I was clean, I dried myself with paper towels and pulled on a fresh pair of shorts and a T-shirt. Then I headed back to the car and bundled my dirty clothes into Monique's suitcase, tumbling my loose change and the leprechaun pen onto the ground in the process. Tonight wasn't my night. I scooped up the coins and the pen and shut the boot.

Sidney was already behind the wheel when I slid back into the passenger side. His wet hair indicated he'd paid a visit to the men's room and had taken my face-splashing advice. Meanwhile, Césaire was in his cage, playing with something I couldn't identify in the twilight.

"He looks happy. Did you two bond while I was gone?"

A smug smile spread across Sidney's face, arousing

my suspicions. "I gave Césaire one of your boots to play with. Turns out it makes a wonderful scratching post."

"You're unbelievable," I said, outraged. "Those are my favorite boots. I don't want one covered in scratches."

"Neither boot was in great shape to start with," Sidney pointed out. "You'll hardly notice the difference."

I narrowed my eyes. "This is revenge for you losing your bespoke shaving foam, isn't it?"

Sidney's grin was broad. "Oh, yeah."

I crossed my arms over my chest and glowered at him, but I made no move to retrieve the boot—an occupied Césaire would be a quiet Césaire. "After you entertained yourself by destroying my footwear, did you come up with a cunning plan for dealing with the Césaire situation?"

"I wouldn't call it cunning, but it's a plan." His hand lingered on the ignition, but he made no move to start the engine. "We try to track down Monique Beaufour."

"And say what, exactly? 'Hey, here's the cat. Sorry we stole your identity, your car, and your money.'"

"To be fair, *you* were responsible for most of those crimes."

I ignored this quip. "If Monique has access to a luxury Mercedes and one hundred thousand euros in cash, she's either filthy rich, filthy connected, or both. For all we know, the woman's a P.I. Perhaps even connected to the police. Satnav Dude warned her not to contact the cops, but how do we know she didn't? She never got in the car to hear the drop-off instructions. We did. And we didn't even know the car's end destination until we got to Montpellier."

A frown creased Sidney's forehead. "Has it occurred to you that Monique might be Césaire's owner? Perhaps she was on her way to France to rescue her pet."

I cast my mind back to the woman on the Tube. "It's possible, but I don't buy it. The Monique I encountered was way too calm to be on her way to rescue her stolen pet."

"Maybe they contacted her about the cat after you'd stolen her case."

"I can't rule that out," I admitted, "but I don't think so. I believe Monique was hired to deliver the ransom money and collect the animal. She's got to be some sort of private investigator. It would explain the disguise in her suitcase."

Sidney's eyebrows quirked. "A P.I. who casually chats about fashion shows on her way to deliver ransom money?"

"Why not? If she's a pro, this is all in a day's work for her. And for all we know, her seemingly inane chatter could've been some sort of code."

"So no tracking down Monique." Sidney sighed. "Do you have a better idea?"

"Yeah." I swiped the dashboard screen and brought

up the navigation system. "Head back to the motorway and follow the directions to Aix-en-Provence. Meanwhile, I'll find an address for an animal hospital in Aix."

"All right," Sidney said, gunning the engine. "At least he'll be well cared for at an animal clinic."

While he drove, I searched the navigation for an animal hospital in Aix. It didn't take long for me to hit gold. "I'll reroute us from the town center to a clinic just off the motorway. We dump the cat and get out of Aix. We'll have to keep the car a while longer. Maybe dump it closer to Nice."

"What do we do if the clinic's closed?" Sidney asked.

"Then we find another place. There's got to be a twenty-four-hour animal clinic somewhere in town."

We drove a while in silence with just the light of our headlights to cut through the darkness. There were few cars on the motorway, but then, it was nearly ten at night. The outside temperature still hovered at a sticky thirty-three degrees Celsius, and I was glad the car came equipped with excellent air-conditioning.

I was half asleep when Césaire let out a high-pitched howl, jolting me back to consciousness. Sidney and I swung around in our seats to check what was up. The cat peeked out of my boot and bared his sharp teeth in a snarl.

"What's your problem, little guy?" I asked. "Are

you hungry? The people at the animal clinic will give you a good feed."

Césaire's only response was a menacing hiss.

"Friendly creature," Sidney said, returning his attention to the road. "He reminds me of my grandmother's cat. Actually, he reminds me of my grandmother. Similar personalities."

I bit back a laugh. "When we get to the clinic, you should stay in the car, preferably with the engine running."

He shot me an amused look. "Have you cast me in the role of your getaway driver?"

"Think of it as material to draw from at your next audition."

"I'm touched by your consideration for my acting career." He flipped the indicator and took the exit for Aix. "What's your plan, exactly? Walk into the clinic and dump the cage at the reception?"

"Pretty much. I'll put on Monique's wig and sunglasses and perform a quick drop and run."

"And then we take off in the car, tires screeching?" He cast me a long look. "Sounds like a terrible idea, Angel."

"I'm not wild about it, but do you have a better idea up your sleeve? I'm on the run from gangsters, using a stolen identity and a nicked car. We've both delivered ransom money to kidnappers and ended up with a cantankerous cat. A cat whose owner was willing to pay a small fortune to get him back. At this stage, a trip to the cops won't be pretty for either of us."

"All right." Sidney slowed at the traffic lights and pushed a stray strand of hair off his forehead. "What about spending the night in Aix? Is that still on the cards?"

"I don't see that we have a choice. We'll be lucky to find a vacancy this late at night, and we'd be pushing our luck if we continued to Nice. I say we take the first hotel we find with rooms available."

The lights changed, and Sidney hit the gas. He slid me a look of concern. "Cheer up, Angel. In a few minutes, this'll be over. Césaire will be in safe hands, and we'll leave the car wherever we park it. It won't solve your Monty Carlyle problem, but at least Monique Beaufour and her cohorts will be out of the picture."

A visceral premonition of doom crawled over my skin, leaving me queasy. Could it be that easy? Or had my lifetime's supply of luck run out during last night's shootout at the hilariously misnamed pub, The Lucky Charm?

I tamped down my fears, squared my shoulders, and forced a smile. "You're right. We're due a lucky break. Everything's going to be fine."

10

Sidney followed the satnav's directions to the animal hospital. The hospital didn't appear to have its own car park, but there was a public one directly across from the building. Once we'd parked, I hopped out of the Mercedes and fetched the wig and sunglasses from the suitcase. I contemplated getting back into the hideous maternity jumpsuit, but dismissed the idea as a waste of time. Although I needed to conceal my identity from the security cameras, I was anxious for the drop-off to be over. I wanted to get as far away from the cat and the car as possible.

While I donned my disguise, Sidney dragged the cat cage out of the back. "We've struck gold." He pointed to the glowing lights inside the animal hospital. "It looks like they're open."

"If so, that's the only stroke of luck we've had all day." I adjusted the pink wig and tucked a stray strand of hair under it. "I have no idea how actors cope with wearing wigs for hours on end. They're sweaty and itchy."

"Good ones, properly applied, are fine," Sidney said. "I had to wear a long, powdered wig when I played King Louis XVI of France. It all went swimmingly until we reached the scene where I was guillotined. My wig and the severed head rolled in opposite directions while I was still reciting my death speech."

"Sounds like an award-winning performance."

"Oh, it was. I was crowned Best Comedic Actor of my year. Which would've been a great honor had the play I won it for not been a tragedy."

I tugged at my T-shirt. "I'll have to try to channel a bedraggled version of Monique."

"A bedraggled Monique, complete with livid scratches down her face that absolutely no one will notice."

"Can the sarcasm, or I'll make *you* go in with the cat." I slid on the sunglasses and picked up the cage.

Sidney eyed me critically. "You'll fall on your face wearing those shades in the dark."

"I'll be careful. As you oh-so subtly pointed out, I need to hide as much of my face as possible. The shades help."

"Do you think I could sneak in and use their

toilets?" He bounced from one foot to the other. "I have to pee."

"Seriously, Sidney? Couldn't you have gone at the rest stop? Or find a bush? We don't have a disguise for you to wear, and we don't want the security cameras picking you up for the police to find."

"If we part ways in the car park, it won't be an issue. If the police check the security footage, they'll focus on the person carrying the cage, and you're in disguise."

"You're not in disguise, though."

He indicated his newly purchased outfit. "I beg to differ. Under any other circumstances, I wouldn't be seen dead in these clothes. Besides, I'm an actor. I don't need a costume. I can change my walk and accent at will."

I didn't like this plan, but if Sidney wasn't willing to whip out his boy bits and pee behind the car, I sure didn't want him wetting the seat next to mine. "Okay, but don't be long. I want to get out of here, pronto."

"Okay." He leaned down and peered into the cage. "Bye-bye, little guy. I hope you're reunited with your parents very soon."

The animal arched its back and hissed.

I rolled my eyes. "*He* might be a *she*."

"True, but I wasn't about to get close enough to find out." Sidney examined my butchered face and shuddered. "Look what it did to you."

As I had similar misgivings about the safety in

manhandling Césaire merely to establish his gender, I saw his point. "All right. If you need to pee, move fast. I'll give you a head start so we're not seen together."

"Okay. Thanks, Angel." Sidney locked the car, pocketed the key, and marched across the car park.

To my amazement, each step seemed to transform him further. He started with Sidney's jaunty step and ended with the beefy amble I associated with jocks. By the time he reached the steps of the clinic, he was unrecognizable from the back. Impressive.

I hauled the cage through the car park. When I hit the pavement, I swung right, heading away from the clinic. I attempted to channel Sidney and tried to become more like Monique with each step. All that my hair-flicking and hip-swaying achieved was to make me feel a fool. Abandoning my terrible efforts at improv acting, I paused at a bus stop. I loitered for a few minutes, pretending to read the timetable and ignoring the yowls from the cage. When I was confident I'd given Sidney a decent head start, I retraced my steps to the animal hospital and stopped on the edge of the sidewalk to let a car pass. After it whizzed by, I stepped onto the street.

And froze.

Cam strolled up to the animal clinic. He clutched a phone to his ear and looked up and down the street, searching for someone.

Searching for *me*.

Shards of panic pierced my lungs. My breathing turned to an ineffectual wheeze. My mind reeling, I backed up. Had Cam seen me? Had he seen Sidney enter the clinic a few minutes earlier? If so, had he recognized him?

I whipped off the pink wig and dropped it on top of the cage. Cam had seen me wear the wig earlier. I was less conspicuous with my natural hair than the powder-pink bob. Walking at an average pace for a woman lugging a cat cage and praying Cam wasn't following me, I retraced my steps toward the car. I gripped the cage's handle hard enough for my fingers to ache.

I had no way to warn Sidney that Cam was here and no key to open the car when I reached it. This was not good. My heart thudded against my ribs. Each step seemed to take extra effort. Despite the cage's weight, I wanted to run, but that was a surefire way to draw attention to myself.

How had Cam found me? Sidney and I had both gotten rid of our phones. The car's registration number? That had to be it. Cam had the know-how to access the police radio. If Monique had reported the Mercedes stolen, the police would be looking for it. Cam could listen in or get a French speaker to listen in for him and translate. And if Monique had reported the theft, where was she now?

I neared the Mercedes. At the last second, I darted between two nearby cars. If Cam came into the car park, he'd head straight for the Mercedes. From this vantage point, I could catch Sidney's attention when he returned and duck down between the cars if Cam showed up.

The cat had grown suspiciously quiet. I peeked inside the cage. The animal had managed to drag my wig through the bars and was busy shredding it with systematic precision. "Better the wig than my face. I can't believe anyone would pay one euro to get you back, never mind a hundred thousand. You're cute, kitty cat, but you're a bundle of trouble."

I shoved my free hand into my pocket to stop it from shaking. My fingers closed around Frank's lucky pen and squeezed it tight. How long would I need to wait for Sidney? Every second we stayed here increased the chances of Cam catching us.

I risked a glance over my shoulder. And exhaled in a whoosh.

Sidney ambled across the road, looking like himself again and as though he hadn't a care in the world. His eyes widened when he saw me standing in the middle of the car park. "What's up? I thought you'd have dropped him off by now."

"Quick," I whispered. "Cam's here. We need to get moving."

His forehead creased. "Cam? But how did he find us?"

"I don't know, but we have to go. He's somehow managing to track this car, but at the moment, it's our only mode of transport, and we need to get away from here."

Sidney's lips formed silent words. His hand shook around the car key. Seeing his naked fear slaked my own, pushing me back into coping mode.

"Here, give me the key. I'll drive this time." When it came to putting distance between Cam and us, I had more faith in my pedal to the metal driving style than Sidney's octogenarian pace. "You take the cat cage. Just jump into the passenger seat with it. We can put it in the back once we're on the move."

Every step we took closer to the car increased my paranoia. The hair at the nape of my neck stood to attention, and I felt invisible eyes boring into my back. Either my imagination was running wild, or one of the twins was lurking in the car park. "Time to run," I whispered to Sidney. "Now."

We legged it across the car park. I pressed the car's unlock button and hurled myself behind the wheel, gunning the engine before Sidney was even in the car. He tumbled into the passenger side, clutching the cat cage, and I speed-reversed out of our space.

In the rearview mirror, a slim shape zipped through the darkness, coming closer. Someone in a hoodie. Cam or one of the twins? Wasn't the person too small to be any of them? I didn't wait to find out. I shifted out of reverse, hit the accelerator, and sped toward the exit.

A shot rang out, followed by the *ping* of a bullet

hitting metal. My heart stopped mid-beat, sending tendrils of pain across my chest.

"They're shooting at us," Sidney cried. "Get us out of here, Angel."

"Believe me, I'm on it." I took the turn out of the car park at full speed, screeched down the street, and whizzed through a red light. Not reducing my speed, I followed the signs back to the motorway. Before my brain registered what I was doing, I took the entrance that headed toward Nice. Not smart. If Cam was able to follow us, I wanted to lead him away from my intended destination.

"What's the plan?" Sidney asked in a wobbly voice. "Are we still driving to Nice?"

"No. Not until we figure out how Cam found us." I switched on the navigation. "Can you check if there's a rest stop coming up? I want to stop and do another search for a tracker. Maybe Cam managed to attach one to the car when he confronted us outside Gare du Nord? And the one I found earlier was put there by Césaire's kidnappers? I didn't think Cam had time to tamper with the Mercedes, but he's keeping tabs on us somehow."

"You're confident Césaire's kidnappers are tracking us through the dashboard computer, though," Sidney pointed out. "Could Cam have access to their information?"

"If he does, it implies he and Monty are in league

with the kidnappers. And of all the people whose suitcases I could've stolen on the Tube, I just happened to steal Monique Beaufour's?" I gave a definite shake of my head. "That scenario stretches credibility."

Sidney fiddled with his seatbelt. "How else could Cam be tracking us? I'm not exactly a surveillance expert."

"Neither am I, but I know quite a lot about it." This wasn't quite an understatement. I'd done a lot of internet surveillance during my dodgy previous jobs, but not using physical trackers. I knew enough to know how much I had left to learn. "The easiest way he could do it would be by tracking our phones. But as we both got rid of ours, I don't know."

He shuffled in his seat and tugged at his shirt collar. "Well, ah, about my phone...."

I whipped around to stare at him. Even in the dim light of the car, I could see his cheeks darkening. A leaden sensation weighed down my limbs. "Please tell me you got rid of your phone, Sidney. You must have. I saw you throw it out the window in Paris."

He squirmed under the force of my laser-sharp glare. "What you saw was my phone *case* taking a flying leap into the traffic. I kept the actual phone."

"Why would you do that?" My voice came out in a screech. "I told you to get rid of it."

"I know you did, but my whole life is on my phone." He cast a quick glance at me. "Besides, I'd just been threatened by a knife-wielding lunatic who's apparently your ex. I wanted to hedge my bets and have a way to get help if you turned out to be a crazed nutcase."

"I can't believe you were so stupid! If Cam has your laptop, he can access your phone locator. Give it to me right now."

"But my laptop is password-protected," he protested. "Surely, Cam can't just access my stuff."

"Oh, please. Cam Carruthers is almost as good a hacker as I am. What sort of password do you use? The name of your hamster?"

"I don't have a hamster," he said, defensive. "As I said, I'm a pet-free zone."

"Then I bet you use your birthday or the name of your favorite song."

He scratched the back of his neck. "Well—"

"Regardless of how strong your password is or isn't," I continued, "it wouldn't take Cam long to get past it. Now, for the last time, give me that bleeding phone. If you won't, you can get out of this car and walk back to Paris. You're putting both our lives in danger."

"Okay, okay. I'm on it." He fumbled in his pocket and handed me his smartphone.

I opened my window and threw it onto the motorway. "I'll take you as far as Nice, and then we part ways, Sidney. I'm sorry you got dragged into this mess, but you're a liability. I told you Cam could use your laptop to track your phone. If you don't listen to me, you're going to get us both killed."

"I'm sorry, Angel. I screwed up. In my defense, I'm not a techie. I thought you were just freaking out and paranoid."

"You could've asked me to elaborate." I slapped the wheel so hard it sent a jolt of pain into my wrist. "This isn't a game. Monty Carlyle is a dangerous man, and Cam has a personal grudge against me. You don't want to get caught in the crosshairs."

"I'm already on their radar, Angel. How likely is Cam to let me walk away unscathed?"

We fell silent for a moment, each digesting uncomfortable truths. Sidney was right. He'd pinged Cam's radar the instant he'd defended me outside the Gare du Nord. With access to Sidney's laptop, Cam could find out all about him, including his new address.

"Does Cam know of your connection to Nice?" Sidney asked, breaking our awkward silence.

"Not as far as I know. Cam never met my mother, and I didn't talk about her. He's aware she's French, but that's about it." At his look of confusion, I elaborated. "My mother and I haven't been in touch for a few years. She wasn't a relevant talking point when I was dating Cam. Besides, she's from Marseille, not Nice. She only lived in Nice during one of her marriages. I can't see how Cam could connect those dots."

His brow creased in confusion. "So if you're not

going to stay with your mother, who do you know in Nice?"

"One of my nicer former stepfathers. My mother's a serial bride. She likes the idea of marriage better than the reality."

He nodded. "Okay. Then let's stick to the plan of going to Nice tomorrow. If you still want me to go back to Paris, I'll catch a train from Nice. What about tonight?"

"Now that we know how Cam was tracking us, ditching the car is less urgent. I suggest we keep driving for a while to put distance between Cam and us, and then find a rest stop, preferably one with a service station this time. I need antiseptic cream for my wounds, and we should buy cat food and a scooper to clean out Césaire's cage. We'll have to look after the cat until the morning, and we can't leave him to starve in his own filth."

"Sounds good. Well, not good," he amended. "Nothing sounds good tonight. But it's a decent plan."

An hour later, we exited the motorway at a service station. The cat had tired itself out with Operation Wig Destruction and had gone back to sleep. I envied him the luxury. Despite my exhaustion, I was too wound up to sleep, even if I hadn't needed to drive. A dull ache nagged at my temples.

Before we got out of the car, I stretched my neck from side to side. "I have the start of a headache. Do you have painkillers on you?"

Sidney shook his head. "Sorry, no. They might have some for sale in the shop."

I closed my eyes and dredged up a memory from this morning. It felt so long ago. "If I remember correctly, there's a box of Tylenol in Monique's toiletry bag. I'll check."

"Want me to deal with the shopping? I took your advice and withdrew cash in Montpellier. Even after our shopping spree, there's plenty left."

I had cash left too, but, unlike Sidney, I had no credit card or a rich daddy to fall back on. I needed to make Monique's money last. "You put our lives at risk by not jettisoning your phone in Paris. You owe me. So, yeah, you can take care of the shopping. Don't forget my antiseptic cream. Oh, and mineral water. And can you hang on a sec? I want to see if I can find those tablets. If not, you can add them to your shopping list."

He gave me a mock salute. "Yes, boss."

I experienced a pang of guilt at being hard on Sidney. My searing anger had simmered to exasperated vexation. I would calm down enough by tomorrow morning to give him a friendly farewell at the train station in Nice, but I wasn't at that stage yet.

I got out of the car and walked around the vehicle. Courtesy of Cam and his friends, the Mercedes now had two bullet holes—one lodged in the right-back door, and the other had clipped the left-wing mirror. Still, it could've been worse. A bullet might've hit one of us.

I went to the back and pressed the button to open the boot.

And stared down into the unseeing eyes of one very large, very dead Terrible Twin.

oly smoke. A Terrible Twin was in the boot. A terribly dead Terrible Twin.

I stood stock-still behind the car and sucked air like oxygen was going out of fashion. The ground tilted, shifted, tipped me forward, brought me close to face-planting on a corpse. "Sidney?" My high-pitched tone sounded like a rusty hinge.

"What's up? Did you find the Tylenol?" He poked his head out of the car window and stared in question.

"We have a problem." The statement was ludicrously inadequate, but I was in shock. Despite my less-than-squeaky-clean past, encountering dead bodies wasn't on my daily schedule.

Surprise, then resignation, spread across Sidney's face. "We have many problems, Angel. Can you be more specific?"

"Is a corpse in the boot specific enough for you?"

His mouth opened and closed on repeat, reminding me of a startled carp. "You're pulling my leg."

"I wish." I pointed to the half-open boot with a shaky finger. "Come here and take a look for yourself. One dead dude, complete with a stab wound to the chest."

Sidney tumbled out of the car and lurched to my side. He leaned down and peered into the boot with exaggerated caution. When he clocked eyes on the dead Russian, he emitted a high-pitched squawk that woke the cat. Their combined caterwauling earned us curious glances from the truckers outside the service station.

"Shh." I pressed a finger to his lips. "We don't need to advertise the fact that we're driving an accidental hearse."

Sidney slammed the boot shut and stepped back, breathing hard. "Who is that guy? And who put him in our car?"

"His name is Boris or Ivan, and he, like Cam, is one of Monty Carlyle's muscle men."

"Boris *or* Ivan?" Sidney's voice rose falsetto-high. "Not Igor or Alexei or some other random name of Russian extraction?"

"He has an identical twin brother." I struggled to keep my voice steady. "I call them the Terrible Twins. I can't tell them apart, but our corpse is definitely one of them."

Sidney jerked his head from side to side, an emphatic denial of this undeniable reality. "If that's one twin, where's the other? In the back seat? On the roof? Can we expect to be knee-deep in dead Russians by sunrise?"

I ignored his hyperbole. As so often happened, seeing someone else panic had prodded me out of a state of fear and back into coping mode. "Both twins were at the Gare du Nord with Cam."

"You mentioned Cam wasn't alone, but I didn't see his companions. Isn't this the bloke who fell onto the kid's trike outside the station? I passed him when I was bringing you your suitcase."

"Monique's suitcase," I corrected. "And, yeah. Either it's him, or it's his twin brother. As I said, I can't tell them apart."

"I didn't realize the trike bloke was with Cam, but it makes sense. The same Popeye muscles, the same pervading sense of menace. How did he wind up dead in our car?"

"I don't know. One thing I'm sure of, the body was put there while we were at the animal clinic."

His eyebrow formed a question mark. "How do you know that?"

"When I opened the boot to get the wig and sunglasses out of the suitcase, he wasn't here. Now we have a dead body, and the suitcase is gone. Along with our new clothes, Monique's passport, her Tylenol, and most of her money." I wanted to scream, to run, to hit someone. "Curse Cam and the twins to Hades."

"They swapped our clothes for a corpse?" Sidney staggered back from the car and had a close encounter with a metal garbage can. The impact had to have hurt, but he didn't seem to notice. "This can't be happening. I wanted an adventure, sure, but I didn't sign up for a kidnapped French cat and a dead Russian mobster."

"And you think I did?" I placed my hands on my hips. "If you recall, I didn't want you tagging along. You insisted on staying with me, even after we heard Satnav Dude's instructions. And you kept your phone, even after I told you to get rid of it. If Cam and the twins hadn't been able to track us down, we wouldn't have this creepy corpse in our car."

He stared at me through tired eyes that had probably seen more of life's seedy side during the past few hours than in the twenty-six years he'd lived before. "I'm sorry I kept the phone. I thought the whole situation was a prank. I didn't want to throw away a pricey smartphone for a reality TV stunt. By the time I realized it was the real deal, I'd honestly forgotten I still had the phone."

"I wish this were a prank, and I wish I could press rewind and erase last night." My laugh was rough and acid-tinged. "Irony is, it wasn't even my night to work at the pub. If I'd refused to cover Becky's shift, I'd never have gone to The Lucky Charm. And if I'd never gone to The Lucky Charm, I'd never have seen Monty

Carlyle kill Frank, or shot a ketamine dart into Monty's arse."

"We can't turn back time, but we can try to figure out why this man wound up in our car." Sidney searched my face for answers I didn't have. "What do you think happened? Did they kill each other?"

I took a breath, held it for ten. "You don't get it, do you? It doesn't matter *who* did the killing. What matters is *we've* been framed."

"What?" His body jerked like I'd zapped him with a taser. "No way. The police would never think we killed him."

"Of course, they'll think we killed him. He's dead in our car." I clasped my hands to stop them from shaking. "This is Monty's doing."

"I thought you said Monty was still in London. If this is anyone's doing, it's Cam's."

"Monty doesn't need to leave London to be responsible." I paced a jagged zigzag around the car. I needed to keep moving, or I'd fall apart. "As for Cam stabbing the twin, I'm not sure. Cam's a nasty piece of work, no question, but he's more the hired hacker type than hired killer."

"Cam attacked me with a knife," Sidney pointed out. "And you've indicated he'd kill you in a heartbeat."

"Yes, but he has a personal reason for wanting me dead. I have to assume that's why he's working with Monty. And he'd take you down to get to me. But killing one of the twins?" I shook my head. "It doesn't make sense. Cam knows Monty would go ballistic if he killed one of his favorite minions."

"If Cam isn't the killer, who offed the guy in our boot? His twin brother?"

"That's even more unlikely. The twins are devoted to one another." I released a long breath, feeling my headache increase in intensity every second. "It's time for you to call the embassy and bail. Leave me to deal with this mess."

"Absolutely not." He sounded appalled at the suggestion. "I'm in this just as deep as you are. I'm not leaving you to cope with a feral cat and a dead body on your own."

"I'm serious, Sidney. This situation has gotten way out of hand."

"I'm serious too. I say we call the police. Tell them the whole story. Even if Monty Carlyle has British police officers on his payroll, surely his influence doesn't extend to France."

I scowled at the uneven tarmac. "I wouldn't bet on it. Monty's tentacles extend far and wide."

"Okay. How about I buy the cat supplies, snacks, and other items on our list, including your painkillers. We'll deal with the cat, raise your sugar levels, and then we'll call the cops."

I sagged against the side of the Mercedes, too exhausted to argue anymore. "All right. Maybe an energy drink will revive my fighting spirit. And yes to contacting the police. I don't see how I can avoid it now. I've tried running, and what has it achieved? A boatload more trouble."

Sidney took a step toward me and placed a hand on my shoulder. Its weight was warm and comforting and made me feel less alone. "Wait in the car, Angel. And try not to worry. Once I've taken care of the shopping and Césaire, we'll call the police."

Despite the inappropriate timing, I yawned. "Thanks, Sidney, but I prefer to stay out here. The idea of getting into the car with the corpse freaks me out, even if he's locked away in the boot."

He squeezed my shoulder. "Understandable. I'll be back in a few minutes."

After he left, I peered through the back seat window. The cat glared at me through the bars of his cage, a snarling ball of aggression. "Only the fact that you're someone's much-loved pet is stopping me from dumping you here, cage and all. I like cats, but you're not a nice kitty."

Ignoring the cat's yowls from inside the vehicle, I leaned against the side of the car and tried to make the jigsaw puzzle make sense. Was Sidney correct? Had Cam killed the twin? If so, why? Cam was the kind of dude who preferred to use his fists on people who were no physical match for him. Neither twin fit that category. They could beat the living daylights out of Cam, singly or working as a demonic duo.

Yet one of the twins had wound up with a dagger in his chest. And as I'd seen no sign of any other members of Monty's gang, apart from Cam and the twins, I had to assume Cam was responsible. Framing me after the fact fit Cam's vicious personality. Had he planned to kill the man? Or had it happened during a violent dust-up between villains? And where was the other twin? Was he dead too? The Terrible Twins were tight. There's no way one brother would stand by and let the other be murdered.

I rubbed my eyes. They were sore and dry and felt like I'd scratched them with sandpaper. I couldn't face food, but I needed water, and I needed sleep. But first, we needed to deal with the dead body.

"Hey. Start the car."

I whipped around at the sharp sound of Sidney's voice. He hurried across the parking lot, lugging two large bags and clutching a newspaper under his arm. His face was scream-mask white and just as scary.

My stomach went into free fall. "What happened? Did you see Cam?"

He wrenched open the driver's door and hurled the carrier bags over his seat and into the back, precipitating another yowl fest from the cat. "Get in the car, Angel. Now."

Something in Sidney's tone made me obey. I'd barely clicked my belt into place when he gunned the engine and speed-reversed out of our spot. We shot out of the service station car park. Seconds later, we hit the motorway.

I slid a glance at his face. His profile was rigid with

tension. "No more grandma-speed driving? Now you've got me worried. What's up, Sidney?"

"This is what's up." He tossed the newspaper onto my lap.

The paper was an English tabloid, the sort that specialized in sex, scandal, and sport. I unfolded it, and my breath caught, my stomach roiled, and my head exploded with a silent scream.

The front-page headline didn't hold back: *Buxom Barmaid Murders Boss.*

Underneath those life-changing words was an overblown photograph of me.

Me.

I was the prime suspect in Frank's murder.

12

"This can't be happening." My words seemed to come from someone else, someone far away.

Ignoring smart night-driving protocol, I flipped on the passenger seat light and scanned the article. As I read and reread the words, a hard knot of panic-tinged rage formed in my stomach. My fingers curled into a fist, crushing the paper. "Becky says she saw me shoot Frank? And attributes my act to a lover's tiff? That's crazy. If either of us was interested in Frank, it was Becky, not me."

"Isn't Becky the girl whose shift you covered at the pub?" Sidney asked. "I think you mentioned her earlier."

"Yeah. Becky's a single mother from the Scottish Highlands. She moved to London a few months ago, started working at The Lucky Charm, and attached herself to me like a limpet. I thought she was clingy but harmless." My lips curled into a mockery of a smile. "I wonder how much she got paid to frame me. I knew she was strapped for cash, but I had no idea she'd throw me to the wolves to solve her financial problems."

"I'm sorry, Angel. That's awful. Won't there be security footage to back up your version of events?"

"Not a chance." My voice sounded dull, echoey. Like it belonged to someone else. "The gang will have made sure the security cameras were conveniently broken, and any recordings destroyed."

"What about fingerprints or other DNA evidence?" he pressed. "Surely there's got to be something to prove you're telling the truth?"

"It's a pub, Sidney. There'll be an abundance of fingerprints in the joint, including mine and the murderer's, but they'll have no bearing on the case. Neither Monty nor his men physically touched Frank. They didn't have to. They barged into the pub, shouting accusations and brandishing firearms. Frank didn't need much persuading to back away."

"And then they shot him," Sidney finished for me, as if sensing my reluctance to say the words out loud again.

"Yes." I stared through the window at the near-empty motorway, struggling to breathe, trying to process this fresh disaster. "How will I explain this to the police? With all that's happened over the last twenty-four hours, they'll lock me up for life."

"No police," Sidney said, delivering the words with a vehemence that surprised me. "Not tonight."

I blinked in confusion. "I thought you wanted me to contact the cops right away?"

"I did—before I spotted your photo on the front page of that rag. You've been framed for one murder, and now you're probably being framed for a second. We need to figure out what's going on and lawyer up before we approach the authorities. And as neither of us is in a fit state to think straight, we need sleep first."

"What about the dead body in the boot?" I asked. "How will we explain the delay between us discovering him and reporting his death?"

"Who's going to know when we opened the boot?"

"There's bound to be security cameras in the service station's parking lot," I pointed out. "If the police retrace our journey, they'll check them."

He flicked a hand in a dismissive gesture. "We'll let our lawyer deal with that minor detail."

"Our lawyer?" I couldn't help but smile. "Any lawyer with sense will contact the British Embassy and have you whisked out of the situation and leave me to rot."

"I won't let them." He shifted his gaze from the road to me. "I mean it, Angel. I'll do whatever I can to help you."

"Thanks, Sidney, but you barely know me."

"I know you well enough to be confident you didn't kill anyone." He swiped the dashboard screen. "Can you suggest a destination? I'm just following road signs."

I scrunched up my forehead and considered our options. This late at night, they were limited. I sighed. "Let's head for Nice after all. We've come this far. Might as well go all the way. We can find a hotel and look for Jerry in the morning."

"If we're going to Nice, why don't we break the laws of hospitality and head straight to your stepfather's house? Once you explain the situation, he'll understand."

I sighed. "No can do. I have a rough idea where Jerry works, but I don't have his home address. And even if I did, I don't want to roll up to his house in the middle of the night with a kidnapped cat and a corpse."

"Fair enough. Nice, here we come." Sidney pressed the button to activate the satnav. "One point confuses me."

I raised an eyebrow. "Only one? I have a whole list."

"You say Monty Carlyle is the vindictive type. However, would he go to the trouble of framing you for not one, but two murders, just because you shot him with a ketamine dart?"

"I also witnessed him kill a man in cold blood. Monty doesn't like witnesses. And then I humiliated him in front of his men by plugging his behind with a ketamine dart. So, yeah, I believe he'd come after me with full force."

"To the extent of framing you for two murders in less than a day? Even with his connections, that's quite a feat."

This was an excellent observation and one I'd have thought of myself had I been in possession of a functioning brain. I rubbed my aching head and breathed out a sigh. Sleep deprivation sucked. If I wanted to stay alive, I had to rest, recharge, and recalibrate. "I have no answers, Sidney. I don't even have the energy to come up with the right questions. I don't know why Boris/Ivan was killed or who killed him. I don't know why Cam is working with Monty's gang. For all I know, Monty framing me for Frank's death gave Cam the idea to frame me for the twin's murder."

"Who does Cam usually work for?"

"For his father, Sandy Carruthers."

"Why does that name sound familiar?" Sidney drummed the steering wheel. "I'm sure I've heard it in some context."

"Possibly the news," I said. "Sandy Carruthers is a loan shark from Glasgow who muscled his way onto the London scene a few years back. In addition to lending money for exorbitant rates, Sandy runs several backstreet gambling clubs. Despite his fists and his swagger, Cam's role was strictly office-related. He's a computer whiz and can hack into just about any system. That proved invaluable to his father for gathering dirt on borrowers who'd defaulted on their payments."

"Hacking, loan sharks...this sounds familiar. What did they do to make the front page?"

"An MP killed himself. It came out he'd borrowed a large sum of money from Sandy that he couldn't repay. When he defaulted, Sandy threatened to expose him for taking bribes from foreign governments."

Sidney whistled. "You're referring to the Alan Armitage case."

The story had been splashed across the news for months, helped by Armitage's squeaky-clean image and photogenic family. I wasn't surprised Sidney had connected the dots. "Correct. Cam created deepfake video recordings of Armitage allegedly meeting with foreign politicians and exchanging classified information for cash. They were convincing enough that Armitage felt he had no way out. But before he took his own life, he left a letter detailing the blackmail, and this led to Cam and me being hauled in for questioning."

"You? Surely you weren't involved in blackmail." Sidney's incredulity was oddly touching.

"No. I wasn't being targeted for the Armitage case. The police couldn't get charges to stick against Sandy Carruthers, so they went after Cam for the deepfakes. They knew I was Cam's girlfriend and correctly guessed I was aware of the work he did for his father.

While I hadn't known the content of the deepfakes, I could verify he had the technical know-how to create them."

"Why did you agree to help the police? Weren't you afraid Cam and his father would retaliate?"

"At the time this all went down, I wanted to get away from Cam. I'd tried to leave him a couple of times, and it hadn't gone well." The memories flooded back in a caustic wave of anger, self-loathing, and humiliation. I barely recognized the person I'd been back then.

"I'm sorry, Angel," Sidney said gently. "My brief encounter with Cam was enough to convince me he's not a good person."

I swallowed past the hard lump in my throat. "Yeah, well. He can be incredibly charming and vulnerable when he wants to be. Actually, those are his default behaviors. Most people never see his violent streak."

He quirked an eyebrow. "Should I consider myself privileged?"

His teasing tone made me laugh. "I wouldn't go that far. But to get back to my story, I'd been involved with depriving an online jewelry store of a certain quantity of stock—"

"Depriving?" Sidney snorted with laughter. "You have a way with words, Angel."

"—and the police used this as leverage to persuade me to copy files from Cam's computer. They were sure the computers they'd seized during their raids on our apartment and Cam's dad's office weren't the only ones Cam owned. And they were right. I was able to provide them with evidence that Cam had hacked into various government offices and used the information to splice and dice those videos to frame Armitage."

"Wow, Angel. That's deep. Weren't you scared to speak out about him?"

My laugh turned into a hiccup. "Petrified. But I was in a no-win situation. If I refused, the police had enough evidence against me to get me a prison sentence. Cam's dad wouldn't want to risk me making a plea bargain. He'd have ensured I left in a body bag."

"And by agreeing to help the police, you still landed on Cam's and his father's hit list?"

I nodded. "That about sums it up."

"Why weren't you placed in witness protection? Surely you'd have been a prime candidate."

"That was the carrot they dangled in front of my nose, but it was all hogwash." I gave a wan smile. "Outside of fiction, few witnesses get protection. I was neither saintly enough nor important enough to qualify. No, I agreed to cooperate because Alan Armitage's family deserved justice. I didn't approve of the man or his politics, but Cam's deepfakes led to him being accused of treason. After Armitage's suicide letter was made public, Sandy Carruthers went after his wife and kids. I couldn't let more innocent people get hurt."

"So you helped the police and started afresh?"

"Yeah. I figured my best bet was to lie low for a while and hope my dad smoothed things over with Carruthers."

Sidney's look of sympathy was gut-wrenchingly real. "That didn't happen?"

"Apparently not. I bounced around a bit after Cam was taken into custody. I spent a while in Ireland, then on the Isle of Man. I came back to London a few months ago when Frank offered me a job. Frank knew my dad, but he was never part of Sandy's crew. He agreed to give me work in the pub, and I agreed to keep a blind eye to his less-than-kosher dealings."

"If Cam got a prison sentence, what's he doing chasing you all over France? Why isn't he behind bars?"

"That's what's confusing me. He got a five-year sentence, and that was because he had a good lawyer who got the most serious charges dropped. Cam must be out on parole, either for good behavior or, more likely, because he cut a deal."

"Would the deal explain him hunting you down? Could he be a plant in Monty Carlyle's operation?"

I massaged the back of my neck. "It doesn't seem likely. Cam doesn't do subtle, and Monty's paranoid. Also, Sandy's line of business is totally different from Monty's. Monty specializes in heists. Think art thefts and jewel robberies. Sandy is a loan shark who runs gambling dens on the side. No, if Cam's working for Monty, it's a legit job in an illegal business."

"Maybe this is a one-off assignment," Sidney suggested, "because Cam has a grudge against you."

"Perhaps. He has a reason to want me in hot water. I'm just surprised he went from hacking to hanging out with the twins."

The satnav instructed Sidney to take the next exit. Soon, we were off the motorway and winding into the outskirts of Nice. Ordinarily, I'd have been straining to catch my first glimpse of the sea, but tonight, I was indifferent to the beauty of my surroundings.

"There's a hotel sign." Sidney pointed to a building to our right and flipped on the indicator. He pulled into the small parking lot and found a space. "I'll see if they have a vacancy. In the meantime, can you deal with the cat? I don't know if they'll let us take him into the hotel, but we need to get him fed and watered. I stocked up on snacks and drinks at the service station, and the shop assistant helped me find cat food."

The cat had quieted down during the journey from the service station to Nice, but he'd maintained a low-level mewling of discontent. In this heat, we couldn't leave him in the car overnight, regardless of the hotel's pet policy.

We got out of the car. Sidney hauled the shopping bags from the back seat and dumped them beside me. "If the hotel doesn't allow pets, we'll sneak him in. I suggest we deal with his needs before we go in, just in case. There's a pooper scooper in one of the bags, plus dried cat food. The other bag contains snacks for us and bottled water." He made a mock salute. "Good luck."

I pulled the pooper scooper out of the bag and eyed the cat, who stared back at me with slit-eyed defiance. "Is landing me with our feline friend revenge for the corpse?"

A hint of a smile broke through Sidney's somber expression. "Maybe."

"Go get us a room. I'll tackle the cat. He likes me better than you."

The cat was positively friendly this time, confining his attacks on me to a couple of half-hearted swipes across my arms. He remained quiet and cooperative while I cleaned his cage and refilled his bowls with fresh food and water. He was tucking in to a packet of kibble when Sidney exited the hotel and jogged over to join us.

"We got a room," he announced with an air of triumph, "and they accept cats. Even better, the receptionist sold me a bunch of travel-sized toiletries we can use until we can replace the ones that disappeared with the suitcase. The price was exorbitant, but I was desperate."

"We can shower," I said, glowing at the idea of this simple pleasure. "And brush our teeth."

"Your latest alias is Anne Marchand, by the way. Mine is Paul Edwards."

I frowned. "Didn't they check your ID?"

He grinned. "I flashed it in front of the receptionist, but he barely glanced at it."

"Awesome. Thanks for sorting that out."

His grin widened. "I doubt you'll be thanking me when you see the state of the room. They only had one with a double bed left, so I'll take the floor."

"Are you looking out for my virtue?" I asked archly. "If so, you're too late. No, I don't mind sharing the bed with you. I trust you to keep your paws to yourself, and you can trust me to knee you where it hurts if you don't."

Sidney winced. "I hurt just thinking about that."

He helped me get the cat back into his now-clean cage and clear up the rubbish. We hauled our sorry collection of belongings into the hotel, where the receptionist didn't bother to look up from his computer screen.

Our room was on the top floor, under the gabled roof, and didn't have air-conditioning. Césaire refused to get back into his cage and curled up on a pillow at the foot of the bed. I was too tired to object. After a quick shower, I put on my T-shirt and washed my underwear in the sink. In this heat, they'd be dry by morning. I'd have to wear today's clothes again, but at least I'd have clean undies.

Sidney consumed half the contents of the snack bag before he had his shower. I couldn't face the limp sandwich he'd tried to persuade me to eat. I shoved a few nuts into my mouth for energy and washed them down with water.

"Let's sleep until we wake," Sidney said, carefully positioning himself as far away from me as the cramped bed would allow. "The cat's happy, and Boris/Ivan will still be dead in the morning. Then we can find your former stepfather. What does he do for a living, by the way? Your vague description of him made me think of a vicar. Or a scholar. Or a failed politician."

"None of the above. Jerry runs a theatrical costumier."

Sidney perked up at the mention of costumes, leaning on his elbows. "Seriously? Do you think he's hiring? I have experience repairing costumes. I can knit, sew, and I'm a dab hand with a steam iron."

I cocked an eyebrow. "Are you planning to jettison your promising career in diplomacy for a job sorting tatty rental costumes?"

"If Jerry is willing to pay me, then absolutely. I adore costumes. There's something magical about slipping on a costume and instantly becoming someone else."

I thought of my hideous pastel pink outfit. I hadn't felt the least magical pretending to be Monique Beaufour. "Whatever floats your boat, I guess. I've never been interested in performing."

"What do you like?"

"Hiding behind a computer screen. I'm not a people person. I like that layer of distance. The bar job was bearable because I mostly got to stay behind the counter and pull pints."

"I can't imagine life behind a screen. I thrive on interacting with people."

"I have no idea if Jerry's looking for staff. You can ask. Only wait until after we've hit him with the news that we're traveling with a kidnapped cat and a dead body."

Sidney's face fell at my blunt reminder of our second unwanted traveling companion. "It's not a great impression to make on a prospective employer. However, it's not like we killed the man."

"No, but rolling up and announcing we've got a corpse in the car is on the unorthodox side of normal."

He shivered and drew his arms around him, finally showing signs of flagging energy. "I can't believe all that's happened today."

"I can believe it, unfortunately." I stifled my yawn in the crook of my arm. "Let's get some sleep. I'm beat."

"Angel? It'll be okay. I don't know how, but I truly believe we'll get this mess sorted out."

I gave him a shaky smile. "Sure we will."

If I repeated this enough times, I might start to believe it.

13

In the last twenty-four hours, I'd witnessed a murder, rescued a cat, and discovered a dead dude in the boot of my car. And a fitting end to my day? Making it onto Europol's Most Wanted list.

It was two fifteen in the morning. We'd switched off the light an hour ago, yet I still hadn't fallen asleep. Sidney, in contrast, had conked out mid-sentence. His soft snores reverberated from the pillow beside mine— a pillow that encroached onto my side of the bed. I gave him a shove. He snorted, stretched out an arm, and continued to snore.

With a sigh of resignation, I shifted position on the hotel's thin excuse for a mattress, shivering despite the heat. Without air-conditioning, the atmosphere in our cramped attic room was sweltering, yet I couldn't make my limbs stop shaking. My nonstop shivering was due to shock, as were my stomach cramps. But knowing their cause didn't make them go away.

I put my pillow over my head, huddled under the thin sheet, and tried to sleep. It didn't work. Thoughts raced through my mind, too fragmented to make sense. Questions tumbled by in quick-fire succession. How had Cam wound up joining Monty's motley crew? Why had the twin been killed? And by whom?

Only one fact was crystal clear. Monty Carlyle wanted me dead. And not just for plugging his behind with a ketamine dart. He was framing me for Frank's murder and making sure I never had the chance to mount a defense.

I curled into a ball. My mind needed an off switch. I was bone-tired, zapped of all energy, brain too fried to devise a brilliant plan to stay alive. On impulse, I swung my legs out of bed and scooped up Césaire from his pillow. The cat greeted me with a sleepy purr and a quick lick. "Wanna bunk down with me for the night?" I asked, stroking his soft fur. "I could do with snuggles."

He gave a soft meow. I took this to be an agreement. Back in the bed, the cat nestled close to my chest, his throaty purrs calming me. I closed my eyes and tried to block Sidney's snores, the light from the streetlamp, and the memories crushing my skull. I was pretty sure the mattress came with tenants, but I was too tired to care about bug bites.

I expected sleep to elude me. Instead, I dozed off within seconds. When the cat woke me, demanding his breakfast, it was shortly before seven. The sun streamed through the thin curtains, bathing our shabby hotel room in the warm glow of Mediterranean light. The temperature was lower than it had been during the night, but this brief respite from the heat wouldn't last. The French Riviera in July was sweltering.

I sat up and moved my neck from side to side, stiff from yet another stint of sleeping in a less-than-ideal position. At this rate, I'd need a deep-tissue massage to feel human again.

Once I'd persuaded my neck to move again, I rolled out of bed and took care of the cat's needs. Then I took a lukewarm shower in our pitiful excuse for a bathroom. After my shower, I blasted my hair with the hairdryer and dressed in the outfit I'd worn yesterday. At least the red scoop-necked T-shirt matched my purloined lipstick.

I completed my morning ablutions with an application of sunscreen from the tiny travel-sized tube Sidney had purchased at reception. I'd inherited my dad's pale Irish skin. Without protection, I'd fry. And with the scratches on my cheek, I needed to be doubly vigilant—antiseptic cream was a must-buy item.

When I emerged from the bathroom, Sidney was still asleep. Unbelievable. We had bad guys on our tail and a corpse in the car, and he was still in the land of Nod. I gave him a shake. "Wakey wakey, Sleeping Beauty."

Sidney opened his eyes and sat straight up in bed.

"Good morning, Angel. Did you sleep well?" His tone was upbeat and perky. Sidney, it seemed, was a morning person.

"I slept," I muttered. "Eventually. Did you know you snore?"

He looked genuinely shocked. "No way."

"Like a foghorn." This was an exaggeration, but I enjoyed watching his mouth gape in horror.

"No way. You must've imagined it." Dismissing my accusation with a cheery smile, Sidney swung himself out of bed and gave me a quick appraisal. "You have curls."

I fingered my damp hair and grimaced. "Yeah. I don't have my sprays and hair straightener."

"Curly hair suits you."

"Just as well. I need to look as unlike my usual self as possible, and wearing wigs in this heat isn't happening."

"We could dye it." He reached out and examined my hair. "I take it the jet black with magenta tips isn't your natural hair color?"

I laughed. "Hardly. I'm a strawberry blonde."

He cocked his head to the side, considering. "We could dye it blond. Or light red to get it close to your natural shade. That'll make it harder for Cam and his pals to recognize you."

I glanced at my watch. "Let's hit the pause button on my makeover, shall we? I'm not ruling out a new color, but we don't have time to bleach and re-dye my hair even if we had the tools. I want to catch Jerry when his shop opens for business."

"Do I have time to shower?" He fingered his T-shirt. "I'm a sweaty mess."

"Okay, but make it snappy."

"What about breakfast?" He stared at the snack bag with a forlorn expression. "I don't operate without breakfast."

"You snooze, you lose, man. You can eat in the car."

He grumbled but complied. Twenty minutes later, we were back at the Mercedes. We both hesitated before getting in the car, our attention fixed on the boot.

"Should we check on the corpse?" Sidney asked, making no move to do so.

"Check what, exactly? That he's still dead? No way are we opening the boot until we absolutely have to. We can't risk someone seeing the dead body and alerting the police before we've lawyered up."

"If we have to drive with him still in situ, I'm spraying the car with deodorant. In this heat, he'll start stinking soon."

After I'd stowed Césaire's cage in the back, I slid behind the wheel. And inhaled the result of Sidney's spraying frenzy. "Whoa, dude," I exclaimed, gasping for air. "You went way overboard on the deodorant."

"Better than the smell of death," Sidney replied between coughs. "But, yeah, I may've been overly enthusiastic with the trigger."

"May have? My lungs are burning." I rolled down my window and took a gulp of fresh air. Then I started the car. I drove considerably faster than Sidney's grandma pace, and we zipped through Nice. As it was a Saturday, the city was just waking up when we reached the center. I cruised down narrow backstreets, craning to read the signs over shop doors.

"Do you know where your stepfather's place is?" Sidney asked when I'd taken us down the same street for the third time.

"Jerry's a *former* stepfather, two marriages back. I saw the address on a Christmas card he sent me a couple of years ago, but I guess I misremembered it. It's got to be somewhere near the Russian Orthodox Cathedral. Look out for a sign for Jerry Gallo, Costumier. Or J. Gallo, Costumier."

I took the next left and plunged down a winding street peppered with people starting their day. Locals lounged in the sun in outdoor cafés, and early-bird tourists headed to the beach.

"Over there on the left." Sidney waved a frantic hand in front of my face. "Next to the bistro. Gallo Costumier."

I checked it out. Sure enough, the gold lettering on the burgundy sign proved he was correct. "Excellent work. Now we just need to find a place to park."

I found a spot in a public car park a few streets away from Jerry's place.

When we got out of the car, Sidney wiped the back

of his hand across his forehead. "This day is shaping up to be a scorcher."

"Yeah." It wasn't yet eight o'clock, and sweat was already trickling down my back, making my T-shirt stick to me like glue. "We'll have to take Césaire with us. We can't leave him in the hot car." Especially not with a decaying dead body. I left that thought unspoken.

Sidney grabbed the cage and pulled it free from the back seat. The cat peered between the bars and gave a half-hearted snarl. "I think he's warming to us," Sidney said.

I suppressed a smile. "He's warming to *me*. Not sure about you. Let's see how he behaves the next time you're on cage-cleaning duty."

We trudged back to Jerry's street, dodging delivery bikes, street cleaners, and tourists. I had the eerie feeling of being shadowed. Yet every time I swung around to see who was there, all I saw was normal people doing normal things. I shook myself, physically and mentally. It was paranoia. No one but Sidney knew I was in Nice.

When we reached the costumier, the door was locked. According to the sign, it wouldn't open until ten. My stomach sank. I should've considered opening times. I didn't want to wait another two hours to find Jerry. The clock was ticking. We had a corpse rotting in the back of the car and no clue how long it'd take before the police or Monty's men caught up with us.

I stood back and surveyed the street. The costumier was wedged between a café-bistro and a yarn shop. The other buildings on the street appeared to be a mix of offices and residential. Like the costumier, the yarn shop wouldn't open before ten, but the café already had patrons seated at its few street-side tables. I reached for the door handle. "Wait here with Césaire. I'll see if anyone knows where I can find Jerry at this time of day."

The air-conditioning hit me the moment I stepped inside the café. I basked in its welcome coolness and surveyed my surroundings. The place was a throwback to an earlier time. Wooden tables and matching fold-down chairs were crammed close together. Vintage advertisements hung on the walls, depicting products ranging from soaps to petticoats.

The indoor tables were deserted, as were those in the walled garden at the rear of the café. Two tourists speaking Spanish left as I came in, armed with takeout coffees. The door swung shut behind them, leaving me alone with the café's sole occupant.

The man behind the counter had his back to me, grinding coffee beans. The rich aroma was pure sensory bliss. Unfortunately, my enjoyment of the cozy morning scent was dampened by a prickle of uneasiness. Even with his back turned, the café's lone occupant dominated his surroundings. He had close-cropped dark hair, skin tanned a rich brown under his tattoos, and was constructed of pure muscle. He looked exactly like the kind of guy Monty or Cam's dad would hire to do their dirty work.

When the man turned to face me, the prickle of uneasiness crystallized into a crackling panic. I breathed through my fear. This man was no threat to me. He had no idea who I was. He just happened to have the build and attitude of men who'd hurt me in the past.

After my mental pep talk, I turned a steady gaze on him. His eyes were a startling blue against the deep tan of his face. He was good-looking in a rugged kind of way, with high cheekbones, a strong jaw, and a nose that had recently been on the receiving end of a fist.

"How's the other guy looking?" I asked in French. The words tumbled out before I had a chance to engage my brain.

His expression didn't alter one iota. "The other guy's dead."

Something told me he was serious. Something also told me that there was context here and I didn't need to panic. At least, not yet. And honestly, with a corpse in the back of my car, who was I to judge?

The man's eyes flickered over me with a cool disinterest I'd have found insulting under other circumstances. "You're not looking too hot yourself." He gestured to my cheek. "Did you have a close encounter with a razor?"

"No. I enraged a cat."

"That figures. Do you want to order a coffee? Or

are you just here to exchange insults?" His gravelly voice sounded like he gargled with whiskey and pebbles. The tone was heavy with sarcasm.

I met him stare for stare. "I'm looking for your neighbor, Jerry Gallo, but his place doesn't open until ten. Do you know where I can find him before then?"

The man didn't answer, but those intense blue eyes seemed to bore into my soul. The seconds ticked by in a loaded silence.

Finally, I could take it no longer. "It's a simple question. Do you know where I can find Jerry? Yes or no?"

"Knock on the side door in the lane between the costumier and the yarn shop. Jerry's usually in his office by this time." Having honored me with a response, the man turned back to the coffee machine. I'd been dismissed, and I didn't like it.

If he'd been less obnoxious, I'd have ordered a cup of that delicious-smelling brew. But I had no desire to prolong this encounter. I'd had my fill of arrogant alpha males. With a muttered thanks, I turned tail and left the café.

Out on the pavement, Sidney sweated under the rapidly rising heat and the weight of Césaire's cage. "Do they serve iced coffees?"

"I don't know, and I don't care." I jerked a thumb at the costumier. "Apparently, there's a side door."

Three young men on motorbikes whizzed down the street. As they neared a corner, one of the bikes backfired. The crack sounded like a gunshot. I was pretty sure several of my internal organs were no longer in their original positions.

Césaire arched his back and yowled. Meanwhile, Sidney clutched his stomach and groaned. "I just retasted my breakfast. And it didn't taste good the first time around."

If the non-reactions of the other people on the street were any indication, backfiring motorcycles were a known quantity. "Not so much as a backward glance," I murmured. "I wonder how long it'd take people around here to notice gunfire?"

"It's the heat," he said. "It's melted their minds. It's sure melting mine."

After the backfiring motorbike incident, the feeling we were being followed returned in full force. I whipped around several times but saw no one suspicious. I quickened my pace. The sooner we got off the street, the safer I'd feel.

We passed the costumier's shop front and entered a side lane so narrow that I hadn't noticed it when we'd first walked by. It was a single-file affair that divided the costumier from the yarn shop by a razor-thin margin.

"Does this even qualify as a lane?" Sidney asked, huffing under the weight of the cage. "It's more like an accidental gap between buildings."

"It's a lane of sorts, and it's got a door. That's all I care about."

I hovered my hand over the bell, index finger outstretched. I couldn't bring myself to press it. What in the world was I doing here? I barely knew Jerry Gallo. He barely knew me. My story was wild, even if it was the truth. Would a quiet, unassuming guy like Jerry help a wanted woman, her zany sidekick, and a kidnapped cat?

"Angel?" Sidney placed a hand on my shoulder. "It'll be okay. One way or the other. We'll find a way out of this mess."

Tears stung my eyes. I blinked them back and swallowed past the lump in my throat. Sidney was kind, a good person. He'd been an idiot to keep his phone after I'd told him to get rid of it, but he'd done so out of cluelessness, not recklessness. He didn't deserve to be hurt by Cam and his pals. I hadn't wanted him along for the ride, but right now, I was glad of his company. I'd helped get him into this mess. It was up to me to get him out.

I took a deep breath and pressed the bell.

14

―――――

*A*fter a couple of minutes, the door opened a crack, the security chain still in place. A heavyset woman wearing a purple turban and a tangerine maxi dress peered at us through the links of the chain. She had the world-weary expression of someone who'd seen a lot, had done more, and wasn't impressed by any of it. Her wary expression softened when she saw the cat. "We're not open yet." She delivered her French in a rasp that spoke of cigarettes and hard living. "Come back at ten."

"We're here to see Jerry," I replied in the same language. "I'm his stepdaughter." Okay, *ex*-stepdaughter, but there was no need to split hairs.

The woman's heavily kohled eyes widened. "Angélique?"

"You know my name?" I examined her more closely. No bells rang. Had I met this woman before?

"Of course, I know who you are. Hang on a sec." She released the chain and opened the door wide, ushering us into the dimly lit hallway. Her long earrings jangled when she moved, delighting the cat. "I'm Francine. Don't you remember me?"

I took her in again, memories cascading through my mind in a mad kaleidoscope. My mother had had a friend called Francine, a stripper at a nightclub. Her trademark had been to never wear many clothes, on or off the clock. They'd met on the set of an adult movie. Francine had got both of them fired after demonstrating her self-defense skills on the director's crotch.

As if reading my mind, Francine laughed. "It's me, all right, but with more padding and more clothing. Twenty years will do that to a girl." Her attention shifted to Sidney. "Who's your handsome friend?"

Sidney held out a hand, ever the gentleman. "Sidney Foggington-Smythe. Pleased to meet you."

My jaw descended in slow-mo. "Whoa, friend. Mind. Blown. What did I just hear?"

"Peregrine Sidney Roland Foggington-Smythe, to be precise." His lips twitched. "What can I say? The British upper classes love to saddle their offspring with pompous monikers."

I shook my head in wonderment. "And I thought my name was bad." Francine looked confused, reminding me I'd reverted to English. "Sorry," I said in French. "An in-joke."

She dropped her gaze to the cage. "Is this your cat?"

"Oh, no. He's not our cat. We're just—" I shot a desperate glance at Sidney.

"Cat-sitting," he finished for me. "We're just cat-sitting."

The woman cooed at the animal. "Are you getting in practice for when you have your own little ones?"

My cheeks grew warm. Sidney was good-looking in a scrawny, '70s rocker kind of way, but I hadn't considered him in a romantic light. I wasn't even sure he was into girls. Sidney flashed me a wicked grin. Clearly, he wasn't going to help me out of this one.

Moving on from our reproduction plans, Francine led us down the hallway, pausing before a door to our left. "I would've recognized you anywhere, Angélique," she said over her shoulder.

My blood ran cold. Had Frank's death hit the French news? It was only a matter of time, especially if there was an international warrant out for my arrest. "That's impressive," I managed. "You haven't seen me since I was a kid."

"There's a photo of you upstairs. You must've been fifteen or sixteen at the time it was taken."

I slow-blinked. Jerry kept a photo of teenage me? I could barely remember what the guy looked like. I had a vague memory of a stocky man with silver-streaked dark hair and a mustache worthy of Tom Selleck. His quiet, serious demeanor had been no match for my exuberant mother's drama. She'd totally overshadowed him. Jerry'd been kind to me during the couple of summers I'd spent with them during their short-lived marriage, but I hadn't expected his affection to extend to keeping a photo of me years later. I wasn't sure how I felt about this revelation.

Francine opened the door, and we stepped into the shop. Its space was more extensive than it had looked from the outside. Every spare inch was packed with racks upon racks of colorful costumes. Some stands were labeled according to time era. Others according to theme.

"Wow. This place is amazing." Sidney put the cat cage on the counter and checked out the tightly packed racks, pausing to exclaim over a pair of garish sequined pants. "All these gorgeous outfits."

"We pride ourselves on being the premier theatrical costumier in the area," Francine said. "All the best theater companies come to us for their outfits. Some TV and film productions, but mostly opera and theater." She turned to me. "This is a wonderful surprise. He'll be delighted to see you."

Heat spread up my cheeks, and my insides squirmed. Would Jerry be happy to see me? I wasn't convinced, especially not once I'd told him my reason for arriving on his doorstep unannounced. "If Jerry's busy, I don't want to disturb him."

"You won't disturb him, honey. Go on up to his office. It's the first door on the right." Francine bent down to the cage and loosened the latch. "Meanwhile, I'll let this little creature stretch his legs."

I exchanged a look of alarm with Sidney. "Is that wise? His claws are responsible for our shredded arms and the state of my cheek."

Francine, holding the cat tenderly in her arms, stared at me in surprise. "This little darling? But he's a perfect pet."

As if on cue, the cat snuggled against her chest and purred.

"Unbelievable," Sidney exclaimed. "That cat hates me."

I stifled a grin. "He's not wild about me, either. But Francine's right. He'll benefit from a little freedom. For all we know, his bad behavior yesterday was due to being cooped up in that cage for too long."

Sidney's eyes grew saucer-large. "Are you insane? You saw what that creature did to your wig. He'll wreck the place."

"He's much calmer today," I said, not sounding convinced. "Aren't you, sweetheart?"

Césaire stared back at me with large, innocent eyes. Had our night of snuggles softened his attitude?

"You're not fooling me," Sidney told him, stern-faced. "Not for one second."

The cat yawned, displaying an impressive set of teeth that were as sharp as its claws.

Sidney took a step back, colliding with a clothes

rack. "Did you see those teeth, Angel? If I have no face left by the time you return, it's on you."

I grinned. "He seems happy with Francine. Let him do his thing and don't get too close."

I left the shop and took the creaky wooden stairs up to the next floor. The hallway was deserted and smelled faintly of mothballs. A few faded posters hung on the walls, curling at the edges. All were from old theatrical productions. Despite Sidney's enthusiasm and Francine's pride in the place, I got the impression that Jerry's joint had seen better days.

As instructed, I paused outside the first door on the right. There was no sign to indicate I'd reached Jerry's office, but then, the costumier appeared to be run on a skeleton staff. Perhaps there was no need to put a sign on the boss's office door. Maybe Jerry liked the anonymity.

I knocked and waited for him to respond.

He didn't.

I waited for a full minute, counting the seconds, and then knocked again. Still nada. Maybe Jerry was on a toilet break. Perhaps he'd nipped out without telling Francine. But I didn't think so.

A leaden uneasiness settled in my stomach. I didn't believe in the sixth sense, and I definitely didn't think I had one. What I did have was a finely tuned gut instinct. Right now, my gut was telling me to turn tail and run.

Pity I'd never been good at following my own

advice. I reached for the handle. The door was unlocked, so I opened it and stepped inside.

The first thing that hit me was the smell. An acrid rusty scent warred with an overabundance of musk and jasmine to create a nauseating olfactory overload.

My second impression was that my Spidey-senses had been right. Jerry Gallo's lousy start to the day eclipsed even mine. In addition to the unfortunate '70s-style decor, his office looked like a tornado had passed through. Filing cabinet drawers were open, the contents spilling out. Random papers covered the floor. A picture on the wall was askew, revealing an unopened safe.

In the middle of this maelstrom, the man I'd hoped would bail me out of my mess lay sprawled across his desk, face down on a pile of papers. Protruding from his shoulder was a gold-hilted dagger. And beside him, her hands covered in blood, stood my mother.

15

We blinked at one another in terrified disbelief as mutual recognition dawned.

"Maman?"

"Angélique?" Her gaze darted from me to Jerry before dropping to her hands, as though seeing the blood on them for the first time. Her rosebud lips parted, forming an elegant O. "Did you do this?"

The accusation had a triggering effect. Raw anger surged through me at lightning speed. Desirée Chablis would never win Mother of the Year. We hadn't seen one another in four years, barely kept in touch, and her first reaction upon seeing her only child was to accuse me of killing a man? After being framed for one murder and presumably a second, I was done being everyone's default villain. "I just walked in. Did you hurt Jerry? You're the one with blood on your hands. Literally."

My mother's baby-blue eyes widened, registering a mix of shock and hurt. "Of course not. He was lying there when I came into the office. I touched him, and —" she broke off on a sob. The bosom of her plunge-necked, figure-hugging dress inflated, charting the progress of her deep intake of breath. And then she emitted a wail worthy of a banshee.

The noise rose to operatic proportions. Unless the entire neighborhood was hard of hearing, we'd have company before my mother ran out of oxygen. Sure enough, the sound of movement came from downstairs —the scrape of a chair on wood, followed by the scramble of feet.

I didn't have time to wait for backup to arrive. I grabbed a vase of roses from the windowsill and hurled the contents over my mother. "Put a sock in it and call an ambulance."

The shock of being drenched in a floral arrangement cut short my mother's impromptu concert. Ignoring her spluttered indignation, I pushed past her and bent over the fallen man.

Jerry sported an impressive gash on the side of his head, in addition to the blade sticking out of his shoulder. The cause of the head wound wasn't hard to find. A blood-smeared blue Murano paperweight lay next to him on the desk. And now that I was eyeballing it close up, what I'd taken to be a dagger was a fancy letter opener. The use of office implements indicated this was a spur-of-the-moment crime. Did that make it more or less likely that my mother was the culprit? And if she wasn't, was the perpetrator still lurking in the building? I glanced up at my mother. "Did you at least check him for a pulse?"

"I didn't have a chance. I'd just found him when you appeared." She brushed a rose off the front of her dress and reached for the telephone on the desk. Her hands were unsteady and she fumbled with the old-fashioned rotary dial.

Swallowing past my revulsion at touching a potential corpse, I placed two fingers on Jerry's neck. I was no first aid expert, but I'd acquired a trick or two over the years. I'd had the opportunity to brush up my skills during my recent Irish adventure with my P.I. cousin and an ever-growing stack of dead bodies. I closed my eyes and focused.

At first, I felt nothing. Then a gentle beat pulsed beneath my fingertips, faint but steady. I blinked and released a ragged breath. "He's still alive."

"Thank goodness." My mother connected with the dispatcher and rattled off instructions.

I hoped to goodness the ambulance would get here fast. Jerry was breathing, but barely.

The thunder of feet on the wooden stairs grew louder. A moment later, the office door burst open. Sidney tumbled in, Césaire attached to his head, making them look like a prehistoric monster. Francine staggered into the office behind Sidney, panting from the exertion of her run up the stairs. Her gaze swept the wreckage of the room, coming to rest on Jerry's slumped form. She let out a squawk and doubled up as though an invisible force had punched her in the solar plexus. "*Mon Dieu.*"

Horror, disbelief, and then resignation flickered over Sidney's face in rapid succession. "Seriously, Angel? Not another corpse. We still haven't gotten rid of the dead Russian."

"What dead Russian?" My mother hung up the telephone receiver and pivoted to face me. "Is that why you're in Nice?"

"It's a long story." I silently cursed Sidney for mentioning our corpse.

Francine backed toward the door, her gaze fixed on me. "Did you kill Jerry, Angélique? Are you a hitwoman? Who hired you?"

The questions spilled out in a rush, each one blending into the other, flaying my already raw nerves.

Sidney gaped at Francine. "Why would you think Angel's a hired killer?"

"You talked about a dead Russian. Did Angel kill this Russian? Did she kill Jerry?"

"No," Sidney said. "And neither did I. We just found his body in the boot of our car. Well, it's not exactly our car, but—"

"Leave it, Sidney. Now's not the moment for this conversation." Sharp prickles of anger spread down my neck. My mother hadn't stood up for me against Francine's accusations, leaving it to a virtual stranger to defend me. So much for family loyalty. "Jerry's alive, Francine. And if the ambulance gets here fast, he might stay that way. Do any of you know first aid? I'm afraid to move him in case the blade goes in deeper, but I don't know if this is the correct position to keep him in."

Radiating distrust, Francine snatched a cushion off the window ledge. Then she eased Jerry's head off the desk and angled the cushion under it so he had more room to breathe. I was still smarting over her wild allegations, but at least the woman seemed to know what she was doing.

The wail of sirens sounded in the distance, growing louder by the second. I prayed they were heading our way.

"That'll be the paramedics." My mother wiped her damp face dry with a wad of tissues from the box on Jerry's desk. "Angel and her friend should wait upstairs. We don't want them involved."

Francine, still bending over Jerry, shot me a look of undiluted venom. "Don't we?"

"No, we don't." Just three words, yet my mother infused each syllable with subtext.

The women exchanged loaded looks. My mother—stony and steel-eyed. Francine—resentful and belligerent. What was going on here? Why did Desirée want Sidney and me out of the way? If she'd been a better mother, I'd have chalked it up to a maternal instinct to protect her child. However, given her lack of interest in me and my welfare, that can't have been the reason.

Their exchange couldn't have lasted more than a couple of seconds, but those seconds passed in slow motion. The peal of the doorbell signaled an end to their cold war.

Francine's lip curled. "All right. Sidney and Angel can go up to the apartment as long as they promise to stay put. Once Jerry's in the care of the paramedics, I want a word with your daughter and her friend."

With a silent nod, my mother disappeared into the corridor, followed by the clickety-click of stilettos on wood as she descended the stairs.

Francine reached into her skirt pocket and pulled out a key. "Jerry's apartment is on the next level. I'll be up as soon as the paramedics take over. If you pull a Houdini, I swear I'll hunt you down and make you regret you ever showed your faces in our shop."

I held up my hands in a gesture of surrender. "Chill. I promise we'll stay in Jerry's apartment. Frankly, we have nowhere else to go."

With a labored sigh, she handed Sidney the key. "Be quick. The paramedics are coming up the stairs."

Sidney didn't need to be told twice. He detached Césaire from his head and thrust the cat into my arms. Then he darted out of the room with the speed of a gazelle on amphetamines.

Césaire squirmed and whined, struggling to get free. "Hang on, kitty cat. You can roam when we get upstairs."

I looked over my shoulder at poor Jerry's broken body. Hot tears stung my eyes. I hadn't seen the man in years, but he'd always been kind to me. "Hang in there," I whispered. "Please don't die."

Francine didn't say another word to me. She didn't have to. The power of her glare on my retreating back pricked me with pins as surely as if I were a voodoo doll.

Sidney and I passed my mother and the paramedics on our way to the staircase, but no one paid us any attention. The staircase narrowed the higher we climbed. At the top, we didn't need to wonder which door was Jerry's. There was only one.

The welcome hum of a well-tuned air-conditioning system greeted us when we stepped inside the apartment. Jerry's open-plan home was surprisingly modern compared to the rest of the building. Instead of the frozen-in-time look of his office, the apartment hinted at a recent renovation. Sparkling white walls, sleek furniture, and a marble-and-chrome kitchen. The polished wooden floor had several luxuriant rugs thrown about in deceptively haphazard fashion, and framed prints of famous paintings of the Impressionist era decorated the walls.

I sat Césaire on the floor. He leaped onto a rug and dug his claws into the fluffy material. I didn't have the energy to stop him. Instead, I collapsed on a black-and-white sofa and wrapped my arms around myself. "Please tell me I'm having a nightmare. This can't be happening."

"You're not, and it is." Sidney cast me a look of concern. "I'm sorry your stepfather got hurt, Angel. His injuries looked bad."

"The letter opener in his shoulder looks dramatic, but it won't prove fatal. I'm less optimistic about the gash on his head." I put my head in my hands and groaned. "I'm starting to feel cursed."

"There was nothing supernatural about Jerry's injuries. Any idea who attacked him?"

I released a shuddery breath. "I'm as much in the dark as you are. I don't understand why anyone would want to hurt Jerry. Unless he's had a personality transplant since we last met, he's a quiet, unassuming man. If my father were attacked, there'd be any number of suspects to choose from. But Jerry's not like my dad. He earns his crust by renting out theatrical costumes, for heaven's sake. Who'd want to hurt a guy like that?"

"A disgruntled ex-employee? Someone with a personal grudge?" Sidney rubbed the back of his neck and loped over to the kitchen. "I need a coffee, and I bet you do too."

"Sorry to disappoint you, but unless he's mended his ways, Jerry's a notorious tea drinker."

Sidney screwed up his nose. "I don't do tea. Very

un-British of me, I know, but I've never been able to stand the stuff." He opened the fridge and examined its contents. "There's a pitcher of lemonade. Want a glass?"

"Sure." I didn't care much what I drank, but I sensed Sidney needed to keep busy. "What next?" I asked when he handed me my glass of lemonade. "We can't stay here. With Jerry out of commission, he won't be able to hook us up with a lawyer. We're on our own."

"I agree that we need to leave, but we'll have to get past Francine." Sidney sank onto the sofa beside me. "I can't get over her one-eighty. She went from over-friendly to hostile in the blink of an eye."

"Yeah. It gave me emotional whiplash. I guess seeing Jerry shook her up."

"Why did she accuse you of being an assassin, though? Even with Jerry lying injured, that seemed excessive."

"How should I know? Everyone else seems keen to pin murders on me. Why not Francine too?"

"Who was the blonde in the office? The one covered in water and flower petals?" A line formed between his brows. "She looked familiar, but I can't place her. It's driving me bonkers."

If my mother had been naked, Sidney might've recognized her. I quashed the snarky comment that sprang to my mind. My relationship with my mother—

or lack thereof—was my business. "She's not important."

"Are you sure? She was standing right next to the desk. I think she had blood on her hands, but from the angle I saw her, I might've imagined it."

My response was a noncommittal grunt. I drained my glass and set it on the frosted glass coffee table. "We should get going before the police show up."

"We'll have to face them soon, though. Any idea how we'll find a lawyer?"

I scanned the apartment. "Do you see a computer anywhere?"

We got up and searched the apartment, coming up empty.

Sidney scratched his chin. "That's weird. There's not so much as a tablet up here."

"No sign of a phone, either." I sighed. "Never mind. Cracking the password would've taken too long, anyway. No, we'll have to go the old-fashioned route and find a library. They'll have computers we can use to access the internet. Perhaps even an old-school telephone directory. What's your cash situation like?"

"I have several hundred euros left." At my raised eyebrow, he added, "Hey, you told me to withdraw plenty of money in Montpellier."

"Okay. That might swing a down payment with a lawyer." I scooped Césaire off what remained of the rug. The cat wasn't happy to be removed from his new favorite toy, and punished me by adding a fresh scrape across my forearm. I winced, but kept moving.

Sidney reached for the handle, but the door swung open before his fingers made contact with the metal.

Francine's bulk filled the doorframe, wafting patchouli oil and righteous indignation. In her right hand, she held a pistol. "Going somewhere?"

16

Sidney and I scrambled back from the doorway, putting distance between us and Francine. In her floaty dress and purple turban, she seemed an unlikely gunslinger. But if you'd asked me two days ago, I would've said I was an unlikely murder suspect. Times changed. And the pistol in her hand looked the real deal. Especially when she lowered the muzzle and aimed it directly at my heart.

"Nice try, but you work with costumes. I presume you have theatrical props on hand too." My voice was steady, but the pulse in my neck pounded a painful rhythm. I'd tussled with tougher broads than this woman, and I refused to be intimidated.

My resolution lasted all of five seconds. The familiar click of a safety catch being released shattered my illusions of being in control.

"Do you want me to put it to the test? I'm happy to use you as my target. Or would you rather I demonstrate on your friend?"

Beside me, Sidney squeaked something unintelligible.

Sensing the charged atmosphere and wanting no part of it, Césaire hissed and bucked in my arms. I released my grip on the cat, letting him jump free and return to what was left of the rug. If Francine got trigger-happy, I didn't want to put him in danger. "What in the blazes is wrong with you? I get that you've had an awful shock, but threatening us with a pistol is uncalled for." I leaned to the side, trying to see past Francine's hips. "Where's my mother?"

"Your mother?" Sidney sounded confused, but I didn't enlighten him that the blonde in Jerry's office had given birth to me. Plenty of time to deal with the topic of Desirée later. Or there would be, assuming Francine didn't shoot us first.

"Desirée's dealing with the paramedics." Francine advanced into the apartment and kicked the door shut, blocking our escape route.

My gaze darted to the window, but we were three floors up and facing the street. I'd seen no fire escape on this side of the building. Sweat snaked down my spine. "The police will be here any minute. Unless France has changed its strict gun laws, the cops will take a dim view of your pistol."

Her wheezy laugh sounded anything but funny. "They'll take a dimmer view of you attacking Jerry."

"For the seven millionth time, I had nothing to do with Jerry's injuries. My only physical contact with the guy was when I checked him for a pulse."

She swung the pistol in Sidney's direction and then back to me. "Sit down, both of you. Keep your hands where I can see them." Francine wielded the weapon like an amateur. Her awkward two-handed teacup grip and shaky trigger finger were more terrifying than a lineup of pro shooters.

I held up my palms and backed toward the sofa, keeping an eye on the pistol. In his haste to put distance between him and the gun, Sidney stumbled over the cat. Césaire arched his back, hissed, and moved himself and his claws to one of the rugs he had yet to destroy.

After a near encounter with the coffee table, Sidney and I made it to the sofa unscathed. We sat as instructed. I stayed on the edge of the seat, heels up, toes down, ready to spring into action. Now that the adrenaline spike had ebbed, I was convinced Francine was bluffing. Why would a fifty-something shop assistant keep a loaded weapon? This wasn't the Wild West. Law-abiding French civilians didn't carry firearms. No, the pistol had to be a prop. A convincing prop, but a prop nonetheless. And yet... A niggling doubt kept me on my guard. That click had sounded just like a real safety catch.

She sank into the armchair opposite, keeping the pistol trained on me. "Who do you work for, Angélique? I want the truth."

I thought of Frank and the pub and of Monty Carlyle. "Let's just say I'm between jobs at the moment."

She swung the gun toward Sidney. "And you? Who do you work for?"

He and I exchanged a look I prayed was more loaded than Francine's pistol. Why was she concerned about our employers? And why was she clinging to the pretense that the gun in her hand was real?

"Technically, I'm also between jobs," Sidney said after an uncomfortable pause. "As of Monday, I'll be an employee of the British Embassy in Paris."

The woman sucked air through her teeth. "You're a spy?"

Sidney's face registered momentary surprise. "Do I strike you as the James Bond type?"

His body language underwent a metamorphosis. The cock of his head, his wicked little smile. I practically saw the shaken-not-stirred martini in his hand.

"You strike me as a typical English buffoon," Francine said with devastating frankness. "But you're with Angélique, so I'm reserving judgment."

Sidney's debonair flair wilted in an instant. "That's not nice."

"Dude, she's aiming a pistol at us," I said. "I think

we can conclude that being nice isn't high on Francine's priorities."

We heard the ambulance roar into action and take off with screeching tires and blaring sirens. An icy prickling sensation spread across my shoulders. We needed to get out of here before the next set of blue lights arrived. The paramedics had no interest in talking to us, but the police most assuredly would.

Francine's gaze swiveled to me. "Why'd you two pick today of all days to come to the shop? Did your mother hire you to kill Jerry?"

"Enough already. I don't know what you've been smoking, but if it's convinced you I'm a gun-for-hire, you need to flush the rest."

"But you—"

"I haven't killed anyone—neither for hire nor for personal pleasure. But keep calling me a killer, and I might be tempted."

"Then why are you here? You barge into the shop after a decade, demand to see Jerry. Next thing I know, he's got a knife in his back."

"He has a letter opener stuck in his shoulder and a nasty head wound. I'm responsible for neither. I didn't hurt him, and I didn't barge anywhere. I knocked on the door, and *you* let me in." I held her gaze, steel on steel. "If you insist on giving me the third degree, can you lower that pistol? I'd rather not add a bullet hole to my list of woes."

Francine's jowls wobbled, and her eyes blazed. Whatever allegation she intended to hurl next was cut short when the apartment door burst open.

My mother stood there, swaying dramatically in that soft, clingy, low-cut dress. "What an awful thing to happen. Poor, dear Jerry." She sashayed to the drinks cabinet next to the sofa, leaving a trail of musky perfume in her wake. She moved like a movie star at the Oscars, too self-absorbed to notice the pistol aimed at her only child. "After all that drama, I need a drink."

Francine heaved her big behind out of the chair and switched her attention—and her aim—to my mother. "What are you doing here, Desirée? I didn't hear you arrive this morning."

"That's because I never left." My mother selected a bottle of vodka and splashed a generous serving into a shot glass. She knocked it back in one gulp before turning slowly to face her friend. "I spent the night with Jerry."

A series of emotions flashed in Francine's face. Incredulity. Hurt. Fury. It didn't take a psychologist to work out that she and my mother were love rivals. "Jerry slept with you?"

"Why not? When we were married, we must've done it thousands of times." She glanced in the mirror across the room and fluffed her hair, Golden Age starlet style. "And we're good together. Really good."

I watched Francine's internal struggle play out.

Her desire to kill my mother fought with her need to control the room. Her trigger finger quivered, but she restrained the urge. "Jerry's a fool. He never should've contacted you. You're bad news, Desirée. You always were. You come to town, people get hurt. Seems your daughter's no different."

"Leave Angélique out of this." For the first time, my mother looked right at the pistol. "And put that thing down. You don't even know how to use it."

Francine sucked in a breath so deep it sounded like a long hiss in reverse. "You had blood on your hands. Perhaps *you* attacked Jerry." It was an echo of what I'd said to my mother earlier that morning before Francine and Sidney charged into the office.

Instead of the damsel-in-distress routine she'd tried on me, my mother's reaction to Francine—her former friend—was different. She stretched to five feet five inches, five of which she owed to her scarlet stiletto heels. "Don't be ridiculous. I'm in Nice at Jerry's invitation, not to hurt him. He asked for my help, and I came right away."

"See where that got him? On his way to the hospital, half dead." Francine's voice wobbled, and a single tear slid down her face. "If you and Angélique didn't attack Jerry, then who did?"

My mother arched a perfectly plucked eyebrow. "Isn't it obvious? This has to be Rocco's doing. I had the sensation of being watched when I was in the corridor before entering Jerry's office.

Rocco—or one of his people—must have been nearby."

I made a show of checking my watch. "Since you've solved this case, can Sidney and I go now? We can't tell the cops anything relevant."

Francine looked almost amused. "Does your dead Russian have something to do with your desire to avoid the police? No, you're not going anywhere. I'm still not convinced you're innocent."

"I never claimed to be innocent. Just innocent of this particular crime." I shot her a wicked smile. "Seeing as we're flinging accusations around, how do we know *you* didn't attack Jerry? After all, you're the one holding a lethal weapon."

Her face turned an interesting shade of purple, and she aimed the pistol at me again. "I've worked for Jerry for twenty-five years. I've been a loyal employee, friend, and confidante. I'd never hurt him."

"I'm seriously sick of you threatening us. That's enough, Francine. Hand me the pistol. I bet it's just a prop from the shop." I leaped off the couch as fast as the shot Francine fired.

And time went wonky. I swear I saw the bullet in the air. Watched each millisecond of its flight in slow motion. Recognized the horror on Francine's face when she realized she'd actually pulled the trigger. Noticed my mother reach out like she could stop the bullet's trajectory. Watched Sidney slump sideways.

The noise of that shot made my heart freeze and

my ears roar. Three sentences repeated in my head in an endless loop.

Sidney's dead.

My mother's going to die.

It's all my fault.

17

The bullet lodged in the left boob of Manet's *Olympia*. The framed picture hit the floor with a crash, spraying the polished wood with glass.

A shocked silence twanged through the room, broken by Césaire's outraged yowl. He abandoned the wreckage of the rug and shot toward the door, meowing to be let out.

Sidney straightened on the sofa, clutching the side of his ear. A trickle of blood dripped between his fingers and onto his crisp white shirt. "That was no prop," he said, his voice rising with each word. "I've been shot."

His words galvanized me into action. I grabbed a bunch of tissues from the box on the coffee table and held them against his ear. Then I turned to the would-be Annie Oakley. "You. Could. Have. Killed. Him." I punctuated each word with cold precision. "What were you thinking?"

Tears ran down Francine's face, plowing through her heavy makeup and leaving a chalky trail on her cheeks. "It's your fault. I wouldn't have fired if you hadn't jumped at me."

My mother grabbed Francine and shook her. "How could you? You might've killed me. You might've killed us all."

Despite the surreal situation, I almost laughed. My mother's number one concern was herself. Always had been, always would be. She was self-centered and selfish, but at least she was consistent.

Her frenzied shaking loosened Francine's grip on the pistol. The weapon hit the floor and fired a second round. This time, the bullet shattered the coffee table and what remained of my nerves.

Césaire's yowling reached a frantic crescendo. He scratched wildly at the door, begging to be released from this mad circus. I felt his pain. The sooner I got out of here, the safer I'd feel—even with Monty, Cam, and goodness knew who else after my blood.

"Stop fighting," I shouted over the cat's yowls. "If you're determined to destroy Jerry's apartment, go for it, but later. Sidney and I don't want to be used for target practice."

"It was an accident," Francine whined. "First you attacked me, then your mother grabbed me, and—"

I held up a hand to cut short her tirade. "Enough

already. Sidney's hurt. We need to treat his wound. Does Jerry keep a first aid kit in the apartment?"

"There's one in the bathroom cabinet. I'll get it." Her words were pitched so low I could barely hear them. Her hunched shoulders and haggard expression indicated the fight had gone out of her, but I still didn't trust her.

"Oh, no. I'm not letting you out of our sight. Take the spare armchair and stay with Sidney and Desirée. I'll look for it."

My mother bent down, picked up the pistol, and unloaded the remaining bullets with practiced precision. "I'll get the first aid kit, Angélique," she said, placing the now-empty gun on the drinks cabinet and pocketing the bullets.

I slow-blinked. Where had my mother learned to handle a pistol? Her assured motions were in stark contrast to Francine's obvious ineptitude. Despite her high heels, she moved fast—so fast that she was back with the first aid kit while I was still processing what I'd seen.

She handed me the kit, plus a packet of cotton pads. "I figured you'd need these."

"Thanks." I opened the kit and removed disinfectant, bandages, and scissors. Sidney clutched the wad of blood-soaked tissues to his ear, his eyes unfocused. His breathing was deep and deliberate. "Can you pour Sidney a drink, Maman? He's in shock."

"Sure. I'll get him a cognac."

I soaked cotton pads with disinfectant and applied them to Sidney's ear. He winced, but didn't try to pull away. Once I'd cleaned the blood, I inspected the wound. The bullet had nicked the edge of his ear, but the cut was neat and not deep enough to require stitches. Pure, visceral relief rushed through me. "You'll live. It'll bleed like a mother, but it's just a graze."

"That's nice." The poor guy sounded like a tranquilized '50s housewife.

I handed him a fresh wad of tissues. "Hold these against your ear until the bleeding stops. Then I'll apply a dressing."

My mother materialized with a generous serving of cognac. She pressed the glass into Sidney's hand. "You poor dear. You're so brave."

Her seductive purr pulled him out of his daze. He stared at her, transfixed, and blushed like a kid with his first crush.

Unbelievable. I wasn't even sure Sidney was into women, yet my mother had taken all of five seconds to coax him out of his stupor. Not wishing to witness Sidney fawning over my mother, I faced Francine. "You could at least express relief that you didn't take his ear off."

She sat hunched in an armchair, her bluster deflated. "I didn't mean to hurt him. I aimed for the picture, and his head got in the way."

"I can't help being tall," Sidney said.

"If you can't handle a firearm, you shouldn't have one," I said. "What in the world were you doing with a loaded gun, Francine? You work for a theatrical costumier, not a drug lord."

Her high-pitched laugh was the closest thing to a cackle that I'd ever heard outside the cinema. "How can you be so clueless? Don't you know Desirée and Jerry work—"

"I feel faint." My mother put a hand to her brow, in full swooning heroine mode, and sagged against the drinks cabinet. "Between finding poor Jerry, my daughter turning up with dead Russians, and now a shoot-out...."

"This hardly qualifies as a shoot-out." Each of my words was as cold and sharp as an icicle.

"Maybe not," Sidney said, wincing in pain, "but remind me to wear incontinence pants the next time we call on your relatives. I came close to disgracing myself."

"I'm woozy...." My mother wobbled yet retained suspicious control over her movements.

Her plight—fake, I was sure—appealed to Sidney's sense of chivalry. Clutching the tissues to his injured ear, he jumped up from the sofa and took her arm. "You're chalk-white. You should sit down."

He led my mother to the armchair next to Francine's. She sank into it with a dramatic sigh, still clinging to his hand. "Thank you so much. It's good to know there's at least one gentleman left in the world."

I rolled my eyes so hard they hurt. If I tried a fraction of her antics on blokes, they'd bust a gut laughing. "If anyone should sit down, it's Sidney. He's the one Francine shot."

No one paid any attention to me. Francine stared at her hands. Sidney stared at my mother.

"I thought you looked familiar when I saw you earlier, but now I'm sure I recognize you. You're Desirée Chablis." He pronounced the name with reverence, instantly triggering my gag reflex.

I spread my arms wide and bowed. "Sidney, meet my mother, the queen of '90s soft porn. Play your cards right, and she might pose with you for a selfie."

"Given that you tossed my phone, that's unlikely."

I pointed to the sofa. "Quit griping about your phone and sit down. I still need to bandage your ear."

He gave an exaggerated sigh, but obeyed. "Are you always this grumpy?"

My mother's tinkling laugh affected me like an acid bath. "Always," she said. "Even as a baby."

"I'm amazed you were around long enough to notice," I snapped, putting antiseptic cream on a clean cotton pad and pressing it against Sidney's ear.

Francine chuckled but made no comment. My mother didn't dignify my remark with a response.

Sidney let me bandage his wound with no fuss, but

his attention was focused on Desirée. "Are you really Angel's mother?"

She treated him to one of her most alluring smiles, the type guaranteed to seduce people of all sexual inclinations. "It's hard to believe, isn't it? Of course, I was little more than a child when I had her."

"You were twenty-four, Maman, and on your second husband." I dropped my voice to a stage whisper. "In case anyone can't count, that means she turned fifty last April."

My mother waved a regal hand. "Fifty is the new thirty, darling."

I finished bandaging Sidney's ear and examined my handiwork. "The bleeding's slowed, but we'll need to give you a fresh bandage when it's completely stopped."

"Thanks, Angel. You're a surprisingly gentle nurse. I was expecting Nurse Ratched. Or Kathy Bates in *Misery*."

I gave him a playful slap on the arm. "Charming. I can be caring when I want to be."

"Don't forget to treat your scratches," Sidney said, indicating the antiseptic cream.

I took his advice. My face looked a little better today, but I couldn't risk the scratches getting infected.

My mother, never one to tolerate the spotlight staying on anyone else for long, cleared her throat. This had an instant effect on Sidney, who needed no further prodding to switch his attention from me to her. "I'm a huge fan of your burlesque act," he gushed. "I saw you perform in London last year."

A London tour stop during which my mother hadn't bothered to contact me. Yes, it still rankled. What rankled more was watching Sidney ogling my mother like she was the hottest thing on the stage. I wasn't jealous. Well, maybe a little. But it'd be nice, even once, to have a man look at me with the same unfiltered adoration that my mother took as her due. "Can we break up this lovefest and focus on what happened to Jerry? Who's the Rocco guy you mentioned? Any chance he's still lurking in the building? Maybe Francine's pistol will come in handy for more than shooting up Manets and coffee tables."

"If it was Rocco, he's long gone." Francine's tone was back to snappish. "I'm still not convinced you didn't do it."

"I'm beyond caring what you think. Your stunt with the pistol makes me think you're one prop short of a stage set. I have no reason to harm Jerry. Quite on the contrary. I came here because I needed his help."

Her eyes slitted so narrowly I was amazed she could still see. "You wanted help from a man you hadn't seen in years? No, I'm sticking to my theory that you're a hired killer."

"Whatever floats your sinking boat. I've had a varied career to date, but oddly enough, paid assassin isn't on my résumé."

"Given your family background, it's not such a

stretch of the imagination," she replied, her tone defiant.

It was my turn to do the eyes-narrowing routine. "What do you mean? My dad's no killer. He's a two-bit thug for a third-rate gangster."

"Both of you. Stop. Please." My mother's words were blade-edge sharp. "Francine, I didn't hurt Jerry, and neither did Angélique. We need to come up with a plan before the police arrive. Better you and I do that alone."

A look I couldn't fathom passed between them. Francine opened her mouth as if to object, then snapped it shut.

Sirens wailed in the distance. I locked eyes with Sidney. "For reasons I'd rather not get into now, it's wiser if Sidney and I aren't here when the cops arrive."

"They can go next door to Luc's café," my mother said. "He knows how to deal with... delicate...situations."

Luc had to be Mr. Arrogant. Everything about the man screamed guy who knew how to deal with... delicate... situations.

"Any chance he can get rid of the dead Russian mobster in the back of our car?" Sidney asked, only half-joking.

Francine regarded him with triumphant suspicion. "I thought you said you two didn't kill people."

"We don't. Someone else killed him and dumped him on us."

The sirens grew closer, followed by the slam of a car door.

"If you don't want to run into the cops, you'd better go now." My mother rose and smoothed down her skirt. "I'll show Angélique and Sidney the fire escape."

"What about the bloody tissues and the first aid kit?" I asked. "Won't the cops ask about those?"

A pounding sounded on the front door of the building.

"I'll get rid of the tissues and the kit," my mother said over her shoulder. "Now, quick. We need to hurry."

This time, Césaire didn't struggle when I scooped him up. He'd cowered at the door to Jerry's apartment ever since the pistol had fired the first time.

Desirée led Sidney and me down the stairs, past Jerry's office, and through a narrow corridor. A glowing green light hung over the emergency exit. She quickened her pace the closer we got and I was more than happy to follow suit. The sooner we got out of this building, the safer I'd feel.

18

When my mother reached for the fire escape door's handle, a glint of metal snagged my attention.

"Wait a sec." I picked up a metal file and handed it to Desirée. "This is how Jerry's attacker got in and out of the building. The fire door's old. It wouldn't take an expert to break in from the outside. And then they used this tool to wedge the door open so that they could make a quick exit."

My mother's expression grew grim. "You're right. We'll have to beef up security."

Voices floated up from downstairs—Francine and the police.

"We need to hurry, Angel," Sidney said, tugging me onto the rusty metal landing.

My mother pointed to the next building. "Luc

owns the café next door. Go to him and tell him I sent you. If I haven't gotten in touch with you by this afternoon, contact my lawyer. Jacques Fournier. Rue Maccarani. Now go."

Sidney and I didn't need telling twice. We raced down the rickety stairs, one unstable step at a time. I clutched Césaire to my chest, comforted by the vibrations of his soft purrs against my pounding heart. When we reached the bottom of the stairs, we found ourselves in a postage stamp-sized garden. It was scattered with broken furniture, random debris, and potted plants of the half-dead variety.

An iron gate separated this garden from next door's. We ran across to the gate, leaping over plants and dodging stray chairs. When we were safely on the other side, I released the breath I hadn't realized I'd been holding.

The cafe's cramped garden was no bigger than Jerry's, but it was a whole pile neater. Carefully tended flower beds flanked the red-brick walls. Six sets of tables and chairs were arranged on the patio to give each group an illusion of privacy. A rainbow-striped awning stretched over the seating area, providing much-needed shade from the intense morning sun.

Sidney wiped stray strands of fair hair off his face, revealing a fresh trickle of blood from his injured ear. "What now? Do we follow your mother's instructions and talk to this Luc bloke? Or do we go straight to that lawyer she mentioned?"

I stroked Césaire's soft fur and took stock of our situation. "Within the next few minutes, the cops will be crawling all over Jerry's building. I'd rather put distance between them and us, but the fact is, you're still bleeding. We need to stop and put a fresh bandage on your ear. Luc's café is as good a place as any. Doesn't mean we need to confide in the man."

"You don't sound enthusiastic. As I recall, you shot out of this café like a prickly cannonball. Am I right at assuming Luc was the cause of your chagrin?"

"We didn't exchange names, but yeah. The man grinding coffee fits my mental image of the Luc who deals with 'delicate situations.'" I punctuated this last part with air quotes. "He's a stereotypical alpha male. I don't care for guys like Luc. On the plus side, his joint serves coffee. I need a caffeine hit if I'm to strategize our next move."

"No pressure, but I flatter myself that I have a few functioning brain cells." His tone was light on inflection and heavy on irony. "Maybe I can help you formulate our master plan."

I cocked my head to the side. "I'm bossy, aren't I?"

He cracked a grin. "Just a tad."

It was good to see him regaining his jaunty manner. Maybe I wasn't such a lousy nurse after all. "Sorry, Sidney. Force of habit. I'm used to fending for myself. Plus, this morning's adventure has shaken me up—and I'm not even the one who got shot. How are you doing?"

"I'm sore. The cognac your mother gave me helped with the shock. So...I guess I'm hanging in there?"

"It's been a wild morning. Let's get that caffeine hit. And a proper breakfast for you." I hooked my arm through his and steered him toward the patio.

The café had acquired customers since I'd last been inside. Through the floor-to-ceiling windows, I spotted two occupied tables. Only one customer sat in the garden, hidden behind today's edition of *Le Monde*. A half-knit hat lay on the table beside him, still attached to needles and yarn. A customer from the yarn shop? Or its owner? Whoever he was, he didn't show the slightest flicker of interest when Sidney and I claimed a table as far away from him as we could get.

I sank onto my seat and lowered Césaire to the ground. After a careful perusal of the table legs, he curled up at my feet and went to sleep.

Sidney dropped onto the opposite seat. "I can't believe your mother is *the* Desirée Chablis. She's famous. Why didn't you tell me?"

A fiery heat burned across my cheeks. I didn't need a mirror to know I looked like a tomato. Years of teasing in school had made me all too well aware of my tendency to blush vividly. "Isn't it obvious? Every kid in school reminded me on a daily basis. Even if they hadn't seen her films, their parents had. How do you think that made me feel?"

He appeared to give my question serious

consideration. "I don't know. If my family had an assigned color, it'd be beige. Each of us is a stock player, and we know our lines. Having an exciting relative must be fun."

"I have an abundance of 'exciting' relatives. Trust me, it's not all it's cracked up to be. Especially when 'exciting' is synonymous with 'absentee parent.' My dad's an idiot, but at least he was around when I was growing up. All my mother did was provide the schoolyard bullies with plenty of fodder."

"I'm sorry. That must have been difficult." Sidney picked up a paper napkin and wiped his ear. "Am I still bleeding?"

"I'm not sure. Looks like it's slowed down at the very least. Does it hurt badly?"

"Like a thousand tiny paper cuts." He handed me a laminated menu. "Did you see they serve full English breakfasts? I love experimenting with local dishes when I'm abroad, but when it comes to breakfasts, I'm a self-proclaimed cliché. Give me a traditional fry-up every time."

I performed a full-body shudder. "I can't think of anything more hideous than eating bacon and sausages right now."

"In that case, you'll be pleased to know we also serve a range of continental breakfasts."

The hairs at the nape of my neck prickled to attention. The man behind me had spoken in perfect

English, but I recognized the gravelly voice from the growling exchange we'd had in French. This had to be Luc.

I turned and stared up into those electric-blue eyes. "I'll have an espresso. I can't think about food this morning." I gave the order in French, daring him to language-switch on me again. It was the age-old dance for dominance whereby a local (almost always a man) showed off his grasp of a foreign language even though etiquette dictated that everyone stuck to the local language unless they couldn't.

His lips twitched, and a glimmer of humor danced in those intense eyes. "Sure," he replied in French, respecting my preference. "Would your friend like a side order of first aid kit with his English breakfast?"

"Yes, please," Sidney said in French, accompanying his words with a broad smile. "And I'd like my English breakfast with coffee, not tea. *Café au lait.*"

Mr. Arrogant inclined his head but didn't write down our order, displaying yet another alpha male tendency that set my teeth on edge.

I leaned back in my chair and subjected him to a deliberate once-over not dissimilar to the one he'd performed on me earlier. "You've got such a phenomenal memory that you can recall all your customers' orders, right down to the last detail?"

A slow smile spread across his too-handsome face. "If a customer's order is interesting enough to warrant writing down, I've been known to find a pen."

I arched an eyebrow. "A first aid kit isn't an unusual request?"

"Not to me. Nice is a tourist town. I get plenty of patrons with scrapes and bruises and no medicine cabinet to hand, particularly people with kids." His attention shifted to the gate that divided his property from the costumier's. "Did you find Jerry?"

"Oh, we found him all right." Sidney's voice cracked mid-sentence. "That's why Desirée sent us over to the café. Are you Luc?"

"Seriously?" I kicked him under the table. Hard.

Mr. Arrogant studied Sidney for a long moment before nodding. "I didn't realize Desirée was back in town. How do you know her?"

"I don't, actually. I just met Desirée this morning. But she's Angel's mother."

Luc's gaze snapped back to me. "*You're* Desirée's daughter? You don't look like her."

I treated him to what I hoped was a man-part-shriveling glare. "No, really? I hadn't noticed."

"Desirée said you'd help us," Sidney said. "We've got a—"

I kicked him again. Harder. "We agreed not to involve Luc."

"Leave my shins alone." He angled his long legs out of my reach. "*We* didn't agree on anything. *You* indicated you'd rather not involve Luc. But *I'm* the one who got shot, remember?"

"You got shot?" Luc's gaze swung back to me. "I

saw the ambulance pull up outside, and then the cops. What's going on?"

I threw my hands up in the air. "Didn't you hear Francine shooting up the place? Frankly, I'm surprised we didn't attract a bevy of curious neighbors."

Frown lines snaked across his forehead. "Francine? Why? What did you do to her?"

I sat forward in my chair and gaped at him. "Unbelievable. Why would you assume I'd done anything to her? I'm not even the one who got shot."

"Francine's not the type to go around shooting people." Luc examined Sidney's ear. "I take it your injury was collateral damage?"

"Yeah. She fired one shot at a painting, clipping my ear in the process. Then a second shot went off when she dropped her pistol."

Luc's mouth quivered. "Okay, that does sound like Francine."

"How did you not hear the shots?" I demanded. "Jerry's apartment isn't soundproofed."

"We get motorcycles backfiring around here all the time."

This was true. We'd heard one backfire right outside the café. I should've taken it as a premonition of bad things to come.

Luc's frown deepened. "What caused Francine to grab a pistol? Did she think you two had broken in?"

"Worse than that," I said grimly. "Someone

attacked Jerry. Someone who wanted him dead. We had a little trouble convincing Francine it wasn't us."

If Luc was surprised to learn his next-door neighbor had been attacked, his expression didn't show it. "I'm sorry to hear that. Jerry's a good guy. Is he going to be okay?"

"I hope so," I said. "His assailant stabbed him in the shoulder and bashed him over the head. Of the two injuries, the head wound looked worse, but I'm not a doctor."

Luc turned to look inside the café and then back at Sidney. "The police will stop by to see if anyone saw or heard anything. You'll need to change out of that bloody shirt. And wear a hat to cover your ear."

"I don't have a change of clothes. All our stuff got robbed when the dead Russian was put in our car. Speaking of whom"—Sidney dropped his voice to a stage whisper—"Desirée indicated you were the man to go to about our dead body problem."

Luc's eyebrows rocketed skyward. He shifted his gaze to me. "I assume *you're* responsible for the dead body."

I glowered at him. "You assume wrong. Why don't you scram and fill our breakfast order? And supply me paper while you're at it. And a telephone directory, if such a thing still exists."

He regarded me with cool indifference. "No can do on the print phone directory, but I have paper. If you want it, you can come and get it yourself."

Sidney looked from me to Mr. Arrogant. "Whoa, you two. Simmer down."

Luc gave a bored half-shrug. "If she's your girlfriend, you should consider updating your relationship status. She comes with claws."

"She's not my girlfriend. And I've noticed the claws."

I crossed my arms over my chest. "Thanks a bunch, Sidney."

"She needs caffeine," he said to Luc, ignoring me. "And food too, even if she won't admit it."

Luc's face split into the first genuine smile I'd seen him give. It transformed his face from arrogant to boyish. My stomach performed a flip and roll. "Come with me, Sidney. I'll get you the clothes and the first aid kit. You can change in the men's room."

Sidney followed Luc into the café, leaving me to stew in the garden. A light breeze shook the awning, mirroring my mood. Luc was proving to be just as take charge as I'd feared. I appreciated his willingness to help my friend, but I didn't trust the man. And why should I? We'd only just met, and that hadn't exactly gone swimmingly.

Waiting had never been my strong point, and Sidney was taking an age. I ripped a napkin into neat pieces, rearranged the condiments, and read the menu so many times I had it memorized. I glanced down at Césaire. He was still sleeping peacefully under the table in his patch of shade. Careful not to disturb him, I eased my chair back and got to my feet. The man with the newspaper had departed during our exchange with Luc, leaving a twenty-euro note anchored in place by the sugar bowl and his copy of *Le Monde*.

I itched to pocket the twenty, but I controlled the urge. Instead, I grabbed the paper. The front page focused on France's latest political crisis. I flipped through the pages, skimming the headlines. With each page turn, my heart rate kicked up a notch. But I needn't have worried. There was no mention of me or Frank or Monty.

Yet.

I dropped the newspaper and wandered into the café. No one paid me any heed, too absorbed with their coffees and breakfasts to notice yet another pale-skinned tourist.

Luc was back behind the counter, frothing milk. A paper notebook lay beneath the counter, within reach. I was tempted to take it and leave, but I'd antagonized Luc enough for one morning. I had no idea why my mother trusted him, and I wasn't sure I wanted to know. But if he was helping Sidney, he couldn't be all bad, right?

And then he swung around and treated me to a look of amused disdain. "Checking on the progress of your coffee? I'm afraid we're all out of the anti-bitch blend."

"That's okay. I prefer the anti-alpha male variety." I leaned over the counter and snagged the notebook. "I intend to keep this. Feel free to add it to my bill."

His rich rumble of laughter accompanied me all the way back to my seat.

19

Back on the patio, I retrieved Frank's lucky pen from my pocket and divided the first page of the notebook into three columns. I labeled each column with a name, printed in block capitals: Frank, Boris/Ivan, Césaire. Then I flipped to the next page and tapped the pen's nib against the paper, creating a circle of bright blue dots. Should I add a new column with Jerry's name?

Heaven knew Sidney and I had enough mysteries to solve without adding Jerry's attack to our list. Yet we were involved, whether we liked it or not. Something wasn't right at the costumier. The loaded looks between my mother and Francine. Francine's half-started sentences cut short by my mother's theatrics. The women's reluctance to have us around when the paramedics—and then the police—arrived on the scene.

I was under no illusions they wanted to protect Sidney and me. My mother's personality and Francine's pistol precluded that conclusion. So why had they wanted us out of the way before the authorities had rolled up? Were they afraid of what we'd say? Or did they fear what we'd overhear? Regardless, the undercurrents at Jerry's place threatened to suck me under if I wasn't careful.

And that was before I considered Luc's role. Who was he, anyway? I'd bet my left buttock he'd served, and not merely as part of obligatory military conscription. The way he carried himself, his self-assurance, his fluid-yet-restrained motions. I'd been around crooks my whole life, some of whom had spent time in the armed forces, most of whom hadn't. A self-proclaimed hard man walked with a loose-limbed swagger. Not the controlled movements of the ex-soldier.

Scrolling back to Sidney, would his brush with a bullet persuade him to contact the British Embassy? The more I thought about Monty and Cam and the twins, not to mention whatever was going on at Jerry's place, the more convinced I was that Sidney needed to leave.

"The look of concentration on your face is terrifying, as is that garish pen. Are you and the leprechaun plotting world domination? And all before your first coffee of the day?" Sidney slid a tray laden with drinks across the table and flopped onto his seat.

He wore a black polo shirt at least two sizes too large and a wide-brimmed khaki sun hat that completely covered his ears.

"I see you've raided Luc's clothes." I indicated the tray. "Has he conscripted you as waitstaff to compensate?"

"Business is picking up inside. I offered to deliver our drinks. The kitchen's still preparing our food, but Luc says it should be ready in ten to fifteen minutes." He handed me an espresso and an accompanying glass of water. Then he slid a large cup of *café au lait* and a water glass toward his side of the table, plus a blister of ibuprofen.

I pointed to the meds. "Did Luc give you those?"

"Yeah. Anything to take the edge off the pain." He pressed two capsules free from the blister pack and swallowed them with water.

I leaned over the table and tugged up his hat. "That's a professional-looking bandage. More professional than my attempt."

"All Luc's work. He says he has experience dealing with wounds like mine."

"I bet he has." I dropped the brim of the hat like it had stung me.

Sidney dumped two sugar cubes into his *café au lait* and gave it a vigorous stir. "I see you've started making notes. I'm good at figuring out puzzles. Want to brainstorm?"

Yes? And no? My hesitation must've shown on my

face because Sidney's expression turned from open to guarded. "No worries if you don't. I just thought, a problem shared...."

"I'm sorry. I didn't mean to offend you. I didn't answer right away because I was torn. On the one hand, I'd love to get your input. On the other, I'm not used to sharing problems. Plus, there's the not-so-small matter of you getting shot. I feel like the only topic we should discuss is how to get you back to Paris."

He let out a long sigh. "How many times have we had this conversation? I'm not abandoning you with the dead body. He's as much my corpse as yours."

"This isn't a game, Sidney."

"News flash—I already figured that out." He leaned back in his chair and folded his arms across his chest. "We got into this mess together, and we'll find a way out together."

I pretended to bang my head against the table. "You're killing me."

"No, I'm helping us avoid being killed." He jabbed a finger at my notepad. "Come on. I can see that big brain of yours at work. Hit me with your ideas."

My emotional state was pulled between relief that Sidney was staying and frustration that he wouldn't leave. Still, if he was here and willing to act as a sounding board, I needed to reshape my jumbled thoughts into coherent conclusions. I surveyed the still-empty patio. "Okay. But we should keep our voices down, just in case."

"Chill, Angel. No one's interested in us. Not even the police."

My heart punched against my ribs. "They're here?"

"Been and gone. As far as the cops are concerned, Jerry was attacked sometime before eight o'clock this morning. That's when your mother says she found him. Luc was just opening the café then and claims to have seen and heard nothing."

"The police didn't want to talk to the café's customers?"

Sidney shook his head. "What would be the point? The few people who were here at the time Jerry was attacked have already left. One of the customers sitting at the counter mentioned hearing shots a while ago, but Luc said it was just a motorbike backfiring. The police weren't interested because A, the alleged shots were heard after your mother called emergency services, and B, neither of Jerry's injuries were caused by a gun."

My heart rate was slowly returning to normal. "That's a relief. It means they won't be looking for us. At least, not about Jerry's attack."

"Exactly." He pointed to the notebook. "Want to get to work?"

"Sure." I flipped back to the first page and showed him my three columns. "I have a lot of questions and observations about Frank's and Boris/Ivan's murders. If I had a laptop, I'd type my thoughts before we went to see a lawyer. In our current device-free situation, I'm settling for the old-school method."

Sidney cradled his mug in his hands and scanned the page. "You added Césaire's name. Do you want to figure out who kidnapped him and why? Or do you just want to get him back to his owner?"

"The latter, definitely. We have way more pressing problems to solve without adding that mystery to our load."

"What about finding out who attacked Jerry? Francine accused you of the crime. Surely you want to clear your name?"

"Francine was throwing accusations around like confetti. I wish Jerry a speedy recovery and his attacker punished, but we can't get involved. We have enough on our plates." I was making excuses, and we both knew it, but I didn't have the emotional bandwidth right now to address anything involving my mother.

He leaned his head to the side, a half-smile brimming. "Why didn't you mention your mother was in Nice? You specifically told me she wouldn't be here."

"I said I had no idea where she was. Which was true." I scrunched up my nose. "Trust me, if I'd known she'd be at Jerry's, I'd never have suggested we come here."

"Your mother strikes me as less dangerous than Francine." He touched his ear pointedly. "I could've used a heads-up about her."

"I'm so sorry you got hurt, Sidney. I hadn't seen Francine in years before this morning, and I barely recognized her. If I'd known about her trigger-happy tendencies, I'd have bailed at the door."

He dumped another sugar cube into his coffee and stirred with vigor. "Yeah, well. She got a shock finding Jerry. Stands to reason she'd suspect the newcomers."

"That doesn't excuse her shooting you. I'm amazed you didn't bawl her out. She deserved a good tongue-lashing."

This made him laugh. "You took care of that, as did your mother. After this morning's shenanigans, Francine's not on my list of favorite people. However, she didn't mean to injure me. She simply has terrible aim."

"You're more understanding than I'd be if our roles were reversed."

"Speaking of roles—what's the deal with Jerry's costumier? Is the business legit?"

It was a question I'd already asked myself. "Are you referring to Jerry being attacked or Francine possessing a genuine pistol?"

"Yes and yes. But also the general vibe at that place. It's all wrong. Take the costumes I admired, for example. Francine told me they represented some of their most popular rental costumes and reeled off the various productions they'd been worn in. However, each of those costumes was immaculate."

"I don't follow. Wouldn't Jerry and Francine want to keep their costumes in immaculate condition?"

"The shop itself is shabby and careworn. I'd expect the costumes to be in a similar condition. Even the best theatrical costume suppliers will have costumes that show some wear and tear and mending. Also, seams that have been altered to fit different people. I saw no signs of wear and tear on the costumes Francine showed me. There's no way costumes that have allegedly been featured in numerous theater productions can look that good."

I scrunched up my forehead. "Why would Francine lie?"

"Why would she keep a loaded pistol?" Sidney arched an eyebrow. "I don't know the answers to either of those questions, but I'd bet my grandfather's vintage watch that that place is a front."

"A front for what, though?" I mused. "Surely you can't suspect Jerry of being a drug dealer? Or of using the business to launder money?"

"I don't know Jerry. From what you've told me, you don't know him all that well, either."

I sat back and blew out my cheeks. "I agree that the atmosphere at the costumier was strange. My mother's and Francine's behavior was bizarre. And there's no denying that Jerry was attacked. But what any of that means, I don't know." I picked up my espresso cup, took a sip, and moaned in pleasure. "Gosh, this is good. It tastes even better than it smells."

"My *café au lait* is perfect too."

I picked up the pen. "Okay, Sherlock. If you want me to bounce ideas off you, it's time to get to work."

"All right," he said. "Let's start with Frank's murder."

I wrote "FACTS SO FAR" under Frank's name and underlined the words. "I've already told you the basics."

"You told me the bare minimum. I know Monty and his men burst into the pub you worked at and shot your boss, Frank O'Malley. What was the place called again? The Lucky Leprechaun?"

"The Lucky Charm," I said dryly. "That name's more of a misnomer than mine. There was nothing lucky about that pub."

"You got lucky," he pointed out. "You lived."

I glanced up from my notes. "I lived to tell the tale. Which is my whole problem. I saw Monty kill a man, a task he usually leaves to one of his minions. That's why he's chasing me across France."

Sidney grinned. "There's the matter of you shooting him in the arse with a ketamine dart."

"Yeah, there's that minor matter." Despite the serious subject matter, talking to Sidney helped to take the edge off my fear. He was a good listener—a rare trait.

He took a sip of his *café au lait* and licked milk foam from his upper lip. "Why, exactly, did Monty shoot Frank? If Monty usually leaves the killing to other people, it had to have been serious for him to be willing to do the deed himself."

"Yeah, I don't get that part. And Monty went all out. I saw him shoot Frank in the leg, and there were five more shots in rapid succession."

"You didn't see him fire those shots? Why are you sure Monty fired them?"

"No, I'd dropped behind the counter after the first shot. However, I'm certain the others came from Monty's weapon. Like I said, they came in quick-fire. Frank yelled out in pain when Monty hit his leg, but he fell silent after the third or fourth shot."

"What about Monty's motive for killing Frank?" Sidney pressed. "All you told me was that Frank double-crossed him."

"First, a little background info. Frank was one of many local business owners who'd allowed Monty Carlyle to buy a share in his business and use it to launder money. In return, Frank got protection and a cut of the proceeds. So far, so bad. I don't know when or why Frank made the stupid decision to skim money from Monty, but that's what Monty accused him of doing. At least, that's what it sounded like to me. Monty accused Frank of taking what was rightfully his."

Sidney whistled. "Not smart. Monty doesn't sound like a bloke to cross."

"He isn't. Frank signed his own death warrant when he stole from the man. And Frank wasn't stupid.

Which tells me he must've had a compelling need to steal that money."

"But you don't know what that need was?"

I shook my head. "I don't know much about his personal life and even less about his personal finances. Frank liked a flutter at the races, but I'm not aware of any massive gambling debts. His sideline in black-market goods kept the pub afloat, and his deal with Monty must've been an added bonus."

Sidney leaned closer and dropped his voice. "If you wanted to keep your nose clean after you helped put Cam in prison, why did you go to work with Frank?"

"I said I wanted to stay under the radar," I corrected. "That meant staying away from Cam's father and his various criminal contacts. I took the job with Frank because I was desperate, and he wasn't a lecher."

"Did you know Frank laundered money for Monty?" Sidney asked. "Or about the black-market goods he sold?"

"No. It didn't take me long to figure out something was up, though. Frank frequently stored his knocked-off wares in the cellar. But I didn't find out about his deal with Monty until Becky told me."

Sidney pulled a face. "The same Becky who claims she saw you kill Frank?"

"The one and only." My tone was as gritty as my mood. "I don't know why she lied. Either she was threatened or bribed or both. And I don't know why

Monty would want the police looking for me if he sent Cam and the twins to haul me back to London. In fact, there's one thing I'm certain about in this whole mess."

"What's that?" Sidney demanded. "Don't leave me in suspense."

Fear wrapped its evil coils around me, squeezing so hard I could barely breathe. I felt the fear, owned it, let it settle. I had to take agency over my situation. If I wanted to stay alive—if I wanted Sidney to stay alive—I needed to get back behind the wheel of my own life.

I took a deep breath. "The one thing I know is Monty intends to kill me. It's not just that I shot him in the rear end. I'm a witness to him, personally, pulling the trigger and murdering a man. Plus, Cam saw you with me, the woman he's been sent to France to kill. Sidney, you're too dangerous to let live."

20

I'd expected a strong reaction from Sidney. Panic. Hysterics. Maniacal laughter. Instead, I got bored disinterest.

"Nice try with the dramatic delivery, Angel, but you need more rehearsals before opening night." He refilled his water glass from the jug on the table and added a slice of lime, all cool, calm, and collected.

The man was exasperating. "Why won't you take me seriously?"

"Because nothing you said is news. I've known I was in danger ever since Cam pulled a knife on me in Paris." He rolled his eyes to the side. "Well, apart from that brief interlude when I thought you'd set up a prank with my pal Ricardo."

"I'm not trying to persuade you to contact the British Embassy—"

"Good," he interrupted. "Because I will contact them, but at a time when it benefits both of us."

"—but if we're sticking together, we have to figure out how to regain control over our narrative. Every move we've made since we left Paris has dug us deeper into the cesspit. Taking the car. Delivering the ransom money. Keeping Césaire. Finding the corpse. And now we've discovered Jerry, half-dead." I felt sick just thinking about it.

"*You* stole the car. *We* delivered the ransom money. As for the cat, what were we supposed to do? Dump him at the side of the motorway? We didn't actively do anything to the dead Russian, apart from driving around with his corpse." Sidney paused, tapped a finger on his chin. "Yeah, okay. That sounds bad. What I mean is, everything that's happened since you took Monique's car was either decided by or done to *both* of us."

"Mostly 'done to,' which is my whole point. We need to take back control. We've spent the last couple of days reacting to situations. It's time for us to stop reacting and start acting."

He nodded. "If we want to act versus react, a visit to the lawyer your mother mentioned is our number one priority. Even if criminal law isn't his specialty, he'll be able to refer us to a colleague."

"My mother mentioned contacting the lawyer if she hadn't gotten in touch with us by this afternoon," I said. "But I'd rather not wait that long."

"Same. However, it makes sense for us to finish our brainstorming session before we see the lawyer. If our thoughts are clear, we'll be able to express them clearly."

He was right. As I'd known he would be. We'd met less than forty-eight hours ago, yet I trusted his judgment more than I had anyone's in...forever? "Okay. Let's start with Becky. She and I weren't super close, but we got on well. I babysat her daughter, for heaven's sake. I don't even like kids. Why did she say she saw me kill Frank? Money?"

"Was she aware Frank was stealing from Monty?" Sidney asked.

"If she was, she didn't share that info with me." I picked up the pen and finished adding to the column the facts we'd discussed so far. "The good news is, we have a motive for Frank's murder. And we know who killed him. What we don't know is how and why Becky is involved, or how we can get Monty and Cam to slink into the nearest abyss."

"We also have a motive for Monty wanting you to get charged with the murder," Sidney said. "Don't forget to add that to your notes."

"I'm not so sure we do have a motive." I frowned at the page and tapped my pen. "Monty is a vengeful lunatic. It makes sense that he'd want to track me down and punish me for shooting him up with ketamine. What makes less sense is him shopping me to the police, even through an intermediary like

Becky. My name is splashed all over the news as the prime suspect in Frank's murder. That means an official international search for me is underway or will be shortly. How does that serve Monty's interests?"

Sidney spread his palms wide. "I don't know Monty. I don't know how he thinks. You said he had contacts in law enforcement. Maybe he persuaded them to help him frame you."

"Yes, but he tends to use those contacts in less obvious ways. And he won't want me talking to the police. He's got people on the inside, but he doesn't wield the kind of power that'd ensure his name would be kept out of the investigation." I stared at the page, willing the words I'd written to yell out a clue. "Monty's a control freak. He'll want to control the narrative. Launching an official search for me is counterproductive."

Sidney toyed with the rim of his cup. "What are you saying? That Monty didn't use Becky to frame you?"

"When I read the newspaper article last night, I assumed he had. The more I think about it, the less sense it makes." My head shot up from the notes I'd been contemplating. "Who else would pay her to frame me? I've never been Ms. Popularity, but the only other person I know who hates me enough to set me up for murder is Cam."

"Could Cam have done it?" Sidney asked. "Found

Frank dead and arranged with Becky to frame you for the crime?"

"If it benefited him? In a hot second. I just can't see how framing me for a pub landlord's murder works in his favor."

"Does he want to curry favor with Monty? Why did he get involved with Monty in the first place? And how would he know Becky?"

"They're both Scottish, but not every Scot knows the other." I shook my head. "I can buy him wanting revenge, but this scenario doesn't make sense. I doubt his parole conditions allow him to leave the UK. Coming to Paris was a major risk. It's not in his interests to have the police, British or French, chasing after me."

"Okay. Let's put Monty and Cam on the back burner for now. Apart from Monty's crew, who knew you were in the pub the night Frank got shot?"

I shrugged. "Anyone at the pub. My name replaced Becky's on the roster because I agreed to cover her shift."

"The police investigating Frank's murder will have seen that roster." Sidney ran a finger under the relevant note on the page. "They'll have found your phone and the other stuff you left behind in the pub. With Becky claiming she saw you pull the trigger, that's enough to make you their prime suspect without Monty trying to frame you."

He had a point. A valid point. But what did it

mean? "If Becky hadn't accused me of murder, the cops would've wanted to talk to me, but they wouldn't have necessarily suspected me of Frank's murder."

"Exactly. And if Monty wouldn't want the police hunting for you, and Cam is an unlikely suspect, who else could have paid Becky?"

"I don't know. My idea factory is all out of stock. Becky was the closest I'd come to making a friend in ages. Not to the point of me spilling my guts, but we could have a laugh together." Come to think of it, I'd confided more in Sidney over the last twenty-four hours than I'd done in a long time. Certainly more than I had in Becky. The notion should scare me, but I found it comforting.

Sidney leaned back and rubbed his chin. "Becky's motive is a line of inquiry we need to pursue."

Luc appeared at our table, effectively ending our brainstorming session. He carried two plates laden with food, one containing a breakfast galette with cheese, ham, and herbs, topped with a fried egg. Despite my vow not to eat, my stomach rumbled. He shot me a knowing grin. "I thought this might tempt you out of your food funk."

"It looks good," I admitted. "Really good."

He deposited our plates in front of us. "I've arranged for Ben, my assistant manager, to take over for me. He'll be here within the next fifteen minutes. Then we'll head to my place and talk."

My smile faded. Even if his food smelled divine, talking to Luc wasn't on my menu.

Sidney intervened before I could say something we'd both regret. "Thanks, Luc. Desirée said we could trust you."

This was an embellishment of what my mother had actually said, but I let it slide. The implication had been there, after all.

Luc gave us a curt nod and then disappeared to serve other customers.

We tucked into our food. To my amazement, I was ravenous. Clearly, my two days of hell had done wonders for my bounce-back skills. Either that or my survival instincts were telling me to replenish my energy reserves before the next catastrophe hit.

The food more than lived up to its appearance. "Oh, my. This is delicious."

"What did Luc give you?" Sidney asked between mouthfuls of sausage. "Some sort of savory crêpe?"

"It's called a galette. A savory crêpe made out of buckwheat." I cut off a piece and nudged it toward the edge of my plate. "Try some."

Sidney forked the piece and popped it into his mouth. He sat back in his seat and moaned. "This is amazing. I'm ordering one of these the next time we come here."

I raised my eyebrow. "There's going to be a next time?"

"We'll have to eat a few more meals before we leave Nice. Why not have them here?"

Because I don't like Luc? I left the thought unsaid. I had no concrete reason for disliking the man, apart from the fact he was disturbingly handsome. He'd been kind to Sidney, and he'd kept the police off our backs. Yet my warning radars pinged every time he came near me.

Pushing thoughts of Luc out of my mind, I angled my plate so I could eat and write. "Okay. Back to work. We've decided it's unlikely that Monty precipitated an international police search for me. We don't know why Becky accused me of killing Frank, but she must've had a reason. Circling back to Monty, we can safely assume he sent the Terrible Twins after me, and presumably Cam too. I'm not sure when Cam got out of prison, or when he started working for Monty. Maybe finding me is a one-off job arranged between Monty and Cam's father. After all, both men have a reason to want me dead."

Sidney shuddered. "You don't think Monty just wanted them to scare you into keeping your mouth shut? Adding another murder to his crime sheet seems extreme."

"Monty knows that even if I'm on the run now, I'll eventually seek help. He's been on the cops' radar for years, but they've never managed to pin a crime on him personally. And as far as I'm aware, Monty's never been suspected of murder. He can't risk me spilling my guts to the cops." A sliver of fear pierced my newly acquired courage. I shook off a shudder and knocked back the rest of my espresso.

Sidney placed his hand on mine. "It'll be okay, Angel. We'll find a good lawyer. If the man your mother mentioned isn't up to snuff, my brother-in-law's a barrister. He doesn't specialize in criminal law, but he's bound to know someone who does."

"Nice to see you two have kissed and made up."

Luc's sardonic tone and teasing eyes had a sandpaper-on-skin effect on me. Heat rushed up my cheeks. I hated him seeing me upset and vulnerable.

Sidney withdrew his hand from mine. "Hey, Luc. Has your assistant arrived?"

"Yeah." The man cocked his head to the side and examined my plate. "I see you're enjoying your food."

Every pore seemed to react to his presence, making me squirm. "It's good," I admitted grudgingly. "I was hungry."

"Finish your meal and meet me out front." His eyes swept over his surroundings. Satisfied no one could overhear, he lowered his voice. "Sidney gave me the lowdown on the contents of your car. I suggest we drive it to my place. I have an underground garage. No one will bother us there."

I didn't fancy driving anywhere in Luc's company, with or without a corpse in the car. However, I didn't see that I had a choice. "Yeah, okay." I made a show of checking my watch. "Give us five minutes."

His slow-burn grin was irritatingly irresistible. "Take your time and enjoy your food." He turned and strode through the open door, leaving me with a burning desire to stick my fork in his back.

"I don't know why you dislike Luc," Sidney said, his voice brimming with amusement. "All he's done so far is help us."

"In a supercilious manner." Perhaps my prejudice against Luc was irrational and unfair. Maybe it was bitter experience setting off warning radars. Regardless, the man unnerved me.

I finished my galette, and Sidney polished off the remains of his full English breakfast. Césaire hissed when I removed him from his comfortable spot in the shade, but thankfully refrained from adding fresh scratch marks to my arms. "It's your turn to carry the cat."

"Is that so?" Sidney grinned at me. "Funny how often it's my turn."

Still, he took Césaire from my arms without further comment and made the barest of winces when the cat rewarded this gesture with a scratch mark.

Outside the café, Luc chatted with an elderly couple at one of the curbside tables and pretended not to notice the two scantily clad teenage girls giggling at him as they walked by. He said goodbye to the seniors and ambled over to us."Where are you parked?"

"In a public car park a few streets from here," I replied. "Close to the Orthodox Church."

Sidney tugged on his sun hat, making me wonder how much pain he was still in. "Do you have air freshener on you, Luc? Or aftershave? Angel didn't like the deodorant I sprayed in the car earlier."

Luc's electric-blue eyes danced with amusement. "Deodorant in the car? My throat is tightening at the thought."

"It stripped the insides of my lungs," I added. "I'd rather ride with Eau de Corpse than that stuff."

Despite not knowing which public car park we were parked in, Luc strode ahead of us, all long strides and swagger. Sidney easily kept pace, but I was forced to break into a jog. A sarcastic remark sat on the tip of my tongue to object, but Luc seemed to know where he was going. Maybe there was only one public car park that matched my description. Or perhaps he was simply a take-charge alpha male.

When we reached the car park, Luc infuriated me by standing at the driver's door. "Toss me the key," he said. "It'll be faster if I drive."

I puffed out my chest. "I drive plenty fast."

"She does." Sidney made fake retching noises. "She mistook the motorway for a Formula One circuit."

Luc's handsome face split into a grin. "Why doesn't that surprise me? I wasn't deriding your driving skills, Angel. I live on the outskirts of Antibes, and it's off the beaten track. You won't find the address on the navigation."

I grunted but threw him the car key. He caught it

in an easy movement. I climbed into the back with Césaire, letting Sidney take the front with Luc. We were soon weaving our way out of Nice, picking up speed when we reached the road that linked Nice with the beach resort town of Antibes.

Despite my grumpiness, it was impossible not to marvel at the gorgeous landscape of the Côte d'Azur, known in English as the French Riviera. I preferred the French name. On a day like today, the azure sky seamlessly met the azure sea. We wound down the coast road, zipping through several small villages. Some were fashionable and teeming with tourists. Others represented a quiet haven for permanent residents.

If I'd been here for any other reason, I'd have soaked up the sights and smells, made the most of every sunny second. But this wasn't a holiday and I wasn't a tourist. The icky reminder dimmed my enthusiasm for our scenic route.

Luc turned off the coast road before we reached Antibes, driving down a sandy track. The beach at Nice was comprised of stones instead of sand. Some people didn't care for stony beaches, but I'd always loved the sharp sensation of the pebbles beneath my water shoes. However, I had to admit that the golden sand at this beach issued a tantalizing invitation. Part of me wanted to forget my troubles, strip down to my undies, and throw myself into the gorgeous blue water.

We slowed in front of a two-story villa set directly on the beach. It was a sleek, modern new-build, complete with floor-to-ceiling one-way windows, a generous balcony on the upper level, and an underground garage. Either Luc's café was a gold mine, or he had another source of income.

Our host punched a code into the keypad by the garage. The door slid open, and we drove down into the basement parking area. Three cars already occupied parking spaces: a snazzy Porsche, an Audi SUV, and a baby-sized Peugeot.

"Nice car collection." I failed to dilute the acid in my tone. "Who drives the Peugeot? Your maid?"

Luc's expression remained impassive. ""No, I do. It's ideal for parking in Nice, but not as good as the Smart I usually drive to work." He pulled into one of the free spaces, and we climbed out of the Mercedes. Césaire immediately leaped onto the top of the Porsche and began washing himself. I expected Luc to object, but he appeared to take Césaire—complete with claws—in his stride. Instead, he turned to me. "I understand you have an unwanted passenger in the boot of your car. Want to introduce me?"

"Not particularly." I wrapped my arms around myself as a precaution. "Boris/Ivan was no looker in life. I doubt spending a day dead in a hot car has improved his features."

"Unlikely," Luc said dryly, "but we have to open the boot if we want to get rid of him."

I squared my shoulders, fighting my revulsion. "All right. Let's do this thing."

None of us moved. I snuck a glance at Luc. He was pale underneath that tan. Maybe he was less familiar with dead body disposal than I'd assumed.

"We're a brave bunch, aren't we?" Sidney pulled a toothpick he'd acquired at Luc's café from the pocket of his shorts and broke it into three pieces. "Want to draw straws? Whoever picks the shortest has to look first."

"Fine," I said wearily. "Whatever."

Luc and I dutifully drew a piece each of broken toothpick from Sidney's fist. We measured them against one another. Sidney's was the shortest. He turned green around the gills.

I grinned. "Drawing straws was your idea, dude. No backing out now."

Sidney walked in a circle and shook his limbs. "Okay. I can do this. Open that boot."

Luc hit the button on the car key, and the lid rose. Sidney walked behind the car so slowly, he might as well have been going backward. Then he leaned down to take a look at the remains of the twin and let out a noise like a strangled chicken.

"What's wrong?" I demanded. "Is he totally gross?"

In slo-mo, an ashen-faced Sidney straightened and turned to face us. "He's not totally gross, Angel. He's totally gone."

21

Sidney's pronouncement had an instant effect on the atmosphere in Luc's underground garage, and an even more profound impact on me. My internal barometer soared from tense to mega meltdown.

"What do you mean, he's gone? Dead bodies don't disappear." Each word exploded from me like a separate gunshot. I slumped to the ground, breathing hard. To my utter humiliation, I burst into tears. Unlike people on TV, I don't cry pretty tears. This was a full-on ugly cry, complete with heaving, hiccups, and snot.

Luc handed me a clean tissue. "Were you particularly attached to the corpse?" he asked, deadpan. "I have to admit I'm relieved he's chosen to push up daisies at a location that isn't my garage."

I scowled at him and let out a flood of words that

would've filled Granny Doyle's swear jar to overflowing.

He took a step back and held up his palms. "Sorry, but I don't get why you're upset. No corpse, no problem. Right?"

Sidney darted me a look and then focused on Luc. "It's not that simple. The dead body was a guy Angel knew. If he's disappeared from the car, that means someone removed him—someone who may think Angel was responsible for his death."

"Or someone who thinks *you're* the murderer," I pointed out. "Cam knows you're with me. That means, so does the surviving twin."

Sidney's mouth gaped, giving an excellent impression of Edvard Munch's painting *The Scream*. "But I never met Boris or Ivan. Why would I want to kill either one of them?"

"Twins, eh? One dead, one alive?" Luc's gaze swiveled from Sidney to me. "You certainly know how to make a first impression. When you trotted into the café this morning, I had you down as a prickly princess with men issues. I had no idea the men in question ranged from a disappearing corpse to his at-large twin."

His droll demeanor sent my mood nuclear. "Do you make a conscious effort to be obnoxious, or does it come naturally? I don't *trot*. I *never* trot. I'm short, yes, but I'm not a prancing pony."

Sidney put a hand on my shoulder. "Easy there,

Angel. I suppose this new shock has pushed you to the breaking point."

All the pent-up emotion of the last two days poured out of me in a volcanic eruption. "I'm not at the breaking point. I'm taking action. I'm owning my own narrative."

"What's the genre of your narrative?" Luc's tone brimmed with amusement. "Literary fiction or horror? Between the crying and the corpse, it's hard to tell."

I shot him my best death ray glare.

"That's enough." Sidney drew back from me and faced Luc. "Can't you see how upset she is? Stop picking on her."

The two men were around the same height, but Luc's muscular build made him appear bigger. A flash of annoyance passed over the man's face, followed by puzzlement. He scrutinized me from head to toe as though seeing me for the first time. Frowning, he strode to the car and peered inside the boot.

And stood motionless for several elongated seconds.

The tension broke when Césaire vaulted from the Porsche to the Mercedes and leaped into the boot.

Luc raised his head and turned back to me, all trace of amusement erased from his face. "I apologize, Angel. When Sidney said the body had disappeared, I assumed it'd never been there. This dried blood proves otherwise."

"Why on earth would we say we had a dead body

in our car if we didn't?" I spluttered. "It's neither April Fool's Day nor Halloween."

"In my defense, your story is farfetched." He pulled his phone from his pocket and tapped the screen. "Plus, the text message Desirée sent me was a mess. I contacted her after I'd patched up Sidney's ear, wanting to know what the heck was going on. She wrote back, mentioned the attack on Jerry, and asked me to help her two 'friends' who were 'in a spot of bother.' She never mentioned Angel was her daughter."

I snorted. "Typical. Desirée's not the maternal type. She probably forgot we're related."

"I doubt that," Sidney said gravely. "It's more likely she was vague in case her message was intercepted."

I stared at him for a long moment, then burst out laughing. "All this coming from a man who didn't know his laptop could be used to track his phone?"

"Since your motorway freak-out, I've racked my brain for the scripts of every thriller I've ever seen." He turned to Luc. "Do you believe us now? Our story's crazy, but it's our current reality."

Luc exhaled and nodded. "I believe you. Your cat's also of the opinion the blood is real. That's good enough for me."

"What?" I stood, squared my shoulders, and forced myself to look into the boot. Dead Russian? Gone. Césaire licking blood from the carpet? Present and incorrect. I tasted bile. "Oh, Césaire. That's disgusting."

"That's a lot of blood," Luc remarked. "And one weird cat. I don't think I've ever seen one with fur that golden. It's almost yellow underneath the black markings."

Sidney pivoted from his position, moving as far away from the boot of death as he could get. "I didn't know cats liked blood."

"They eat mice," I pointed out. "And birds. They may be domestic animals, but they're still animals."

He put a hand on his brow. "All the same, watching him lap up actual blood is turning my stomach."

I sighed and scooped Césaire out of the boot before placing him on the ground. The animal growled at me, baring his sharp teeth.

Luc closed the boot and handed me the key to the Mercedes. "I'll clean it before we dump the car. First, I want to hear the whole story. If I'm going to make myself an accessory after the fact, I'd like to know for which crimes."

He led us up a flight of stone stairs and into a gorgeous open-plan living and dining space. In contrast to the minimalist look of Jerry's apartment, Luc's villa combined rustic charm with modern comfort. Comfortable chairs in livable colors, enormous glass-fronted bookshelves, and a kitchen even I might be tempted to cook in. The floor-to-ceiling windows offered spectacular views of the sea, and I bet the balcony on the upper level was fabulous.

Sidney whistled. "Nice digs."

"Very nice digs," I said dryly. "And if you want to keep them nice, you'd better give me a wet cloth to clean Césaire's paws. I presume you don't want to add blood to the home decor."

Luc fetched a wet cloth from the kitchen and gently wiped Césaire's paws and mouth. To my amazement, the cat cooperated.

"Usually, I'm the one with the cat-charmer skills," I said, "but that cat blows hot and cold with me. What spell did you cast?"

"No spell. Luck." He pointed to a scratch on his arm. "He gave me this earlier. I hope he plays nicely with other cats. Mélisandre is around somewhere. Probably roaming sand dunes."

Luc finished cleaning Césaire and disposed of the cloth in a plastic garbage bag, presumably destined for the incinerator. He didn't strike me as the kind of man who'd allow any DNA evidence to link him to a crime.

The instant he was free, Césaire made a beeline for an elaborate cat climbing tree, presumably the property of the absent Mélisandre.

"Can I offer you two a coffee?" Luc asked. "Or would you prefer iced lemonade?"

I opted for an espresso, and Sidney chose the lemonade. While Luc fixed our drinks, Sidney and I wandered around the living area, pausing by the bookshelves. Luc had eclectic taste. Thrillers lined several shelves, plus a nice collection of vintage mysteries. On others, romances lined up beside chick lit and historical fiction.

I cast an eye around the furniture. These plump armchairs and sofas were made for style and comfort. The abundance of pale pink cushions surprised me, but why shouldn't a man like pink, even a macho guy like Luc? Unless he hadn't chosen the cushions... "This is a big place for one person."

"Subtle as a boulder," Sidney said under his breath.

I ignored him and focused on Luc. "Do you live here alone?"

"Sometimes." He placed a tray with our drinks on the coffee table and gestured for us to sit. "Haven't you been here before, Angel? It was built, what? Four, five years ago?"

I sank into a blissfully comfy armchair and regarded him with bemusement. "Why would I have been here before? We only met this morning."

Luc blinked. "Because this is Desirée's house. She owns this property, plus two others in Nice."

The words were a punch to my already bruised solar plexus. "This is my mother's house?" I had no idea she owned property near Antibes, let alone a beachside villa. And certainly not two places in Nice. How in the world could she afford them all? She was a faded soft porn star, but she'd never earned the kind of money people had imagined. Hers was a pay-to-play business—innuendo intentional. She'd made a little more than her co-stars due to her popularity, which amounted to selling autographed nude pics at places like video stores (back when they were a thing), and making the odd appearance at sex clubs.

A ripple formed on his forehead. "You didn't know? I got the impression you two weren't close, but I assumed you'd be aware where Desirée lived when she was in this area."

"Keeping in touch with her daughter has never been high on Desirée's to-do list."

Although she'd run through a few husbands, none had been wealthy. Jerry, the best of the bunch, had funded my two-year stint at a third-rate boarding school. I doubted she'd netted a decent divorce settlement from any of them. So, where was she getting the money to fund a beachfront villa?

"I find it fascinating that you call your mother Desirée." Sidney perked up visibly. "I always wanted a mother cool enough to allow me to call her by her first name."

"Mine is so cool she gives me frostbite."

Luc considered me for a moment with what I suspected was pity, making me instantly regret my frankness. "Desirée doesn't strike me as the maternal type," he said.

"Trust me, she's not." I eyed him with renewed suspicion. "If my mother owns this house, are you two an item?"

An annoying cat-got-the-cream grin spread across his face. "You do enjoy jumping to conclusions."

To my intense mortification, my cheeks fired up like a furnace. "It's a logical conclusion. You assumed Sidney was my boyfriend."

"Not really. I just said that to annoy you." He rested his massive tattooed forearms on the armrests of his enormous armchair, making the seat look like an ideal candidate for Baby Bear's chair in *Goldilocks and the Three Bears*. "I'm Desirée's house-sitter— on a semi-permanent basis. Desirée stays here when she's in the area."

This didn't fully answer my question, but I figured it was as much as I was going to get out of him for the moment. The fact that this stranger knew more about my mother than I did stung. The fact that he was probably sleeping with her bothered me way more than it ought to and added a sharpness to my tone. "We should focus on why Sidney and I are here. You want a rundown of what's been going on. Why should we trust you?"

"Angel has a point," Sidney said apologetically. "If the corpse has done a Houdini, we don't need your help. We need a compelling reason to confide in you."

Luc arched an eyebrow so dark it looked inked on. "As you both pointed out in the garage, a missing corpse means someone removed the body from the car. I'd say that's a compelling reason."

"True. But if we talk to anyone, it should be a

lawyer." I glanced at Sidney, and he nodded in agreement. "Desirée mentioned a man called Jacques Fournier. Do you know him?"

Luc's lips quivered. "I ought to. He's my grandfather. But if it's a lawyer you want and not my grandfather, in particular, you're already talking to one."

It took a moment for the proverbial penny to drop. When it did, it was with the force of a grenade. "*You're* a lawyer?"

"Why should that surprise you, Angel? Tut-tut. There you go making assumptions again."

I itched to slap the smirk off his face. Instead, I gritted my teeth and plastered a fake smile on my face. "So you're a lawyer. Good for you. Any chance you specialize in criminal law?"

"That was my specialty when I practiced, yes." His calm demeanor gave little away. "My career took a different path to the one I'd originally intended."

"All the way to running a backstreet café? Impressive." I was being mean, but this man riled me.

"If you're a lawyer, even an ex-lawyer, we'll talk to you," Sidney said, shooting me a warning glance.

"Don't I get a say in this?" I demanded.

"Certainly. I'll tell him the parts that involve me. You can tell him the rest."

Sidney straightened in his seat and regaled Luc with our story, tactfully leaving out the specifics of my relationship with Cam and refraining from using names or place names. I cast him an appraising look. Sidney was cannier than I'd thought.

Luc listened attentively, asking pertinent questions when necessary, but otherwise letting Sidney talk. And as I'd discovered when he first sat next to me on the Eurostar, Sidney Foggington-Smythe had a chronic case of verbal diarrhea.

After what seemed like forever, Sidney's story sputtered to its conclusion.

Luc shifted his attention to me. "You've had quite a weekend."

If he'd shown pity, I'd have despised him on principle. Instead, his quiet respect unsettled me and put me on the defensive. "I didn't ask for any of this to happen."

"I don't imagine you did. The question now is what do we do next." Luc leaned his elbows on the edges of his chair and steepled his fingers in a comically subconscious lawyerly gesture. "First, I suggest we find out more about the case against Angel. So far, all you have is a lurid tabloid article."

"If I had access to the internet, I could take care of that myself."

I expected him to object, but he nodded, his expression thoughtful. "Yes, that makes sense. You can use my laptop to do your research. In the meantime, I'll phone my grandfather. If you need legal representation before you speak to the British police, he's your man."

"What should I do?" Sidney's face was boyish and

eager. "I could type up the notes Angel made at the café and add my own thoughts. Or, assuming you have a second computer, Angel and I could divide the internet research."

"I have a tablet computer. You can use that." Luc got to his feet and wandered to the far side of the room to make his call.

"I don't like this," I whispered. "And I don't like him. Coming here was a mistake."

"I don't trust Luc, either."

"What?" My voice rose, and I quickly lowered it again. "Then why did you spill your guts to him?"

"I didn't tell him anything anyone tracking our movements wouldn't know. And I left out all names except ours. I figured you could add those if you wanted to. What other option do we have but to confide in Luc? Even if you and your mother aren't close, she trusts him. I can't imagine she'd suggest we recruit someone who'd hurt you."

Despite my less-than-charitable feelings toward Desirée, I had to agree. My mother was self-absorbed, but she didn't wish me harm.

"Besides," Sidney continued, "whoever removed the body from the car might be waiting to pounce the moment we leave the villa."

I shook my head. "I don't think so. We can't know *when* the corpse disappeared. The one and only time either of us eyeballed the dude was at the motorway rest stop outside Aix."

"He was definitely dead, right?" Sidney's eyes were wide as flying saucers. "If he was just injured, he might've escaped."

"He was dead, Sidney. No doubt about it."

He gave a shuddery sigh. "I knew you'd say that. Then who took him out of the car?"

"Cam? The surviving twin? The car was parked all last night and again this morning. As it's easier to spirit away a corpse in the dark, my guess is he was gone before we got up this morning."

"Are you saying I nearly killed us with deodorant for nothing?"

"Honestly? The only bad smell in the car was that spray."

A gorgeous long-haired Persian cat slipped through the cat flap in one of the floor-to-ceiling windows. She waltzed through the room and jumped onto my lap, meowing in greeting. "Aren't you a beauty," I cooed, stroking her soft white fur. "You must be Mélisandre."

Mélisandre's reply was a satisfied purr. Perhaps I hadn't lost my magic touch with cats after all. I fussed over her, and she accepted my ministrations with lavish enthusiasm. Our mutual lovefest had barely begun when Césaire leaped onto the coffee table, back arched, and fangs bared. Mélisandre's reaction was electric-shock fast. Her high-pitched shriek enraged Césaire, who went in for the attack.

Luc was upon the combatants in an instant. Hurling his phone onto an empty armchair, he hauled

Césaire off the cowering Mélisandre, who vaulted off my lap and streaked through the room at the speed of sound. She was through the cat flap and down the beach before I could react.

Meanwhile, Luc still held the snarling, bucking Césaire in a firm grip. "I knew this was an odd-looking cat. No domesticated cat has fur this golden. This thing's a wild animal."

Sidney and I took another look at the creature we'd fed, watered, and sheltered for almost twenty-four hours. A creature I'd insisted share our bed.

I pushed back into my chair, wishing the fabric would swallow me whole. "What is it? A lynx? A cheetah? A *tiger*?"

Sidney swiped a finger across Luc's phone screen and held it out for us to see. A photograph of an animal with rich golden fur streaked with black markings stared back at us.

I sucked air through my teeth. "Holy hockey sticks. I slept with an ocelot."

22

S idney backed into the bookshelves, holding the phone up to his face like a shield. "I can't believe we drove across France with a wild animal."

"A wild animal *and* a corpse," Luc said, his tone sandpaper dry. "Frankly, I'm not sure which one scares me more."

Césaire struggled against Luc's firm grip, but he didn't let go. I regarded the animal with renewed interest. "To be fair, he can pass for a domestic cat. His ears are pointier and his markings are unusual, but he's no bigger than a house cat."

Luc examined his reluctant captive. "He's probably a kitten. If I recall correctly, ocelots are small by exotic cat standards."

"No wonder the ransom was so high," Sidney said. "I thought it was a bit much for a cat."

I looked at Césaire, then at Luc and Sidney. "What

are we going to do with him? I don't know how to look after an exotic pet."

Césaire chose this moment to drag his claws over Luc's intricately tattooed forearm. Luc grimaced and lost his grip on the animal. With a parting snarl, the ocelot leaped free. He stalked back to the climbing tree, scaling it with a speed that wasn't normal for a regular cat.

"How did I fail to notice we were harboring a bona fide beast?" I mused. "I'm usually more observant."

"You've had a lot on your mind," Sidney pointed out. "Dart guns. Bodies. Deadbeat ex-boyfriends. You've had quite a weekend."

I crossed my arms over my chest. "Thanks, Sidney. You know how to comfort a girl."

"Are ocelots legal to own in France?" he asked Luc.

"The trade in exotic animals is strictly controlled," Luc replied. "Somehow, I doubt Césaire was imported legally. Otherwise, why would his owner not report his theft to the police?"

"Because the kidnappers told him not to?" I suggested. "But, yes, I agree it's more likely that Césaire didn't enter the country by legal means."

Sidney looked back and forth between Luc and me. "Does this information help us locate his owner?"

"No," Luc said slowly, "but it makes me think your original plan for Césaire is still the best course of action. We'll leave him at an animal shelter where he'll be well cared for and can't hurt any other animals."

"I'm up for that plan," I said. "If Césaire's owner has the means to smuggle an ocelot into the country, plus pay an exorbitant sum in ransom, he's not someone I want to mess with. We have plenty of thugs on our tail without adding an overly wealthy exotic animal nut."

Luc's phone vibrated, indicating an incoming call. He took the device from Sidney and frowned at the screen. "It's Desirée."

My stomach knotted as it always did at the thought of my mother. Sidney and I waited while Luc took the call. His side of the conversation was monosyllabic, his expression inscrutable. After what felt like forever, he disconnected and looked at us.

"Well?" I demanded. "How's Jerry?"

"Lucky to be alive. He's got a nasty concussion, and the hospital is keeping him in the intensive care unit. However, they're confident he'll pull through. Unfortunately, the stab wound caused considerable damage to his shoulder. He'll have to have an operation, but the doctors want to wait until he's stable to proceed."

The tension in my shoulders ebbed. "That's a relief. First good news I've heard all day."

"Desirée has a favor to ask you two. And so do I." Luc's gaze rested on me. "She and Francine are still with the police. As a result, they've had to reshuffle appointments and shifts at the costumier and the yarn shop. Seeing as you don't have a corpse to dispose of,

I've agreed to take care of one of Desirée's appointments. This leaves me short-staffed at the café this afternoon. And Maurice needs assistance at the yarn shop. Would you help us out? Desirée will pay you for your time."

It took me a moment to process the implications of what he'd said. "What sort of appointment would my mother have that you could 'take over?' She's a former porn star turned part-time burlesque dancer. Are you planning to strut your stuff at a strip club?"

A flicker of surprise showed on Luc's face before the shutters slammed down. "That's confidential."

An uncomfortable quiet descended over the room. I wanted to push Luc for more information, but I could tell it was a hopeless case.

"Are the yarn shop and the costumier linked?" Sidney asked, slicing through the tension.

"Jerry owns the majority share in both businesses," Luc replied. "Desirée owns the rest."

I inhaled sharply. "Why would my mother invest in a yarn store? She couldn't craft her way out of a crocheted blanket fort."

"You'll have to ask her that." Luc's tone was clipped and didn't bode well for further interrogation. "And in case you're wondering, the café's all mine."

"We'll help out," Sidney said. "Won't we, Angel?"

"What about the Mercedes?" I demanded. "We need to get rid of it. And we have to deal with Césaire."

"I'll take care of the car now." Luc strode to a bowl

on the polished kitchen counter and took out a car key. "You can take the Peugeot. If I draw you a map to the main road, can you find your way back to Nice from there? I'll write down the address of an animal shelter that'll take Césaire. My cousin works there. I'll call her to give her a heads-up, and she'll make sure no awkward questions are asked."

"We'll have to concoct a cover story," I pointed out. "We can't risk the shelter reporting us to the police."

"That's simple. I'll tell Isabelle I found the animal abandoned on the beach. I've asked you two to drop him off at the shelter. Any follow-up questions her bosses might have will be directed at me."

I turned the plan over in my head and couldn't find fault with it. "All right. I'm in. But on one condition."

Luc chuckled. "Are you in a position to be making conditions?"

"I need a smartphone. One that can't be traced back to me. And a laptop."

"That's a lot of equipment for working one shift. Are you sure you don't want to throw in a new car too?"

"I'm happy to borrow the phone and laptop." I forced a smile. "I need access to the internet."

Luc inclined his head and regarded me thoughtfully. "Okay. You can borrow one of my phones."

"Once we've handed Césaire over to your cousin, what exactly do you need us to do?" Sidney asked.

"The yarn shop job is clear enough. But what about the café? Are we to cook? Wash up? Serve food?"

"Please say it isn't cooking," I interjected. "The last time I cooked a meal for the general public, my hotel guests started dying."

Luc's eyebrows rocketed. "You certainly know how to sell your services to a prospective employer."

"I wasn't the poisoner," I clarified, "but it put me off cooking for life."

"Were you fond of cooking before the Lucrezia Borgia incident?"

"Well, no," I admitted. "I can just about boil water."

"I love cooking," Sidney interjected. "I took a summer course at a cooking school in Paris."

"Okay, you're hired. I need someone to help out in the kitchen." Luc turned to me, his eyes dancing with merriment. "How do you feel about knitting needles?"

"The last time I *felt* a knitting needle was when I accidentally stabbed myself with one during a home economics class at school. But if this Maurice bloke needs someone to unpack stock, I'm willing."

"He mentioned expecting a large order of knitting needles and Peruvian wool. He needs someone to help him unpack the boxes."

"Okay. I can do that."

Once Luc supplied me with his spare smartphone, Sidney and I captured Césaire from his perch at the top of the climbing tree and bundled him into the

Peugeot. Now that I knew he wasn't a domestic cat, I was less freaked out by his un-catlike tendencies, but still unimpressed by his propensity to scratch.

With Sidney acting as the map reader, we found our way back to the main road and zoomed toward Nice. Shortly before we reached the city, I pulled into a public car park next to a beach.

"Why have we stopped?" Sidney asked, looking out the window in confusion. "I thought we were to drive straight to the animal shelter."

"Not until I've done a little research on our new pal Luc. You might take his word at face value, but I don't trust that man an inch. I want to know who Luc Fournier is and make sure his cousin really does work at the animal shelter."

"How do you know Fournier is his surname? He said your mother's lawyer, Jacques Fournier, was his grandfather. That doesn't mean they share the same name."

I patted his arm in mock condescension. "His mailbox, dearie. In France, people include their names on their mailboxes. That's why I slowed the car next to it when we were leaving the villa. I wanted to see if my mother's name was included."

"And was it?" Sidney asked.

"Nope. Just a Jean-Luc Fournier. I'm not sure how much that tells me except that the villa isn't listed as my mother's permanent residence."

I slipped the borrowed phone out of my pocket and

input Luc's name in a search engine. I scrolled through several pages and found him listed as a consultant for his grandfather's legal practice. I clicked on the link to get more info. No photo, but a comprehensive curriculum vitae, including the military experience I'd guessed he'd had.

I sighed. "There's more to the man than these details. Unfortunately, I don't have time to dig deeper. Definitely on my to-do list when I acquire a phone that's not owned by Jean-Luc Fournier or his associates. I'll look up the animal shelter next."

Sidney leaned over to look at the screen. "Does Luc's cousin check out?"

"Insofar as they have an Isabelle Fournier listed as working there."

"Now that you've done your due diligence, are we going to get moving?" Sidney looked over his shoulder into the back. "The sooner we bid adieu to the wild beast, the happier I'll be."

"Césaire's behaved well since we left the villa," I pointed out cheerfully. "He's ripped Luc's back seat to shreds."

"I'm not sure whose claws are sharper—Césaire's or yours."

"Tut-tut. Now, who's the mean girl? We'll be back on the road in a minute. I want to check the news to see if there are any updates on my alleged crime." I scanned the popular UK news sites one by one, followed by the French. "I'm still front-page news at home, but I barely register on the French news sites. They're fully focused on their rogue politician. The only site I found with a photo of me has a lousy, overblown CCTV image that could be of anyone."

"That's good news, right?" Sidney said. "Doesn't it mean the French police aren't looking for you?"

"No such luck. I'm sure they've been supplied with a decent photograph of me. The alleged murder of an anonymous London publican by his equally anonymous employee simply isn't interesting enough to the French public." I placed the phone on the dashboard but kept my hand on it. "I could do a search on Becky. See what bull she's spouting on social media."

"I would if I were you," Sidney said. "You can take screenshots to give to your lawyer."

I picked up the phone again and input Becky's name. "I wish she had a less common surname than Campbell," I muttered. "There are a bajillion people called Becky, Becca, Becki, and Rebecca Campbell. And none appear to be the woman I worked with."

He frowned. "I thought you were friends."

"I said we got on well."

"Aren't you friends with her on any of the social media channels? Or has she blocked you?"

I cast him an amused glance. "I pride myself on my hacking skills, remember? I'm not foolish enough to leave a digital footprint."

"Are you saying you're not on any of the major

social media platforms?" His aghast expression made me laugh.

"Shockingly, some of us can survive—and even thrive—without knowing what the person they sat next to in school fifteen years ago had for breakfast." I input the names of the other people who worked at The Lucky Charm and found their profiles with no difficulty. Then I searched through their friend lists. But no Becky. "That's strange. I can't find any trace of her."

"Maybe Becky is also careful about her digital footprint," Sidney pointed out. "She might not be on any social media channel."

I frowned, remembering my ditsy coworker. "Becky was the type who'd live on social media. Even if she'd closed her accounts since talking to the police, they'd still show up in a search." Had I misjudged Becky as severely as I'd misjudged the airhead who'd sat near me on the Tube?

Sidney tapped his vintage watch. "Regardless of Becky's social media presence, we need to get moving. I promised Luc I'd be at the café by two o'clock, and we still need to drop off Césaire."

Still deep in thought, I slid the phone into my pocket and drove us to the animal shelter. We pulled into the staff car park and double-parked the Peugeot. "I'll deal with the ocelot," I said, feeling generous now that Césaire was about to become someone else's problem. "Want to say goodbye to him first?"

Sidney held up his sore hands and glowered at the cage. "How about, 'Goodbye and good riddance'?"

I grinned. "Point taken."

When I carried the animal to the back entrance, Luc's cousin was waiting for me. She was small and dark-skinned with a friendly smile that drew attention to her gold lip ring. "Hey, you must be Angel. And this must be Césaire."

She took Césaire from me. Now that the time had come to say goodbye to the ocelot, I had a lump in my throat. I wasn't even fond of the animal. He'd peed on me, scratched me, and generally proved to be a pain in the behind. Still, he was a handsome creature.

I scratched him behind the ears, just the way he liked it. Césaire purred with pleasure. And then, a split second later, he pulled a Jekyll and Hyde and drew his claws across my hand.

I withdrew my hand and cradled it. "I don't care where you fall in the cat family, Césaire. You are one bad pussy."

The ocelot turned its back on me and began to clean his paws.

Luc's cousin executed a perfect Gallic shrug. "Ocelots are unpredictable. He'll be delighted when we give him a few toys to destroy."

"Destruction is Césaire's middle name," I said. "All the same, I hope you can locate his owner. Someone out there cares about him."

Isabelle's face grew grave. "If he was imported

illegally, his owner will be difficult to trace. But we'll keep him safe regardless. Worst case scenario, he'll go to a zoo."

I said goodbye to her and got back in the car. We drove to the car park where we'd parked the Mercedes this morning and trudged back to Jerry's street. I took Luc's spare phone out of my pocket. "Can you give this back to Luc when you see him?"

"Sure, but I don't know when he'll be at the café. Why don't you keep it until later? Maybe you can use your staff break at the yarn shop to do more sleuthing."

I hesitated, turning this idea over in my mind. It had occurred to me to do just that, but I was reluctant to hang on to any device belonging to the mysterious Jean-Luc Fournier. Even though I'd deleted the internet searches I'd already made on the phone, Luc could quickly check that information if he had the technical know-how. Somehow, I feared he did. All the same, having internet access allowed me to run a cursory check on Jerry, Francine, and my mother.

"Okay. I'll hang on to the phone. Just until I can get my hands on a new one."

Sidney wagged a finger. "No stealing. We're in enough hot water as it is."

I gave a mock salute. "Yes, sir."

We parted outside the café, and I continued on to La Belle Laine, the yarn shop. As I'd suspected, the man with the newspaper who'd sat near us in the café this morning was the manager. Maurice was a dapper little man with a silver-gray handlebar mustache and a tendency to talk. Within fifteen minutes of my arrival, I'd received a rundown on Maurice's life history, including his various careers. According to him, he'd been everything from a circus performer to an accountant. Running the yarn shop was his wind down to retirement.

As I knew nothing about the various yarns and needles the shop stocked, Maurice took care of the customers. I was assigned the exciting task of unloading a million boxes of wool. In a burst of ill-placed optimism, I created a space in the stock room to continue research during my break. I placed the notebook and the leprechaun pen on a table, debated putting the phone there, too, but decided to keep it on my person.

My break was a long time coming. I spent the next three hours lugging boxes through the shop and arranging their contents in the stockroom. Finally, I was down to the last four.

Outside the yarn shop, the afternoon sun beat down in what felt like a relentless rhythm. No salty breeze blew in from the sea, leaving the air around me sticky-hot and obscenely oppressive. I pushed frizzy curls back from my face. Haircare products were on my must-buy list. Another shower using the cheap shampoo Sidney had picked up at the hotel would turn my hair into a French-fried fright.

Four big boxes of yarn stood stacked next to the

doorway. I grabbed the top one and turned to go back into the shop. I was mid-step when I heard the screech of tires. A van pulled up—hot-pink wheels, blaring hip-hop music, burning rubber scent. A sensory triple whammy. My gaze was fixed on the crazy-colored wheels.

Major mistake.

I should've dropped the box and barricaded myself inside the shop.

Too late.

The van door slid open, revealing a vision in skintight latex flanked by two hulking men sporting shades and the no-neck look. The only way for me to tell them apart was the bandage wrapped around one of the thug's hands.

The wannabe supervillain leaped onto the pavement, roundhouse kicked the box out of my arms, and grabbed me by my collar. From beneath a thick fringe of turquoise hair, defiant eyes burned holes in my retina—eyes I'd last seen yesterday, staring at me from a passport photograph.

23

The pavement seemed to shift beneath my feet. "Monique Beaufour?" My voice sounded sucking-on-helium high. How was I going to talk myself out of this situation?

She narrowed her eyes to serpentine slits and jabbed a finger into my chest, so close her jasmine-scented perfume made my nose itch. "You stole my suitcase. And my car. And my cat."

Her French-accented English was flavored with a similar *ooh là là* lilt to my mother's, but her expression was feral with raw rage.

"You want them back?" Aiming for a nonchalance I didn't feel, I spread my palms wide and made an "oh, shucks" face. "No can do on the suitcase or the cat, but you can have your car back. And as a goodwill gesture, I'll even throw in a corpse. How do you feel about a dead Russian mobster?"

"Shut. Your. Face."

"See, I thought we could have a pleasant conversation over a coffee. Or a cocktail if you want a drink to match your hair." I jerked a thumb at Luc's place. "The café serves turquoise daiquiris."

Apparently, Monique wasn't in the mood for cocktails or conversation. She hauled me to the van. I let out a yowl that rivaled even Césaire's best efforts. The high-pitched noise right next to her ear made her wince. I wriggled out of her grasp and elbowed her in the ribs. Monique grunted, doubled over, but rallied fast. She socked me in the jaw before I could defend myself.

The pain was intense. I staggered back, swayed, and collided with a postbox. I'd always rolled my eyes at cartoon characters seeing stars and weird symbols when they got hit. Yet here I was, watching asterisks and hashtags float before my eyes.

Monique's grip closed around my arm. She yanked me toward the van, then gave me a vicious shove between the shoulder blades.

I face-planted on the floor of the van, my feet still on the pavement.

Monique leaped over me and into the driver's seat, letting the no-necks haul me inside. The vehicle took off before they'd slid the door shut. I pushed myself up and tried to wriggle free from them. I kicked and screamed and bit. I knocked off one guy's sunglasses and smashed the other in the face.

But I was losing, and we all knew it.

The guy with the bandaged hand grabbed a soggy cloth from an open toolbox. "Stay still, and we won't make this hurt—too much."

Unlike Monique, he spoke English with a guttural accent that hinted at Eastern Europe. His words were a surefire way to make me disobey. I bucked and railed against my captors, but the two thugs held me fast. The one with the cloth put it over my mouth and pressed it tight.

The sickly sweet smell of chloroform made me gag. I held my breath and fought them with all my might, landing a blow to one guy's crotch. He crumpled like a rag doll. His reaction brought me immense satisfaction. Unfortunately, I didn't have long to savor the moment.

The second no-neck didn't release his hold on me or the chloroformed cloth. My lungs burned. I couldn't keep fighting. I had to breathe. I sucked in chemical-tainted air. My vision faded, flickered, and then went out as I lost consciousness.

When I came to, my world rocked from side to side. For several minutes, I rocked along with it, too groggy to realize the implications. Finally, it came to me. I was in a boat. The bowels of a boat. I was in a small berth in a cabin so narrow I could almost touch both sides.

I tried to sit up, but a wave of nausea rolled over me. I barely had time to grab the bucket next to my berth before I threw up. After I'd reacquainted myself with breakfast, lunch, and possibly my food intake for the last month, I sagged against the wall.

There was no mistaking the sway of the boat or the porthole that gave a glimpse of the periwinkle blue Mediterranean. I wasn't just on a boat. I was out at sea. This wasn't good.

I grabbed the bottle of mineral water secured in a holder next to the bed, opened it, sniffed, and took a long drink of cold water. I didn't know how long I'd been unconscious, but the water was nice and cool and couldn't be long from the fridge.

Once I'd rid myself of the taste of past meals, I reached into my pocket for Luc's phone.

And came up empty.

I swore fluently in several languages. Naturally, they'd gotten rid of the phone. It would've been my first move in their shoes. Whatever about the no-necked thugs, Monique struck me as a sharp customer.

I checked my watch. The analog dials showed nine thirty. Morning or evening? I groped my way to the porthole and peered through. Yeah, my impression of periwinkle blue had been spot-on. A brilliant orange-yellow sunset was in progress, turning the sea into a shimmering blue-purple. Monique and the no-necks had kidnapped me around three in the afternoon. Assuming today was still today, I'd been out for six, six and half hours. To keep me unconscious for that long, chloroform hadn't been the only drug they'd given me.

What had they given me? Rohypnol? No wonder I felt like roadkill.

The cabin door crashed open, making my upset stomach lurch.

Monique leaned a slim hip against the doorframe and gave me a malicious once-over. "You look like hell."

"I feel worse." I lurched my way back to the bucket and bid *adieu* to the water I'd just drunk. After I was done, I slumped next to the berth. "What in the blazes did you give me?"

Her scarlet lips formed a spiteful sneer. "Trust me, you don't want to know."

I grabbed the edge of the berth and pulled myself to standing. Still woozy, I staggered across the cabin.

Monique blocked my exit.

I met her stare for stony stare. "Thanks for the splendid hospitality, but it's time I was leaving."

She snorted and pointed a perfectly painted talon at the porthole. "We're ten nautical miles from the Port of Nice. I hope you can swim."

"I can, but in my current condition, I'd wind up as flotsam."

Monique's lips quivered and then flattened into a scowl. "Smart aleck. The boss wants to talk to you."

"Is this the boss who paid one hundred thousand euros ransom for his pet's safe return?"

"Yeah." She crossed her arms over her chest, drawing attention to the deep V of her latex catsuit.

"Before we go anywhere, I want to know who you are. Who do you work for? And where's Césaire?"

First Francine, now Monique. Any second now, she'd accuse me of being a paid assassin. I copied her arms-across-the-chest stance. "Thanks to you, I'm currently unemployed. I was working a trial shift at the yarn shop when you and your muscled minions grabbed me. I guess I can kiss goodbye to that career prospect. As for Césaire, he's safe."

"Why should I believe you?" She took a step closer, getting up in my face. "If you've hurt that animal, my boss will hurt you in ways you can't even imagine."

Anyone willing to pay a hundred thousand euros for Césaire's safe return had to be rich and powerful. And as I knew from bitter experience, influential people can get away with murder. Literally.

"Check out my face," I said, edging away from her. "Césaire hurt me, not the other way around. You know he's an ocelot, right? Because when you grabbed me off the street, you accused me of taking *your cat*." I laid emphasis on these last two words.

"I wanted to find out how much you knew about Césaire and his owner." Her nostrils flared. "Who hired you to steal my suitcase and my ride?"

"No one. It's all a massive misunderstanding." I spread my arms as wide as they could go in the tiny cabin. "What can I say? I ran into a spot of bother in London. When you sat across from me on the Underground, I took you for an easy mark. My mistake. If I'd known the complications you and your suitcase would bring me, I'd have hurled it onto the tracks."

"I don't remember seeing you on the Tube," she said in an accusatory manner, as though this oversight were my fault. "I went over the passengers in my head when I realized my suitcase was missing, but the carriage was packed. Why, out of all the people on that train, did you have to rob me?"

Despite the dire situation, I laughed. "I've been asking myself that question for the last two days. Look, you flashed your passport in front of me. I needed to disappear. Simple as that. I had no idea your case contained a ready-made costume and a wad of cash. And the dude dangling car keys in front of my face in Paris? I was being chased by three irate thugs. I needed a getaway vehicle. As for the ocelot, I wouldn't kidnap that thing for a million euros. It's vicious."

She smirked. "So I've heard. Thankfully, I've never met the creature. My boss keeps his pet in his private apartment. No staff allowed."

"So chasing after an ocelot isn't part of your regular job description?"

"If it were, I'd have quit long ago." Monique scratched her right arm, pulling a face as though it was driving her crazy.

"Allergic to latex?" I drawled. "You might want to rethink your choice in outfits."

She dropped her arm and glared at me. "Is there anyone in your life you haven't antagonized recently?"

"I'm not a contender to win a Miss Congeniality award," I admitted. "But even by my low standards, the number of people currently out for my blood is extreme."

A line rippled between her brows, and she scratched her arm again. "So if you aren't connected with Césaire's kidnapping, why did you rescue him?"

"The kidnappers had hacked the satnav in the Mercedes. When I tried to program the navigation, I got a recorded message giving me instructions to deliver ransom money, followed by dire threats about Césaire's fate if I didn't comply. I assumed Césaire was a person. I'd stolen your passport and your car, thus preventing you from rescuing him. I guess I felt it was my duty." I paused to let her process this information. "And, of course, there was the minor fact that I needed transport, had no fixed destination, and half of London's underworld was on my tail."

Monique's gaze sharpened. "If your trip to France was pure chance, how do you explain the man traveling with you? Peregrine Foggington-Smythe?"

The name Peregrine threw me for a moment, but there was no forgetting Sidney's dreadful double-barreled surname. I'd hoped to keep him out of this conversation, but if Monique had tracked me down to the yarn shop, she'd probably been following us for a while. "How do you know about my friend?"

"I saw him with you. Did you know his father works for the British Foreign Office?"

"He mentioned his father was a diplomat," I said slowly, not sure where this was going. "But what does that have to do with me?"

"That's what I'd like to know."

"How did you find me? The Mercedes?"

"Yeah." She pursed her lips. "Armin, the man who gave you the car keys, assumed you were me. The outfit he described you wearing was the disguise I'd planned to wear when I picked up the Mercedes. So I realized at once that the person who'd stolen my suitcase in London was the same person who'd taken my car in Paris."

"How did you know I had Césaire? Did the kidnappers contact you?"

She glared at me. "I ask the questions, not you. Why did you keep the car once you realized it was connected to a kidnapping plot?"

"I'd planned to dump it yesterday evening, but events intervened. When did you get to France?"

"Thanks to your shenanigans, hours later than planned. I've been trying to track the car and find Césaire ever since." Her eyes narrowed a fraction. "You still haven't answered my question about your friend Foggington-Smythe. How do you know him? I assume he translated the ransom instructions for you."

"I managed to get the gist," I replied dryly.

She wrinkled her perfect little nose. "You English

always have such terrible French. I happen to know Foggington-Smythe is an exception."

I regarded her thoughtfully, my mind working overtime. Normally, I bristled when anyone assumed I was English—a typical Irish trait—but that wasn't what was bothering me. I played and replayed the memory of the dark silhouette who'd shot at the Mercedes as we drove away from the animal clinic in Aix-en-Provence. A smaller silhouette than I'd thought likely for Cam or the twins. The jigsaw puzzle pieces began to fit together...until my careful contemplation was cut short by a strong wave that rocked the boat.

Monique grabbed the edge of the door and managed to stay upright. I went flying and landed on the floor. The violent movement triggered another bout of nausea, but the distraction had bought me more time to slot pieces into place.

One such piece screamed loud and clear. Sidney had said he never went by his first name, but his official documents would be under Peregrine. So might his credit card.

From the moment she'd confronted me outside the yarn shop, Monique had spoken to me exclusively in English. She didn't realize I was a dual national who spoke French as well as she did. She was aware of Sidney's identity courtesy of the money machine, but she didn't know mine.

My lips curved into a wicked smile. Monique, the badass supervillain, had no idea who I was.

24

J pulled myself up and looked my kidnapper straight in the eye. "You don't know my name, do you?"

Monique's elfin features hardened to granite. "Shut up. I ask the questions, not you."

I sniffed the air. "Even in my post-chloroformed state, I smell the sweet scent of prevarication."

She took a step toward me, thought better of it, and retreated with a snarl.

"Your English is good enough to understand that word? Impressive. Or do you simply have enough sense to know when you're being baited?"

The V-neck of my adversary's low-cut catsuit inflated to such an extent that I wondered if her boobs would fall out.

"You're pumping me for clues as to my identity," I continued, thoroughly enjoying having her at a disadvantage. "You know my friend's name because he used his credit card. This means you have access to security camera footage from Montpellier. You saw him withdraw cash, noted the time, and checked all the transactions at the ATM. But you haven't a clue who I am. The person who, as you put it, stole your suitcase, your car, and your cat."

"So you're smart as well as a smart aleck." Monique's sneer seemed forced, but the revolver she whipped out of her holster looked real enough. She leveled the gun at me. "You're correct. I don't know your name. Care to share?"

"Not particularly. I never bought into the 'caring is sharing' baloney. Besides, I don't care to share with a woman pointing a loaded revolver at my chest." I gestured to her weapon, amazed at how calm I sounded when my internal organs were engaged in a game of Twister. Perhaps I was getting used to having my life threatened on a regular basis. Or maybe I was fed up with people messing me around.

Monique's dark eyes turned as cold as liquid nitrogen. "Why did you and Foggington-Smythe visit Jerry Gallo this morning? Are you connected to him?"

The intensity of her gaze turned my insides to mush, but I held my ground. "Was that you following us? I had a feeling we were being shadowed."

"Answer my questions," she snapped. "I want to know who you are and who hired you."

"I bet you want to know a lot of things. However, sharing goes both ways. Your name isn't Monique, is it? I bet that's one of the many aliases on your many passports. How else did you arrive in Paris so quickly after I did?"

"Okay, Sherlock. That much is true." Keeping her revolver trained on my heart, she checked her watch. "We'd better walk and talk, Ms. No-Name. My boss gets antsy if he's left waiting."

Battling the urge to hurl, I held her glacial gaze in a deadlock. "Your boss can wait another five minutes. You followed us across France. It was you I saw in the car park in Aix-en-Provence, wasn't it? Did you kill the Russian?"

A spasm of annoyance passed over her face. "That wasn't planned."

"Story of my life. All the same, I want to know what happened. Did he attack you?"

Her jaw jutted forward, and her eyes narrowed to slits that reminded me of Césaire's signature look. "It was more a matter of us attacking each other. I tracked the car to Aix, but you and Foggington-Smythe had already left the car park when I arrived. Instead, I discovered a large man lurking around the Mercedes. When I approached the car, he pulled a knife." She shrugged. "So I returned the favor."

"And your altercation ended in you plunging your knife into him several times," I finished. "Whereas you appear to be unharmed."

Monique's smirk returned. "What can I say? Speed trumps strength."

"Why did you put him in the Mercedes for me to find? Were you trying to frame me for his murder?"

The smirk wavered. "What are you talking about? I didn't try to frame you. Why should I? I need you to help me find that blasted animal."

"You put the dead man in the boot of the Mercedes." I cocked my head to the side. "How did you think that would come across? And what hack did you use to open the boot?"

"No hack needed." Her lips stretched into a humorless gash that bore no resemblance to a smile. "I had a spare key. As for the body, I put it in the boot in case anyone walking through the car park posed awkward questions about the corpse at my feet. I intended to wait for you and your friend to return and tackle you then."

"Unfortunately for you, we scuppered your plans by leaping into the car and taking off."

"With Césaire." Her lips twisted into a painful knot. "Which didn't make me happy."

"A grievance you expressed by firing shots at us as we drove away." I looked her up and down. "Yeah, you were the person I saw in the rearview mirror."

Monique flicked a wrist, dismissing me like one would a pesky fly. "Stop talking and start walking. My boss isn't a patient man."

"I'll walk when you tell me why you removed the corpse from the car."

Her eyes widened in what appeared to be genuine surprise. "What are you talking about? I didn't touch the body after I put it in the Mercedes."

A bead of sweat formed on my upper lip. "Are you saying you didn't take the dead Russian out of the car somewhere between Aix and Nice?"

"Of course not. Why would I? I hadn't intended to kill him, but once you drove off with his body, I figured you could deal with the consequences."

"What about the lumps of lard who helped you bundle me into the van outside La Belle Laine? Could one of them have removed the corpse?"

Monique blinked several times before answering, making me doubt the veracity of her response. "No. They know nothing of this dead Russian. Why should they?"

If she hadn't made the dead man disappear, who had? Cam? The surviving twin?

A big man appeared behind Monique. It was one of the no-necks who'd hauled me into the van. He tapped his watch. "The boss wants you to bring her to the lounge," he said in French.

Monique made a moue of distaste. "She just woke up, Mirko," she replied in the same language. "Give me a chance."

He hovered in the doorway, making no sign of departing. Monique stiffened in his presence and glared at me. "Enough of this nonsense," she said to me in English. "Get moving."

She pushed me out of the tiny cabin and into a long, narrow corridor. I stopped and blinked several times, taking in my surroundings. The boat we were on was bigger than I'd thought. It was a yacht. A superyacht. Maybe even a megayacht. Courtesy of summers spent on an Irish island, I knew how to sail, but my experience began with a rowing boat and ended with a clapped-out, fourth-hand speedboat.

Monique jabbed me in the back with the revolver. "Stop dawdling."

She prodded me down the corridor, followed by Mirko. We climbed three flights of narrow stairs, each culminating in a deck more luxurious than the one below. The third staircase brought us up to a sprawling lounge with floor-to-ceiling windows, a fully-stocked bar, a hot tub, and a retractable skylight roof.

Three nape-challenged dudes loitered with intent. One was the man with the bandaged hand—the guy who'd held the chloroformed cloth over my mouth. Mirko joined him, muttering something I couldn't make out. The no-neck with the bandage darted a lovelorn glance at Monique and looked crestfallen when she ignored him.

I nodded to the thugs. "Gentlemen." With the impassivity of Buckingham Palace guards, they all stared through me.

In the center of the lounge, a bald man sat cross-legged and barefoot on a rug. He seemed as wide as he was tall, and he appeared to be meditating. This guy was the closest thing to a Buddha that I'd seen in real life.

"I take it you're the boss man," I said in English, determined to maintain the impression that I didn't understand French. "Nice yacht, but I can't say I'm impressed by your hospitality. I feel like a third-class passenger aboard the *Titanic*."

The man opened his eyes. His zen vibe ended the instant his gaze locked with mine. His bushy white eyebrows formed a vicious V, piercing my bubble of self-control. His small, raisin orbs were the meanest I'd ever eyeballed.

Bad Buddha.

"I am Mr. Christianopoulos." He spoke in deliberate, heavily accented English, each syllable requiring great effort. "You stole Césaire."

Not waiting for an invitation and not expecting one, I dropped onto a plushly upholstered seat opposite Bad Buddha. I leaned back and jerked a thumb at Monique. "I stole her suitcase. That set off a chain reaction that led to me stealing her car. But I didn't steal Césaire. I rescued him. You should be praising me, not drugging me."

The man's wheezy laugh made me wonder if he needed an oxygen tank. "Nice try, English lady, but I don't believe you."

In common with every self-respecting Irish person,

I itched to correct his assumption that I was English, but common sense prevailed. Much better to let him make assumptions. "I don't care what you believe, but this happens to be the truth."

"Where is the money we left in the car?" he demanded, stabbing me with his cold eyes. "What did you do with the briefcase? Where is Césaire?"

"If you wanted to interrogate me, drugging me was a bad move." I made a revolving finger gesture at the side of my head. "I'm woozy and confused."

"Unless you want to be dead, you'd better start talking."

"I left the ransom money at the drop-off point, just like the kidnappers instructed." I pointed at Monique. "I already told your lackey all of this."

Bad Buddha's beady gaze fixed on his employee. The dude made my skin crawl. Judging by the flash of disgust that flickered over Monique's face when she looked at him, she felt similarly.

"What did she tell you when you questioned her?" the man demanded in French. "How is she connected to the kidnappers?"

Monique replied in a language I didn't understand. Greek? Bad Buddha's name sounded Greek. Whatever she'd told her employer didn't please him. He turned up the volume and gesticulated wildly, pointing at me, the no-necks, and Monique in no particular order.

She stood in stoic silence during his harangue. Her only movement was to reach under the sleeve of her catsuit to scratch the spot that had been bothering her earlier. Why she'd opted for a long-sleeved latex outfit in this heat was beyond me. After enduring a rapid flow of what sounded like abuse, she snapped a response, thus sending Bad Buddha into a frothing fury.

Their tense exchange lasted for a few minutes, giving me an opportunity to search for an escape route. Despite my *Titanic* quip, I was confident that a yacht this size would have smaller boats on board—in case of an emergency, as well as an easy way to go to shore. My rusty sailing skills might stretch to a small speedboat. Gaining access to one would be the issue.

I studied the no-necks. Their number had doubled since our first encounter in the van, and I was sure more thugs lurked unseen on board the yacht. A man wealthy enough to have his own mini-*Titanic* would have a legion of security guards at his beck and call.

Finally, Bad Buddha finished chewing out Monique, and her rigid posture relaxed a fraction. He turned those evil eyes on me. "Where is my little Césaire?" he demanded in English. "You must tell me at once."

I threw my head back and laughed. "How stupid do you take me for? If I tell you where Césaire is, you have no reason to keep me alive. I have no intention of ending up as fish food."

The man's growl was as fierce as his expression. "I'll find Césaire with or without your help. But know this: if you've hurt him, I'll make your death slow and painful."

A ripple of revulsion coursed through me. "I haven't hurt your pet. Césaire is safe. Like I said before, I rescued your pet. I'm not responsible for his kidnapping."

"If you rescued Césaire, why did you not bring him to me?"

"I didn't know who *you* were. I wanted to return Césaire to his owner, but I had no easy way of finding out who he belonged to. Also, I had more pressing matters to deal with than tracking down an overly rich exotic pet owner."

Bad Buddha's lips moved, and he emitted a bark that bordered on laughter. "Monique mentioned you had a selection of villains in pursuit. What have you and the young Englishman done to be so unpopular among the criminal classes?"

I shrugged. "It's our natural charm."

Bad Buddha shook his head. "You're brave. I'll give you that. Stupid to anger me, but you bear up well under pressure. I don't suppose you're looking for a new job?" His gaze swiveled to Monique, who refused to make eye contact with either of us. "I'm displeased with some of my current employees."

"I'm deeply flattered," I said dryly, "but I don't accept employment from people who kidnap me, drug me, and then threaten me with a torturous death."

The man's laugh turned into a coughing fit.

Whatever he'd intended to say next was interrupted by the roar of an approaching speedboat. I whipped around to see a white-and-blue blur zipping through the darkness. The glaring lights reflected on the now dark sea made it impossible for me to see their faces, but there was no mistaking the shape of a submachine gun.

The no-necks' hands went to their holsters. My heart went to my throat. I was done with adrenaline-fueled action, but was it done with me?

25

"Prepare to attack," Bad Buddha shouted in French. "It might be the kidnappers."

The no-necks got into position, weapons cocked. The two who'd helped kidnap me moved to the sides of the yacht while the other men flanked their master.

With the threat of an imminent bombardment, Monique snapped out of her sulk. She made for the bar, deliberately kicking my shins on her way. Sensing it would be worth my while, I followed her, pushing past the pain with each step I took.

My instinct was rewarded. Monique tapped a code into a security panel embedded into the bar's wooden counter. I memorized her finger movements—another trick taught to me by my dad's dodgy pal Jimmy the Rat. Once she'd input the sixth digit, the wooden panels retracted, revealing an arsenal worthy of a Jason Statham movie.

"Overkill much? You see one speedboat and freak out." I was careful to speak in English, maintaining the impression that I was a proud monolinguist. I squatted and examined the contents of the cache. "Nice collection. Can I snag one of the SIG Sauers?"

"No," said everyone else in unison.

Glaring at me, Monique whipped out an MP5, ammo, and field glasses. She hit a button to close the cache and then strode to the windows. She peered through the binoculars and released a string of words I guessed to be Greek swear words. "It's the *Aurora*."

"The *Aurora*? Are you sure?" Bad Buddha straightened his legs and allowed his bodyguards to help him to his pudgy feet. "What can they want?"

They spoke French, not Greek, presumably for the benefit of the no-necks.

"Her, presumably." Monique indicated to me. "We picked her up outside La Belle Laine. I was careful to toss her phone into the sea when we were still in port, but someone will have seen us outside the shop."

Bad Buddha's beady eyes sought me out. I adopted a bland expression and checked out his impressive array of vodka bottles. If they assumed I couldn't follow their conversation, they'd keep speaking in French. I didn't want them to switch to Greek again. I had few advantages in this game of cat and mouse, and I had no intention of blowing those I had.

"La Belle Laine? Why didn't you tell me this before?" Bad Buddha glared at Monique, his round face turned an interesting shade of puce. Then he rounded on Mirko. "Why didn't you inform me where you picked her up?"

Mirko slid Monique an ominous look before answering. "Elektra said she'd bring you up to speed."

Monique's real name was Elektra? My wannabe supervillain description hadn't been far off the mark.

"A misunderstanding, sir," Elektra said smoothly, not meeting Mirko's accusing stare. "I told you we should have kept the collection team to two. Adding a third person to the mix always causes confusion."

"After you failed to rescue my little Césaire? And lost me one hundred thousand euros? I sent Mirko to supervise." Bad Buddha's voice rose in volume with each sentence.

"It would have been more efficient to let me and Ladislav go on our own," Elektra insisted, keeping her tone neutral.

"Ladislav is a fool," Bad Buddha snapped. "I wanted someone I could trust in charge. Mirko has never messed up a job." He left the "unlike you" unspoken, but the meaning hung in the air like a bad smell.

I checked out Mirko, the alleged supervisor of my kidnapping. He was sallow-skinned and huge—well over six feet four. Despite his size and supposed seniority, he'd let Elektra walk all over him.

"Seeing as we found the girl outside La Belle

Laine," he said to his boss, "she must be connected to Gallo's operation. Maybe Foggington-Smythe too. You read my report?"

Bad Buddha's bushy white eyebrows formed a V of concentration. "Yes. The boy speaks many languages, including Russian. His grandmother is ex-KGB. That would interest the Omega Group."

Operation? The Omega Group? Ex-KGB? This was fast turning into a bad action movie. Had the drugs they'd pumped me with given me paranoid delusions? Or was this conversation all too real?

"Have you heard any rumors about the Omega Group expanding their team?" Mirko asked Bad Buddha and Elektra.

Both shook their heads.

"Have you heard anything, Ladislav?" Bad Buddha barked across the deck.

The thug with the bandage pivoted from his position at a starboard side window. "No, sir."

"I'd be surprised if they wanted to add any new players right now. Not after last week's fiasco." Elektra checked that her MP5 was fully loaded. "Gallo's deal with Rocco Casetti went south in a spectacular fashion. He'll be too busy dealing with the fallout to think about new hires."

Bad Buddha grunted in agreement before turning his reptilian gaze back to me. He subjected me to a scrutiny so intense it felt like a prison strip search. I returned the favor, using the current stalemate to process what I'd learned.

Rocco Casetti had to be the Rocco my mother had mentioned—the man she suspected had been responsible for the attack on Jerry. And the Omega Group? Was that Jerry's company? And if so, were Bad Buddha and his cohorts implying that Jerry was involved in organized crime? Poor, boring Jerry who was so bland and unassuming that I'd barely remembered what he looked like?

One of the unnamed no-neck's walkie-talkies crackled into life. He held it to his ear, listened, and grunted. "They want permission to come on board."

Bad Buddha shrugged and switched to English. "Okay. We have visitors. Maybe they'll tell us what happened to my little Césaire."

And maybe they'd distract Bad Buddha long enough for me to steal their speedboat and escape. Hey, I was due a lucky break, wasn't I?

The no-neck muttered into the walkie-talkie. A few tense moments later, three people emerged at the top of the stairs. Luc—cool, calm, collected. My mother —elegant, poised, sexy. And then came Sidney, resplendent in a neon-orange life vest. His hair stuck up wildly after his ride on the speedboat, and his new sunglasses were held together by duct tape. A large bruise was forming on his forehead.

"An accident on the speedboat?" I asked in English, my tone dry as the Sahara.

"Those things move fast." Sidney removed his wrecked shades and blinked owlishly at his surroundings, finally focusing on me. "You didn't tell me you were going sailing."

"It was all rather spur of the moment," I replied in a tone that was more lemon than lemonade.

Luc placed his submachine gun at his feet. It was an open gesture of peace. Although Elektra and the no-necks didn't reciprocate, they lowered their weapons.

Without looking at me, my mother swanned across the deck. She'd changed out of the clingy dress she'd worn this morning. Instead, she wore a charming vintage sailor suit. She'd arranged her blond hair in a '50s-style high ponytail, held in place by a scarf decorated with anchors. Her dainty blue and white ballet shoes matched the nautical theme.

She stopped in front of Bad Buddha and held out her hands. "Giorgios," she said in her best husky stage voice. "How are you? It's been forever since I last saw you."

Bad Buddha bowed to my mother and kissed her hands, clinging to them longer than I'd have tolerated if I'd been in my mother's dainty little shoes. "Desirée, my dear. Enchanted, as always." He indicated Monique. "You know Elektra, my PA?"

Desirée pasted on her most charming smile, the one that didn't quite meet her eyes. "Elektra. Of course. We met at the ball in Venice. You had lavender hair on that occasion."

"And you were Rocco's date," Elektra replied with a smirk. "I'm sorry to hear things didn't work out between you two."

My mother's smile didn't falter. "How sweet of you to say so, but Rocco was strictly business. Given your own history with him, I'm sure you'll understand why I wanted to keep our interaction on a professional footing."

Elektra's lips drew back in a snarl.

Miaow. These two had claws sharper than Césaire's.

Bad Buddha cleared his throat. "Kind of you to pay us a visit, Desirée. And Fournier, too."

Luc inclined his head but remained as impassive and silent as Bad Buddha's no-necked bodyguards. What role did he play in Jerry's business? And in my mother's life?

"When we learned the *Aurora* was approaching, I was expecting Fournier." Bad Buddha regarded my mother through slit-like eyes. "I didn't realize you were back in Nice."

"A flying visit, darling. I'm heading to Monte Carlo in the morning."

Bad Buddha's snake eyes settled on Sidney. "You've brought the English boy with you, Desirée. Is Mr. Foggington-Smythe your new recruit?"

"New recruit for what?" Sidney, who'd been rubbing his sore forehead, perked up instantly.

My mother's tinkering laugh made my teeth

vibrate with unfilial feelings. "Oh, no. Sidney doesn't work for us. He and my daughter are just helping out at the café and the yarn shop."

"Your daughter?" Bad Buddha's fleshy forehead folded into a frown. "I thought she was away at boarding school."

"I was," I said in French, enjoying his and Elektra's matching slack-jaws when they registered my language switch. "However, the nuns were disinclined to keep me beyond the age of eighteen. That was several years —and several careers—ago. And speaking of careers, my mother was being discreet."

Desirée's smile stiffened into a rictus.

Dared I do this? My impetuousness had gotten me into trouble in the past. However, it had also gotten me back out. Apart from Sidney, everyone standing on this deck had riled me in some way today, ranging from Luc irking me in the café, to Bad Buddha imprisoning me on his yacht. The invisible daggers my mother was aiming my way decided my fate.

"Come now, Mother dear. We're all friends here, right? All the kissing, and the pawing, and the military-grade weapons? Why don't we let Mr. Christianopoulos into our little secret?"

"What secret?" Bad Buddha demanded, his serpentine gaze swiveling from me to my mother and then back again.

"There's no secret." Desirée's voice had turned

from husky to harsh. Her femme fatale act was slipping.

I held out my hand to Bad Buddha. "We haven't been properly introduced. I'm Angel Doyle, and this is my associate, Sidney Foggington-Smythe. We're the Omega Group's new dream team."

26

Desirée's exhale reminded me of a deflating balloon. Her expression contorted before she regained control of her emotions. She turned a simpering gaze at Bad Buddha. "What Angélique means is—"

"I'm delighted to meet you, sir." Sidney's booming voice eclipsed my mother's dramatic efforts. He stepped forward and pumped the bemused Bad Buddha's pudgy fist. "New job, new start. I'm thrilled to be part of the Omega Group."

I'd known he could act, but I wasn't sure how he'd cope without a script. Realizing he could pull off improv was a huge relief.

"I knew you two had to be part of their crowd." Elektra stalked over to me, jabbing a finger in an accusatory fashion. "And you speak French. Why did you let me think you didn't?"

"In English, we have a lovely saying involving the word assumptions. If you were determined to make them, why would I stop you? Besides, I rather enjoyed listening in to your conversations—all of them."

I let the implication sink in, enjoying the flicker of panic on her face, and Bad Buddha's obvious consternation. I had no clue what they'd said to one another when they'd conversed in Greek, but if they wanted to leap to the conclusion that I'd understood them, who was I to correct this impression?

"I'm delighted we're all getting to know each other," my mother purred in a desperate attempt to draw our attention back to her. "However, our visit isn't a mere social call, Giorgios. I believe Elektra and my daughter had a communication problem. How can I help to redress the issue?"

Elektra snapped to attention. "Your daughter screwed up my mission to rescue Mr. Christianopoulos's pet. She's an absolute menace."

My mother fluttered her eyelashes. "I'm sure Angélique wouldn't do anything to endanger an animal. It must have been a misunderstanding."

Elektra's face turned puce. "She stole my stuff. Then she snuck into France using *my* passport."

"Using your *fake* passport," I pointed out. "*One* of your fake passports. We've established your legal name isn't Monique Beaufour."

"No." My mother's tone was saccharine-sweet. "That's one of Elektra's favorite aliases. It's so quintessentially French. But then she does speak French like a native. I can allow her the presumption."

"Nevertheless," Bad Buddha cut in, visibly irritated to have lost control over the proceedings, "your daughter and her friend have caused me considerable distress. From what Elektra has told me, they impeded my efforts to rescue my pet ocelot. And they stole my money."

"That's not true." Sidney's voice was firm and projected beautifully. All that time in drama school had stood him in good stead. "Angel and I intervened in a kidnap plot and saved your pet."

Bad Buddha scowled. "If this is true, then where's my money? And where's Césaire?"

"Safe," I said. "Probably having a grand old time ripping the skin off the poor unfortunates who work at the animal shelter in Nice. Ask Luc. His cousin works there."

Bad Buddha looked to Luc for confirmation. "Is this true?"

Luc nodded. "Your pet will be well looked after. Now that I know he belongs to you, I'm sure we can arrange for you to collect him quietly."

"In other words, we've guessed you imported Césaire illegally." I shot Bad Buddha a challenging look. "And you won't want any awkward questions or pesky paperwork."

"This is all very well," the little man said, "but what about my money?"

"We don't know where it is." I held his reptilian gaze, praying I wouldn't flinch. "Give us time, and Sidney and I will find out."

"What she means," my mother cut in, her voice unnaturally high, "is that Jerry and I will be happy to help you look for the kidnappers."

"Exactly. They'll oversee our work during our probationary period. However, with Jerry in the hospital, Sidney and I will be your points of contact."

"Jerry is in the hospital?" The little man's bushy eyebrows snapped together and his surprise seemed genuine. "What happened?"

"Someone broke into his office this morning and attacked him," Luc said. "We're assuming Rocco was responsible. Unless you know different?"

"Of course not," the little man shouted. "Why should I attack Gallo? I have no beef with the man."

My mother patted Bad Buddha on the head as though he were a dog. "Luc wasn't accusing you, darling. But you may have heard rumors. We'd be grateful for any information you might have."

"I know nothing about Gallo's attack," he snapped. "This is the first I've heard about it."

I glanced at Elektra. Like the no-necks, she'd lowered her MP5 when Luc had put his on the floor. However, she still held it in a white-knuckled grip. Elektra knew Sidney and I had been in Jerry's building this morning. She'd been following us, waiting to pounce and get Césaire. Had she left before the paramedics arrived?

She'd tracked us all across France. Why would she get as far as the costumier and then give up? A retreat would only make sense if she'd seen paramedics arrive, closely followed by the police. But if so, why hadn't she informed her boss that there'd been an incident at Jerry's place?

"Jerry will be fine," my mother said with forced breeziness. "A couple of days in the hospital, and he'll be back to work."

This wasn't the impression Luc had given Sidney and me, but I wasn't about to argue the point with her. I focused on Bad Buddha. "When was Césaire taken? That information will help us track down the kidnappers."

"Yes, please fill us in on all the details." My mother's breathy voice was starting to sound less affected and more oxygen-deprived. "Jerry and I will be happy to help you track down the kidnappers."

The old man scowled. "Very kind of you, Desirée. I know you and Jerry provide excellent services, with or without your new recruits. However, I prefer to manage my own affairs."

"How's that worked out for you so far?" I couldn't resist asking. "You needed us to tell you where Césaire was, and you appear to be clueless about the kidnappers' identities."

"You must forgive my daughter," my mother said soothingly. "Angélique has always been impulsive."

I opened my mouth to object but caught Sidney's slight shake of the head. I snapped my lips together and ground my teeth to the point of pain. I didn't like Bad Buddha, but I liked his armed security team even less.

"I thought your daughter was still a child," the man grumbled. "Why is she suddenly in Nice and joining the Omega Group?"

"You flatter me, Giorgios. Angélique is over twenty."

"I'm twenty-six," I corrected. "That's closer to thirty than twenty."

Bad Buddha laughed his wheezy laugh. "So it seems. And you speak excellent French, my dear. My mistake for underestimating you."

"That's okay," I shot back. "Smarter men than you have underestimated me in the past. Bearing that in mind, why don't you tell us about Césaire's kidnapping? After all, Sidney and I have a vested interest in helping you figure out who took him. As long as the kidnappers remain at large, we'll be your number one suspects."

Bad Buddha released a long sigh. "All right. Sit. All of you."

"I prefer to remain standing." Luc made no move to retrieve the weapon at his feet but established his desire to stay near it.

Our host flicked his wrist. "If you must. But the

rest of you, sit. Ladislav, make us a jug of strawberry margarita. I know it's Desirée's favorite. Mirko, fetch snacks from the galley."

"You're always the perfect host, Giorgios," my mother simpered as the two men lumbered off to do their boss's bidding.

"The guy had me hauled off the street, chloroformed, and drugged. I don't call that stellar hospitality." I flopped onto a seat and maintained eye contact with my erstwhile captor.

"Tell me exactly how you found my pet." He delivered this a command, not a request.

Sidney darted me a glance and then addressed Bad Buddha. "I can fill you in," he said in his suave, shaken-not-stirred voice. "I was with Angel the whole time."

He outlined our adventure in a few succinct, un-Sidney-like sentences, starting in Paris and ending in Nice. He provided more details than he had to Luc but still refrained from mentioning the specifics of my run-in with Monty Carlyle.

"So you see," he finished, "I'm just as involved as Angel. Neither of us stole your money. We obeyed the kidnappers' instructions and left the briefcase in the Château d'Eau. In the meantime, they left Césaire in the Mercedes for us to find. Not knowing what to do, we looked after him before dropping him to an animal shelter in Nice this afternoon."

"You left the briefcase at the Château d'Eau in

Montpellier?" Luc gave a crack of laughter. "Why didn't you mention that to me earlier?"

"I was trying to be discreet," Sidney said with dignity. "Why are you laughing?"

"Yes," Bad Buddha demanded. "I don't see anything funny in his story."

His shoulders heaving, Luc's hand strayed to the pocket of his combat pants. "May I take out my phone?"

The Greek's eyes narrowed. "All right. But do it slowly. My men tend to get trigger-happy."

A moment later, Luc, still grinning, held out his phone to Bad Buddha. "See this article?"

The man took the device and examined the screen. He jerked as though he'd been jolted with a stun gun. "You think this is my money?"

"The description fits, doesn't it?"

I looked at Luc. "I'm still in the dark. Can you fill us in, please?"

"Yesterday evening, a tourist in Montpellier reported finding an abandoned briefcase in the Château d'Eau. Fearing a terrorist attack, the police notified the bomb squad. They performed a controlled explosion. Instead of defusing a bomb, they discovered cash to the sum of one hundred thousand euros."

Bad Buddha swore once more. "I'll never see that money again. What I don't understand is why the kidnappers didn't collect it? They went to a lot of trouble to hack the satnav, provide the burner phone, and all the rest. I was told exactly which car to choose from my fleet and send to the Gare du Nord to meet Elektra."

"I was in London on a business trip," Elektra said, reading the unspoken question from my expression. "Mr. Christianopoulos ordered me straight back to France. I've worked for him for several years, and he's known me my whole life. He grew up with my father on Corfu. Naturally, he put me in charge of the rescue mission."

"A rescue mission which you messed up," Bad Buddha growled. "And then you blamed your failure on these young people."

Elektra's mouth opened and shut like a carp.

If she hadn't riled me, I'd have pointed out that I'd been at least partially responsible for her screwed-up rescue mission. Instead, I focused on her boss. "What confuses me is why the kidnappers put Césaire in the Mercedes. They didn't collect the briefcase, but they returned the ocelot? That doesn't make sense." I sat back in my seat, sifting through the facts. An idea floated at the back of my mind, too nebulous to grasp. It'd come to me eventually. They always did, given time. Unfortunately, time was a commodity I didn't have.

Luc took his phone back from Bad Buddha. "It sounds to me like the kidnappers had a plan, and that plan went wrong."

Ladislav trundled across the deck, carrying a tray

with our drinks. The memory of him holding the chloroformed cloth over my mouth made me see red. Every fiber of my being tensed, wishing I could go for the jugular. I shook my head when he tried to press a glass into my hand. "No, thanks. I'm still recovering from the last substance you gave me."

The man's thick lips quivered, and he kept his eyes lowered. "Would you like a jug of mineral water, sir?"

The question was addressed to Bad Buddha, but the words echoed in my head. My heart flip-flopped, then beat a little faster.

Seated across from me, Elektra shifted position and slipped a finger under the arm of her latex suit. She must be itching like crazy. And sweltering in this heat. In my post-drugged state, her decision to wear long sleeves hadn't made an impact on me. Now that I was semi-sober, it struck me as hella strange.

"What's the ocelot's name, Ladislav?" I posed the question as casually as I could manage.

The thug stared at me, confusion written across his thick features. "What do you mean?"

"I'd like you to tell me the ocelot's name," I repeated. "I've forgotten."

"Césaire." He frowned. "But you know this. You've said his name several times."

"Césaire." I pronounced the name as he had, imitating his heavily accented French. "Indeed."

A slow, sick certainty spread through my body, paralyzing me temporarily. I knew that voice. I'd heard it in the Mercedes, shortly after Sidney and I left the Gare du Nord. And I'd heard it again when we'd reached Montpellier, on the other end of a cheap burner phone.

Beside me, Sidney sucked in a breath and grabbed my arm.

"He's Satnav Dude," we said in unison.

27

*E*lektra whipped around and darted a fearful glance at the man I was now certain had been the voice on the hacked navigation system. "What are you talking about? What dude?"

I pointed to her right arm. "Pull up your sleeve, Elektra."

Fear, then hatred, burned in her dark eyes. "What nonsense is this? Why should I strip for you?"

"I'm not asking you to strip. Just to show us your right arm." I pointed to my cheek, still livid with Césaire's scratches. "I'm guessing it'll look a lot like my face."

"And my scalp." Sidney bent his head and showed us where Césaire had scalped him.

"Ocelots have extremely sharp claws," I said, "and they like to use them."

"What's this she's talking about, Elektra?" Bad

Buddha stared at his PA. "I thought you said you hadn't found Césaire."

"I haven't. Not yet. That's why I'm going back to Nice to collect him from this animal shelter. I can leave right now." Her tone was somewhere between seductive and plaintive. From the expression on Bad Buddha's round face, he'd picked up on the discrepancy.

I didn't take my eyes off Elektra. "You don't want her going anywhere near your pet again, Mr. Christianopoulos. She'll only demand another hundred thousand euros for his 'safe return.' She and her neckless accomplice stood to make a lot of money from the staged kidnap. Only Sidney and I inadvertently wrecked their perfect plan, and now that cash is in the hands of the police. The voice on the hacked satnav was Ladislav's. And he answered the call I made on the burner phone."

"It's not true," Ladislav whined. "They're trying to frame me."

"You're saying that Elektra and Ladislav faked Césaire's kidnapping to get money out of me?" Bad Buddha's raisin eyes burned with rage. "How do you know this?"

"Because they're amateurs," I said. "They didn't even bother to use a voice changer when Ladislav recorded his message for the hacked satellite navigation system in the Mercedes. He has a distinctive way of pronouncing Césaire's name."

Elektra's hiss brought back happy memories of our road trip with Césaire. Seriously, those two had a lot in common.

"I assume they only made the recording as a precaution in case you sent one of your other security guards to accompany Elektra," Sidney said. "They had to make it look like she was following the kidnappers' instructions."

"Ladislav is right. This is a trap." Elektra rounded on me. "You set up this whole farce. You took Césaire. You demanded the ransom money and set up Ladislav and me to take the fall."

"We have an accusation and a counter-accusation." I addressed Bad Buddha. "Who are you going to believe?"

His furrowed brow told me I'd struck a chord. "If Ladislav and Elektra concocted this plan, where was Césaire from the time he went missing to when you say you found him in the Mercedes?"

"We don't know." Sidney looked at the now quaking Ladislav. "Elektra was in London when Césaire went missing. Correct?"

Bad Buddha paused as though uncertain. "She left the night before Césaire disappeared. Also, Elektra doesn't have anything to do with my animal collection. I keep them all at my home, and I don't like to mix business and pleasure."

"I can only reiterate my request that Elektra shows us her arm. She may have said she left France the night before Césaire went missing, but are you certain of that?"

"Your theory doesn't make sense." The man's words were harsh, but I could see he was wavering. "Ladislav can't have been involved. He was with his sick mother in Marseille until this morning."

A sickly shade of green spread across Ladislav's face.

"Marseille is only two hours from Montpellier," I pointed out. "He could've easily driven there and back. My guess is, he was responsible for the ocelot, and Elektra was to take care of the money. No one was actually meant to leave that briefcase unattended."

"Precisely," Sidney picked up the story in a laconic drawl. "Elektra was the brains of the operation. The plan fell apart when she didn't make it to Paris in time to collect the Mercedes."

Bravo. For an overindulged rich boy, Sidney was as sharp as a blade. I took the invisible conch and continued our tale. "With Elektra not physically present in Montpellier, Ladislav was on his own. And that's where the plot began to unravel. He was too stupid to realize that the person calling him on the burner phone wasn't Elektra. Concluding that you'd sent one of your other security guards to assist her, he kept up the pretense. Ladislav put the ocelot in the Mercedes when the call was over, just as she'd told him to do. I suspect he'd had an unpleasant time in Césaire's company and was relieved to get rid of the animal. He assumed Elektra would pretend to drop off the ransom money at the Château d'Eau, but in reality, have it hidden for them to collect later."

"Your story is ludicrous." Elektra pushed a strand of turquoise hair out of her face and rounded on me. "Why would I pretend to kidnap Césaire?"

"I can think of one hundred thousand reasons why." I raised an eyebrow and looked straight at Ladislav. "Sorry, dude. Elektra had no intention of sharing the ransom money with you. If I hadn't stolen her suitcase, she'd have collected the Mercedes from Armin, driven to wherever she had another car waiting. Then she and the briefcase would have driven off into the sunset."

"None of this is true." Elektra whirled around to her boss. "She's lying. She stole Césaire, along with her Russian spy friend."

"You think I'm a Russian spy?" Sidney looked delighted.

"Apparently, your grandmother is ex-KGB," I said, watching his reaction.

He digested this information. "I hadn't known that, but it doesn't surprise me. She invokes terror wherever she goes. She's the one with the attack cat."

"I figured."

"Roll up your sleeve, Elektra." Bad Buddha glowered at his PA. "If you've had no contact with Césaire, you have nothing to worry about."

"See? Even Césaire's loving owner acknowledges

his tendency to shred skin." I turned to Ladislav. "While Elektra's showing us her arm, why don't you show us your hand? I bet Césaire is the reason you're wearing a bandage."

The thug cradled his injured hand. "It wasn't my fault. She put me up to it. I just did what I was told. She must have taken down the wrong phone number."

"Shut up, you idiot," Elektra growled at Ladislav.

I pounced on this information, slotting it into the jigsaw pieces I already had and winging the rest. "Ladislav gave Elektra the wrong number for whatever burner phone he was using. He probably left his work phone at his mother's house, in case he was linked to Césaire's kidnapping and Mr. Christianopoulos checked on his whereabouts. When I stole her suitcase, and Elektra missed the train to Paris, she tried to contact Ladislav, but couldn't reach him. And Ladislav, being a fool, failed to realize I wasn't Elektra, thus putting the final nail in the coffin of their get-rich-quick scheme."

"The voice changer was faulty. I couldn't get it to work." The words exploded from Ladislav, ushering forth a torrent of garbled excuses.

Elektra quivered with rage. "Don't you see this is a plot to discredit me? They're all lying. Ladislav, too. They're attempting a coup. They want to take over your business."

Bad Buddha ignored her, fixing his terrifying stare on me. "Continue, young lady. Why should I believe that two of my long-term employees are plotting against me?"

"I'll answer your question with one of my own. Why didn't Elektra tell you Jerry Gallo had been attacked? When my mother mentioned it, your surprise was genuine."

The man blinked. "Well, yes. But why should Elektra know of the attack?"

"Because Elektra tracked Angel and me to the costumier," Sidney said. "And at the time, we still had Césaire with us. Did she mention this to you?"

Bad Buddha's face was now so purple that I expected him to have a coronary at any second. "No. She mentioned none of this to me. She told me she'd tracked the Mercedes to a Peregrine Foggington-Smythe who was with a female accomplice who'd stolen her passport."

"Peregrine is my first name," Sidney said with an air of apology. "Terrible, I know."

"So Elektra shared information about Sidney but never mentioned seeing us with Césaire this morning? What about the incident in Aix-en-Provence last night? Did she tell you she killed one of the men who was chasing me and put his corpse in the Mercedes?"

Bad Buddha snapped his lips together. "No, she did not."

"It wasn't relevant," Elektra said quickly. "I was focused on retrieving Césaire and then finding the ransom money."

"No, you just wanted the money. You didn't give a hoot about the ocelot. You wanted us to lead you to the cash. That's why you were looking in the Mercedes when the Russian approached you." I took a step closer to Elektra, who was perspiring visibly. The scent of her jasmine perfume mixed with fear and sweat. *Jasmine...*

I'd always had a good sense of smell. When I'd walked into Jerry's office this morning, I'd noticed three warring scents: blood, musky perfume, and a lighter jasmine scent. The acrid blood scent was Jerry. The cloying musk was my mother's signature scent. And the jasmine?

A smile spread across my face. "I know why Elektra didn't tell you she'd been outside the costumier this morning. Because she wasn't outside the costumier to retrieve Césaire. She was there to kill Sidney and me."

"Of course." Sidney snapped his fingers as though an idea had just occurred to him. "With us dead, we wouldn't be able to contradict whatever lies she concocted to cover up her involvement in the botched kidnapping."

I looked right at Bad Buddha. "Elektra wasn't pleased to have Mirko tagging along this afternoon when you sent them to Nice to track down Sidney and me. If Mirko hadn't been there, she and Ladislav would have killed me and then found Sidney and killed him. And I bet Elektra would have made sure I met with a nasty 'accident' on the yacht if you hadn't sent Mirko below deck to hurry us upstairs."

"Sounds like Jerry is lucky she didn't kill him," Sidney said.

"What?" My mother whipped around to look at him. "What are you saying?"

"That Rocco Casetti didn't attack Jerry. Elektra did."

"Exactly," I said. "Elektra wasn't just *outside* Jerry's building this morning. She entered it via the fire escape and hid in his office. He must have come into the room, sat down at his desk, and then noticed her. In her panic, she attacked him, using the paperweight and letter opener on his desk."

If looks could kill, my mother's would have caused Elektra to spontaneously combust.

Bad Buddha turned to her and then to Ladislav. "Is this true? Did you betray me? Endanger my little Césaire? Try to trick me out of my money?"

Ladislav began a spluttering, incoherent explanation that consisted of excuses, his sick mother, and blaming Elektra.

Cool as a cucumber, Elektra drew out her revolver and plugged two shots into her now former co-conspirator. Ladislav hit the deck and lay still. Blood pooled from his prone form, soaking the deck.

Luc, Mirko, and the other guards all grabbed their weapons.

Elektra laughed in their faces. She reached behind

a cushion on one of the seats and whipped out a grenade. In an instant, she pulled the pin and tossed it onto Bad Buddha's ample lap.

Then she fired at the lounge windows, shattering the glass. She leaped through the opening and plunged into the sea. Before any of us could react, a speedboat roared to life, and the *Aurora* shot away from the yacht, leaving a plume of water and a live grenade in its wake.

28

Luc was the first to react. He bounded across the deck, barking orders at Mirko and the other no-necks. Mirko gave instructions through his walkie-talkie, and the yacht's engine purred to life.

"Everyone hit the deck." Luc scooped the live grenade from a stunned Bad Buddha's lap, raced over to the shattered window, and hurled it through the opening.

Sidney and I synchronized our inelegant deck-hitting efforts, face-planting on the floor just as the explosion rocked the boat. Luc's excellent throw and the crew's quick action in getting the yacht moving minimized the aftermath of the explosion.

My mother pushed herself up on her elbows. "Is everyone okay?"

Sidney sat up and examined the remains of his

sunglasses, which were now broken in three places. "These are the only casualty."

I grabbed the edge of a seat and crawled on it. "Way too much drama for one weekend. Maybe I'll have that strawberry margarita after all."

Sidney poured me a glass from the jug Ladislav had made before he'd gone to meet his maker. I downed the contents in a few long gulps.

Luc and the no-necks rushed around, checking that Elektra hadn't left any more unwanted surprises for us. Mirko and one of the other guys removed Ladislav's body from the deck. A cleaning team materialized from below deck to deal with the mess. Clearly, calling the cops wasn't high on anyone's agenda. Why wasn't I surprised?

While Luc and the gang did their thing, my mother helped Bad Buddha back to his seat and took the one opposite mine. "You owe us a speedboat, Giorgios."

"Also compensation for rescuing Césaire and unmasking his kidnappers." The alcohol was helping to restore my equilibrium. "Not bad for our first assignment for the Omega Group. Right, Mother?"

Her only response was a lightning-bolt glare directed at me. I smiled back at her, enjoying every millisecond of her barely concealed anger.

If Bad Buddha picked up on the tension between us, he chose to ignore it. "I'm impressed, Desirée. Clearly, your daughter takes after you. Naturally, we can come to a financial arrangement. And I'm willing to make said financial arrangement more interesting if you agree to help me track down Elektra."

"Certainly," my mother purred. "If she attacked Jerry, we have a particular interest in making sure she's apprehended. And once we reach Nice, Luc will arrange Césaire's collection."

I glanced through the window. Night had fallen in earnest, but the twinkling lights in the distance indicated we were heading back to port. I rubbed my eyes, feeling the nauseous headache of earlier return. After the cocktail of substances Elektra and her cohorts had given me, downing a cocktail of the alcoholic variety hadn't been a smart move.

While we purred across the Mediterranean and back to Nice, I worked my way through a bottle of mineral water and let my mother entertain Bad Buddha. Once they'd hammered out the specifics of Césaire's retrieval, they switched to gossiping about people I didn't know. Now that their conversation didn't concern Elektra or the ocelot, I switched from soaking up information to processing it.

I'd claimed to be a member of the Omega Group partly to put Bad Buddha in his place but mostly to infuriate my mother. I hadn't expected Sidney to back me up with such aplomb. He'd been so self-assured he'd almost convinced me our fictional careers were the real deal. What was the Omega Group, anyone? Some kind of murky crisis management firm? An organized crime syndicate? Or an off-the-books investigation agency? What role did my mother play?

I was still mulling over these questions when the yacht's engine stopped close to the port.

Mirko got to his feet. "I'll escort you to shore in our speedboat."

Buddha pumped my hand and Sidney's before handing us over to Mirko's care. "Thank you both for your help," he said in French. "You're excellent additions to Jerry and Desirée's team." To me, he added with an oily smile, "No hard feelings, I hope. You seem to have recovered from your ordeal."

My facial muscles twitched. "Add a nice tip for me onto whatever arrangement you're making with my mother, and there'll be no hard feelings."

The little man threw back his head and laughed. "So like you, Desirée." He patted my hand. "Of course, my dear. I'll make sure you get your tip."

Mirko operated the speedboat and steered us into port less than ten minutes later. Luc helped me out of the boat and onto the pier. We all walked down the dock in silence. Had the circumstances been different, I'd have absorbed all the sights, sounds, and smells of Nice's famous Old Port and the glimpse of the city in the throes of a summer Saturday night. As it was, I could barely keep one foot in front of the other.

When we reached the car park, Mirko stopped in front of a dark SUV and turned to Luc. "Want to take my car to the animal shelter?"

Luc nodded and dug in his cargo pants pocket for a key. He tossed this to Sidney. "You can take the Peugeot back to Jerry's building. Is it okay if they spend the night in Jerry's apartment, Desirée? Angel looks ready to collapse."

My anti-take-charge-males radar beeped, then spluttered into silence. Luc was right. I was dead on my feet. I needed a shower, and I needed sleep, and I suspected I was too tired to have them in that order.

"That's fine." My mother took a key out of her purse and handed it to me. Her eyes snapped with a warning, but I was too tired to care. "You can let yourselves in. I'll give Francine a heads-up in case she decides you're up to no good again."

At my horrified expression, Luc added, "Don't panic. You won't have to share with Francine. Her apartment is on the floor below Jerry's."

"What about Césaire's cage?" Sidney asked. "Won't Mirko need it to transport the animal? It's still in the costumier."

Mirko's face indicated he wasn't relishing his imminent encounter with Césaire and his claws. "Could you leave it outside for me to collect on my way back to the port? I can manage him on my own that far."

"Certainly." My mother withdrew a second key from her purse and pressed it into Sidney's hand. "This opens the costumier. Get the cage and leave it in the side lane for Mirko to collect. I'll tell Francine to switch off the alarm."

Luc and Mirko climbed into the SUV, leaving Sidney and me with Desirée.

The instant the SUV turned out of the car park, my mother rounded on me. Her suave, in-control mask dropped, revealing a woman on the edge of a meltdown. She grabbed my shoulders and shook me so hard my teeth rattled. "You stupid little fool. What were you thinking? Do you have any idea of the damage you've caused?"

The depth of her emotion shocked me more than the violent shaking. Stunned, I extricated myself from her grasp. "Why don't you enlighten me?" I said coldly. "Start with the Omega Group and go from there."

"You shouldn't even know that name," she snapped.

"No, I suppose I shouldn't. I'll add it to the list of facts I didn't know about you before today. Your multiple properties in Nice, for example. Your work for a mysterious organization that may or may not be on the right side of the law. Your relationship with Luc."

Desirée's agitation was a joy to behold. I'd rarely seen the woman display genuine emotion, and witnessing her lose control was a once-in-a-lifetime experience.

A myriad of emotions flashed in her eyes. "I'm not your father, Angélique. I don't work for criminals."

I arched an eyebrow. "Just with criminals on occasion?"

"You need to leave Nice." She grabbed my wrist, squeezing it tight. "And you need to leave tonight."

Sidney placed a hand on Desirée's and eased her off me. "Leave Angel alone." His voice was firm and controlled and seemed to penetrate Desirée's fog of anger. "Can't you see she's near to collapsing? She's had an awful couple of days, and now this experience."

"Do you even know who that awful man is?" My mother's voice broke with feeling. "He could've killed you, Angélique. He would have if we hadn't shown up and diffused the situation."

"To be fair," Sidney countered, "Angel's improv skills and sharp mind did most of the diffusing. Her deductions were spot on. She figured out who kidnapped Césaire and why, as well as who was responsible for Jerry's injuries."

"I don't know *who* Mr. Christianopoulos is, but I can guess *what* he is. A Greek shipping magnate with ties to organized crime?" I looked to my mother for confirmation. "How did I do?"

"Close. He has a yacht, but that's where his ties to the shipping industry end." My mother scrunched up her nose in distaste. "Let's just say Césaire wasn't his only illegal import."

I crossed my arms over my chest. "And this is a guy the Omega Group 'does business' with? You disapproved of Dad's more questionable associates.

Yet, you earn your crust by selling your mysterious services to a man like that?"

"What was that English phrase you trotted out for Elektra about making assumptions?" Her voice was low and husky, but there was no hint of the coquette in her delivery. "Just because your father is a criminal doesn't mean I am."

"Then what, exactly, does the Omega Group do?" I demanded. "The one thing I'm sure of is you don't earn your living from burlesque shows, and Jerry doesn't earn his from renting out theatrical costumes."

My mother released a long sigh. "I can't share that information with you. Not now. Maybe not ever. Can't you just chalk this weekend up to an interesting adventure and go back to your regular lives?"

"My regular life currently consists of being on Europol's Most Wanted list," I pointed out. "I'm on the hook for a murder I didn't commit, on the run from the gangster who did the deed, and dealing with a mysteriously appearing and disappearing corpse."

"I can help you sort that out. I've already spoken to Luc's grandfather. He's a defense lawyer specializing in criminal law. He asked around, and while you're wanted for questioning in connection with Frank O'Malley's murder, no arrest warrant has been issued. Whatever rag you read that in got that part wrong."

My mother had spoken to the lawyer on my behalf? Did I find her concern more touching or presumptive? "Arrest warrant or not, I'm being framed for a crime I didn't commit. And Frank is dead. His murderer will get away with it, just like he's done countless times before for other crimes."

My mother's phone buzzed with an incoming message. She grimaced, suddenly looking very much like her age. "We'll get this sorted. I promise. Right now, you and Sidney should get some rest. We can talk in detail in the morning."

"What about you?" Sidney asked. "Where are you going now?"

"To meet an acquaintance who can help me locate Elektra." She pivoted and ushered us into motion. "My car is parked near Luc's Peugeot. I want to give you two a couple of safety devices before you go back to the costumier."

"Safety devices? As in guns and ammo?"

"Certainly not. France has strict gun licensing laws. Neither of you has a license." She stopped in front of a red Porsche and opened the passenger door. After a quick perusal of the glove compartment, she withdrew a can of pepper spray and a stun gun. Her lips twisted into an ironic smile. "Not the arsenal you were hoping for, but one that's less likely to get you pulled up on serious criminal charges."

Sidney pocketed the pepper spray. I took the stun gun. "Believe it or not, we would be useful additions to your organization," I said. "Provided you're legit and above board. We're smart, can think on our feet, and we're good with languages. Additionally, Sidney can slip into a role and be convincing without needing a costume or a script. Those are valuable assets to a business like the Omega Group."

I was winging this conversation. Truth be told, I had no idea if I'd want to work for the mysterious Omega Group, nor if Sidney was interested in joining me. However, it sounded more interesting than pulling pints in a pub. What did I have waiting for me back in London, anyway?

A flicker of annoyance passed over my mother's face, followed by amusement. "You don't give up, do you? You haven't a clue what we actually do."

"My boss is dead, and I'm out of a job. Sidney's desperate to get out of starting his new job on Monday. Why don't you give us a chance, Mother, Desirée, whatever I should call you? When have I ever asked you for anything before?"

"You never have," she said softly. "And I know I owe you. Look, let's defer this conversation until the morning, okay?" She withdrew her phone and glanced at her screen. "I need to get moving."

Desirée slid behind the wheel of her Porsche and took off in the opposite direction than the one Luc and Mirko had taken. Sidney and I trudged to the Peugeot and climbed in.

He started the engine and eased us into the traffic. "Do you think she'll bite?"

I shrugged. "Who knows? But probably not. Desirée excels at wriggling out of uncomfortable situations. It wouldn't surprise me if that was the last we'll see of her."

"Surely not." He sounded shocked. "She's your mother. Won't she want to stick around to make sure you're safe?"

The thought that she wouldn't depressed me way more than I cared to admit. I was twenty-six, for heaven's sake. Surely I was old enough to not care about my feckless parent's lack of interest in me and my life?

I slid the stun gun out of my pocket. "She's provided me with a weapon. As far as she's concerned, she's fulfilled her maternal duty." I massaged the sides of my head. "Do you mind if we drop the subject? I still have a headache from whatever concoction Elektra and her friends gave me. Thinking about Desirée makes it worse."

"Sure. Of course."

We drove in silence through the streets of Nice until we reached Jerry's street.

Sidney slowed the car in front of the costumier. "Why don't you go on up to the apartment? I'll park and join you after. You have the key?"

"Yeah. But in that case, give me the key to the costumier as well. I'll take care of Césaire's cage before I go upstairs."

He handed me the key, and I got out of the car, waving him off. I stretched my neck from side to side, feeling the strain in the tired muscles. Luc's café was closed for the night, as were most of the other businesses on the street. Only the bar on the corner was still open, its broken neon lights blinking in the dark.

Apart from the illuminated display window, the costumier was in darkness. I inserted the key into the door and stepped inside. The jangle of the bell above the door made my heart dance a mad jig. I took a deep breath to steady myself. My nerves were shot after my weekend of horrors. Every sound made me jump.

I felt around for a light switch but found none. Swearing under my breath, I groped my way to the shop's counter where I'd last seen the ocelot's cage. I had a good memory for details, and I used the costume racks to guide me. My hands skimmed over soft velvet, smooth silk, and rough sequins.

And then my fingers touched cold flesh.

My nausea returned in full force. I was letting my imagination run wild. Nevertheless, I ran my hand over the object that had caused my revulsion. A chin, a nose, an eyebrow stud. I'd found the missing corpse.

I let out a yelp, leaped back, and caught my foot on the edge of Césaire's cage. On instinct, I tried to grab a solid object to stop me from falling. Unfortunately, the first solid object I found was the dead Russian. He tumbled forward from the clothes rack that had been propping him up. Gravity took its inevitable course. The Terrible Twin rushed to the ground, knocking me over and crushing me under his literal dead weight.

I flailed and pushed, trying to get the corpse off me.

Suddenly, the lights went on. Blinking, I scrambled free from the dead man and strained to see who was there.

And quickly wished I hadn't.

The sight that met my eyes was a scarier prospect than getting cozy with a corpse.

If it were possible to crossbreed a pug with a cut-rate variety show performer, the result might resemble Monty Carlyle. He had a penchant for luridly colored velour suits and bow ties. Tonight's aubergine linen suit was a nod to the heat, but the green-and-white bow tie was true to form. The clashing colors emphasized his green-tinged pallor. Had the ketamine dart affected him that badly? Or was Monty suffering from an illness?

He stepped in front of me, looking like fodder for the undertaker. The revolver he aimed at my chest made me question which of us would make it to the morgue first. "Ms. Doyle, I presume?"

29

Monty advanced on me—until his foot made contact with the dead body lying beside me. When he clocked the corpse, he took a step back and uttered an oath. He pinned me in place with the force of his glare. "You killed Ivan."

In other circumstances, I'd have defended myself against this unjust accusation. But Monty's distraction had bought me a few vital seconds to get my thoughts in order and take action.

My fingers closed around the handle of Césaire's cage. I picked it up and hurled it at Monty's head. However, Monty was quicker on his feet than I'd given him credit for. He dodged the missile, and it crash-landed on the cash register with an almighty clang.

His sweat-soaked face contorted with rage. "Stay down, or I'll shoot you."

He'd do it too, just as he'd shot Frank. My certainty

of my imminent demise was cemented when two clothes racks were pushed aside. The unmistakable forms of Cam and the surviving twin loomed into view.

They looked as though they'd been in a fight, possibly with each other. Cam sported a black eye, a split lip, and moved with a limp. The twin—the bigger of the two—had fared better. He had a massive bruise on one cheek but appeared otherwise unharmed. The men's meaty hands formed fists that could smash my face to smithereens.

Cam's lips curled into a sneer. "Nice to see you again, Angel."

A wave of nausea swept over me. The thugs still hadn't noticed the corpse. Any second now, the twin would notice his dead brother. Struggling for air, I crawled back from the men, seeking an escape route. My options were limited, and all involved getting past Monty and his dudes. Not good. Not good at all.

Cam took a menacing step toward me, his loathing for me palpable. The twin surveyed me with disinterest—until his hard eyes came to rest on his brother's corpse.

A keening sound came from deep within his throat. His expressionless features crumpled and he dropped to his knees. He rolled the body over, revealing the dead man's face. "Ivan? She killed Ivan?" Then he doubled over, sobbing and wailing and rocking his brother back and forth.

The twin's reaction confirmed that he hadn't known his brother was dead. Presumably, Monty and his goons had followed Sidney and me and seen us talking outside the shop. Had they taken the opportunity to sneak in and surprise me? Or had they already been inside, lying in wait to ambush me? If they'd been waiting for me, they couldn't have been here long. Otherwise, they would've found the body. So who'd hidden the corpse in the clothes rack? Elektra? If so, why?

The twin's wails grew louder. "Why did she kill Ivan?"

"I didn't kill him," I said, scrambling back as far as I could go. "I haven't killed anyone."

"Of course, she killed him." Cam's evil grin showed just how little he cared about the fate of his fellow thug. "Who else could've done it?"

Monty let out a roar and fired a shot into the counter, just above my head. "Why are you killing my men? What grudge do you have against me?"

The noise rang painfully in my ears, and the room seemed to shift. I tried to speak, but above the twin's wailing and the ringing in my ears, I couldn't hear my own words. I increased my volume. "I didn't kill Ivan. A wannabe fraudster named Elektra stabbed him and put him in the boot of my car." I paused. "Well, it was her car, technically. Long story. But then, it's been a long couple of days."

Monty's chins strained his polka dot bow tie, and

he pulled it loose. "Why should I believe you? You shot me with a dart gun. And you killed Frank."

I gaped at him, giving the company a front-row view of my orthodontist's excellent handiwork. "What do you mean, *I* killed Frank? *You* killed Frank. I saw you pull the trigger."

"I've never killed anyone," Monty said with impressive dignity for such a ridiculous-looking man. "And I didn't kill Frank. Why would I? The man owed me money. Dead men don't pay their debts."

"But I saw you shoot him." I questioned the words the instant they were out of my mouth. I'd seen Monty shoot Frank in the leg. I'd heard several other shots, but I hadn't actually seen any of those shots go into Frank.

"Yeah, I shot him in the thigh and fired a few warning shots. I needn't have bothered. He passed out with shock before I fired the second time."

"The newspapers said he's dead," I said, searching his face for answers. "Did the shot to the leg kill him?"

"If you've read the newspapers," Monty replied with a snarl, "you know you're the prime suspect for Frank's murder."

"Yeah, because you framed me. You paid Becky Campbell to lie to the police and say she'd seen me kill Frank."

Cam snorted. "Nice try, Angel. Pity no one believes you."

Monty undid the top button of his shirt. He wasn't an attractive man at peak health. Tonight, he looked rougher than I felt. "I don't know anyone called Becky Campbell. Why would I frame you? Frank and I went way back. By one means or another, I want justice for his death. If you killed him, I'll make you pay. If not, I'll hunt down whoever is responsible."

"Wait, what? Are you serious? I saw you shoot him. Then I shot you with the dart gun to buy me enough time to escape. Ever since, you and your muscled minions have been chasing me across Europe, presumably to kill me before I tell the authorities about you killing Frank."

"I've been chasing you to avenge Frank's murder." Monty pointed to his buttock. "And there's the small matter of you attacking me."

"I plugged you with a ketamine dart, but I've never killed anyone."

"She's lying." Cam's hand strayed to his holster. "She killed Frank. She's always had a violent streak."

His words hit me with the force of whiplash. Of all the people present, Cam knew I'd never laid a hand on anyone unless in self-defense. What game was he playing? Did he hope to goad Monty into shooting me? Or incense Boris? The Russian was still weeping over his dead twin, but he'd be baying for blood before long.

"Leave your weapon alone, Cam. I don't trust you not to kill her just to satisfy your own lust for revenge. I hired you to help me find her alive and keep her alive until I say otherwise. So far, all you've managed to do is lose one of my men."

"That's not fair," Cam shot back. "Ivan went missing in Aix-en-Provence. How was I to know she'd killed him?"

"I haven't killed anyone. Not Frank, not Ivan, not any other death you want to blame me for."

Monty shifted his focus to me. "I assumed you'd come back to the pub to finish off Frank and steal my money. Why else would you go on the run?"

"I didn't kill Frank, and I didn't steal your money. When I hightailed it out of the pub, I thought I was the only witness to you murdering a man. And I'd just plugged you with a ketamine dart."

"Yes." Monty regarded me with narrowed eyes. "I didn't appreciate that move. Turns out I'm allergic to ketamine."

That explained his pallor. "If you're sick, why aren't you resting? Surely I'm not important enough for you to personally chase me across France?"

His nostrils twitched, and his jowls quivered. "Why didn't you go to the police?"

"I'm aware you have cops on your payroll. And I've had experience with the police making promises they didn't keep. I needed to put space between you and me and keep myself safe while I thought over my options."

"How'd that work out for you?" Monty's mouth made a scary smiley. "How did you run afoul of a stab-happy wannabe fraudster?"

"If you want to catch up over drinks, can we defer that pleasure to a time when I'm more awake?"

"You've got a smart mouth, girl."

"I'm twenty-six. Hardly a girl." I got to my feet. To my relief, Monty didn't try to stop me. "Seriously, though, you didn't kill Frank?"

"No." Monty delivered the word with a grim-faced finality.

"If you didn't kill him, and I didn't kill him, then who did?" I frowned, turning the facts over in my mind. "Becky? But why? What motive could she have had?"

Monty didn't lower the revolver, but his initial bluster had deflated. Maybe he was starting to believe I was telling the truth. "Money?" He shook his head. "No. The cash from the register was missing, but that's not enough to warrant killing a man."

Boris laid his brother's body gently on the ground and covered it with a velvet cloak from one of the costume racks. He'd stopped wailing, but his silence screamed with pent-up rage. He got to his feet and skewered me with a single look. "Did you kill my brother?"

"No. As I said, I found his body. That's all." In a few short sentences, I summarized my adventure across France, leaving out the details of Césaire and his owner's identity. "So when we opened the boot and found the body gone, we didn't know what to think. I assumed his killer had taken it to prevent the police from finding DNA evidence. But she denies seeing the body after she put it in the boot of the Mercedes.

While she's a certifiable homicidal lunatic, I believe her. I have no idea why Ivan ended up here. Whoever brought his body to the shop hid him in one of the clothes racks, and he fell on top of me."

Cam's hand strayed once more to his holster. "Angel's story has more holes than Swiss cheese. I say we force her to tell us the truth."

"By shooting her?" Monty sounded almost amused. "No, Cam. I've interrogated a lot of people in my time. Her story stretches credibility, but she doesn't. Let her talk."

Anger and frustration played out on Cam's face. He wanted me dead, with or without his boss's permission. I fought past my nausea and pounding headache. If I wanted to stay alive, my only chance now was to keep Monty interested. "How did Cam get involved with your operation?" I asked. "Is hunting me down a one-time gig, or is he your new full-time employee?"

Monty didn't answer immediately, clearly weighing up how much to reveal to me. "When I realized who you were, I put feelers out for information. Cam approached me and offered his services to get you back. I prefer to run my own operations, but he knows you, and he's good with internet-based tracking. I hired him to help the twins find you."

I slid Cam a long look. "An interesting choice of job for a man who's just out on parole. You are out on parole, right? What deal did you broker to pull that off?"

His face twisted into an ugly mask. "The only one here who cuts deals with the law is you."

"I helped put Cam behind bars," I said to Monty, confident that he already knew but keen to give my side of the story. "He was behind the Alan Armitage deepfakes. He's also a woman-beating scumbag. Helping to get him banged up was one of my proudest moments."

Cam took a step closer to me but stopped at Monty's warning growl. "Enough of this nonsense," Monty said. "I don't care about your history with Cam. What I care about is finding out who killed Frank and put my operation at the pub in jeopardy."

"Ah, now we're getting to the pertinent part. Somehow, Frank getting killed impacts whatever scheme you were running out of The Lucky Charm." I smiled at Monty, enjoying the sight of his sweaty face growing purple to match his suit. "Given the extent of your annoyance, I guess it was more than mere money laundering. Am I right?"

"Mind your own business. You're in enough hot water without looking for more trouble."

"True, but I've never been good at taking advice."

"You, come with me." Boris jabbed a meaty finger at me. "You show me where to find this Elektra who killed my brother."

"Now is not the moment, Boris," Monty said in a

soothing tone that appeared to have no effect on his muscular protégé. "We'll find Ivan's killer when the time is right."

Boris pounded a fist into his palm. "Now is the time. I want to find this Elektra."

The door that separated the costumier from the rest of the building creaked open, and two figures stepped inside. Sidney, white-faced and terrified, stumbled into the shop. Behind him strode Elektra, brandishing a flick knife in one hand and a revolver in the other.

30

"Well, well, well. This is quite the little gathering," Elektra drawled, prodding the barrel of her revolver into Sidney's back. "I only swung by to get revenge on you and Angel, and I walk in to find several someones have the same idea. Are you going to introduce me to...?"

The moment Elektra spotted Boris played out like the big reveal in a movie. Her face developed a rubbery quality, flexing and shifting into a variety of expressions. Her grip on the revolver loosened. The weapon hit the floor in harmony with her slackening jaw. "You?" She pointed at the twin. "But I killed you. You're dead."

I didn't know if Boris knew enough French to understand precisely what Elektra had said, but he'd gotten the gist. A menacing rumble came from the man, followed by a deafening roar.

"Boris," I said sweetly, "meet Elektra."

A berserker rage descended over the man. He whipped his own flick knife out of his pocket and advanced on Elektra. "You killed my brother."

Elektra scrambled for the revolver, but Boris was already upon her. In desperation, she flicked her knife open. The opponents plunged their knives into each other's torsos in perfect synchronicity. Grunting, they staggered back, pulling their blades free. They stared at their matching chest wounds in stunned horror. Before any of the rest of us could react, Boris and Elektra collapsed onto the floor.

"Check Boris for a pulse," Monty ordered.

Cam leaned down and did as he was told before shaking his head. "Nothing. He's dead."

I did the same with Elektra and could detect nothing. I hadn't expected to—her lifeless stare told me all I needed to know.

Sidney moved toward the phone on the counter. "We need to call an ambulance. And the police. And try CPR."

"I don't think so." Cam pulled his revolver free from its holster and aimed it at Sidney. "Move away from the phone."

"Lower your weapon, Cam," Monty said in a bored voice. "Let them call whoever they want to call. We'll be long gone before the emergency services arrive."

Cam swung the revolver in Monty's direction, a

blood-curdling sneer spreading across his face. "*I'll* be long gone. *You'll* be part of Angel's corpse collection."

"What do you mean, my corpse collection?" I demanded, my hackles rising. "I'm not responsible for any deaths."

"So what?" he said with a sneer. "The cops won't know that."

My anger formed a cement brick in my stomach. Cam wanted to set me up to take the fall for all the deaths. Did that mean he'd stolen the corpse from the car? How had he managed it without Boris seeing him?

A slash of genuine fear showed in Monty's eyes before his protective armor slammed into place. "Come now, Cam. It's been a long day. Put down the gun before you do something you'll regret."

"What I regret is ever trusting that bitch. She shopped me to the cops. And for what? Creating a few fake videos of a corrupt politician?" Cam focused on me. "I can see the newspaper headline now: 'Buxom Barmaid Turned Serial Killer.' Do you have a middle name, Angel? All the best serial killers have three names."

"And all the best assassins." I inched my way back to Elektra's fallen revolver. "And will I be standing trial for my alleged crimes? Or will I take my own life in a fit of remorse, moments before the cops burst in?"

His lips stretched wider, revealing very white, very sharp teeth. A wave of revulsion coursed through my body. This man was loathsome. How had I ever found him attractive? "Naturally," he said. "You snapped and then came to your senses too late."

"Angel said you were a rotter." Sidney's fingers closed around a fake spear. "I see now she was exercising restraint."

'Who are you, rich kid? Are you supposed to be my replacement?" Cam sneered. "A namby-pamby posh boy who pretends to be an actor? Get a real job, mate."

"Sidney's worth a million of you," I said, sliding another inch toward Elektra's revolver. "And you're a hypocrite. You've never had a real job in your life. You did dodgy jobs for Daddy."

"I learned a thing or two in prison," Cam said, his voice that scary soft tone he'd always used right before he'd hit me. "And the number one thing I learned was not to rely on anyone else for my crust. Not even my father—especially not my father. If he'd hired me a decent lawyer, I'd have gotten off on a technicality. But no. Sandy insisted on using the same doddery fool he trots out for all court appearances."

"You were guilty, Cam. You created those deepfakes. You set the events in motion that led to Armitage's death. There's no point in blaming everyone else for your actions. Not me, not your dad, not your dad's lawyer."

"You're making a major mistake, Carruthers." Monty's voice was deceptively calm, but I sensed the raw rage behind his words. "You'll never get away with killing me. Besides, I still have my revolver. I'm a better shot than you are."

"Do you want to put that to the test?" Cam laughed in Monty's face. "Drop the weapon, old man. I'll shoot you before you have the chance to pull the trigger."

I inched closer to Elektra's revolver. I could barely breathe from the tension and prayed my fingers would cooperate. *Nearly there...*

"Did you remove the corpse from our car?" Sidney asked, still clutching the fake spear. "Elektra insists she didn't touch him."

"Of course. His discovery added a nice touch, don't you think? First, Angel kicked up a fuss when he fell on top of her. Next, that silly cow burst in here like a cartoon villain, thinking Ivan had come back to life."

"When did you remove the body?" I asked, wanting to keep him talking. "While Sidney and I were at our hotel last night?"

"Yeah. I called in a favor and got a mate to run a thorough check on any properties your mother owns. She has quite the collection. Through a process of elimination, I decided we should try Nice. Until we lost track of Posh Boy's phone, you were heading in roughly that direction, and Nice was the only place nearby where your mother had property. We'd have arrived sooner, but Boris insisted on staying in Aix to look for Ivan."

I pointed to his injured face. "Which led to you

and Boris getting into a fight. How did you convince him to accompany you to Nice? Did you tell him we'd kidnapped Ivan?"

"I told him Ivan was with you the moment we realized he was missing, but Boris refused to believe you and your pal could overpower his brother. When we found Ivan's phone in the car park across from the animal hospital, he finally agreed that Ivan had to be with you."

I slid another inch to the left. "Once you got to Nice, you looked in every car park in the city until you found the Mercedes. You and Boris split up to search, right? Otherwise, he'd have been with you when you opened the car boot and found Ivan's body."

"Yeah." A look of revulsion passed over Cam's face. "I checked the boot for cash and weapons. I wasn't expecting to find Ivan dead."

"But why did you remove his body?" Sidney asked. "Why didn't you just leave it there and tell Boris?"

"Leverage. I needed information from Angel. Still do. I figured hiding the corpse would loosen her tongue. I guessed she'd killed Ivan in self-defense and she'd be terrified of Boris finding out. I didn't want her disposing of the body and wrecking my opportunity to squeeze details out of her."

"What information?" I demanded. "What could I possibly know that's worth killing for?"

Cam sneer stretched across his face, making him look like a killer clown. "Don't play games with me,

Angel. You know exactly what I want to know. Where are the files?"

I stared at Cam in confusion. "What files?"

"We can discuss that later." Monty loosened another button on his shirt. "Where did you hide the body, Cam? And when did you put it in the shop? You've been with Boris and me the whole time since you collected me at the airport."

"You flew to Nice once Cam confirmed my whereabouts?" I asked Monty, picking up on his wish to avoid discussing the mysterious files with Cam and willing to play along for the moment.

Monty nodded. "I took my private jet."

I looked at the man's pasty complexion and apparent physical distress. "Are you sure Cam's been with you the entire time? Then he must've kept the corpse with him."

"The boot," Sidney interjected. "I bet he followed Elektra's example and stashed the body in the boot of whatever car he and the twins picked up in Paris."

"Well done, all of you." Cam's laughter had an unhinged edge that made the hairs on the nape of my neck stand to attention. "You're a regular bunch of amateur detectives. Yes, I put Ivan's body in the boot of our rental car. I made sure Boris didn't go near it. The only time I needed to open it was to store Monty's case when we collected him from the airport. I made sure I was the one to deal with the case."

"And then you must've distracted Boris and Monty

long enough to sneak the body in here when you all showed up to lie in wait for us." I addressed Monty. "How did he manage it?"

"Cam volunteered to check the coast was clear." Monty pulled a face and shuddered. "He must've put Ivan in here then, presumably to convince Boris you'd killed his brother."

"But I thought you wanted to keep the body as leverage," I said, turning back to Cam. "What changed your mind?"

He wrinkled his nose, answering my question.

"Ah." Sidney laughed. "Ivan was starting to smell— or at least you knew he would before much longer. The heat will do that. You'd hoped to catch up with Angel sooner than you did and thus needed a new tactic."

My heart pounding against my ribs, I slid the final inch needed to reach the revolver. I held out my hand.

Too late.

Cam kicked Elektra's revolver out of my reach and picked it up. "Nice try, Angel, but you lose. Still think you can outshoot me, Monty?"

"What do you want?" Monty's face beaded with sweat, making me wonder if he'd keel over before Cam had a chance to shoot him. "Money? A ticket to a new life? I can give you both."

"I know you can." Cam's growl had a bear about to pounce quality. "And you will. I want you to tell me where Frank hid his files."

"Do you mean his accounts for his various black-market deals?" I was pretty sure those weren't the files Cam was referring to, but those were the only files I knew about. What else could Frank have been involved in? The man hadn't been stupid, but he was no criminal genius.

"I'm interested in files worth a lot more than Frank's side business." Cam regarded me thoughtfully. "So you don't know anything about his real money-maker. In that case, there's no reason for me to keep you alive."

Files...alive...Becky... The pieces finally slotted into place.

The realization hit me with the power of a blow to a vital body part. "It was you," I whispered, sagging against the counter. "You killed Frank. Not Monty. Not Becky. You."

Up until this point, Cam's talk of my corpse collection had consisted of people he hadn't killed. Elektra had killed the twins. Boris had killed Elektra. As far as I'd been aware, Cam hadn't killed anyone. For all his bravado and threats, I hadn't believed he'd actually shoot any of us. Now I knew I'd been dead wrong.

Cam inclined his head. "Congratulations, Angel. You finally figured out the obvious."

"Angel said Becky's Scottish," Sidney said, sounding far calmer than I felt. "Is she a friend of yours? Or a relative?"

"She's my cousin." Cam twirled the revolver,

toying with our emotions, relishing our fear. "When I told her Monty was planning to confront Frank, she asked you to swap shifts with her. The rest was a piece of cake. Monty went in, firing shots. Angel shot Monty with a dart gun and fled the scene. All I had to do was wait until Monty and his men left. Then I went into the pub and finished the job."

The casual way Cam referred to murdering a man didn't make me optimistic about our chances of getting out of here alive.

From Monty's strangled intake of breath, he'd clearly had a similar train of thought. "Why, Carruthers? Why did you kill Frank? I get why you paid your cousin to help you frame Angel. You had a history with her and wanted revenge. But killing a pub landlord for a few hundred quid? It doesn't make sense."

Cam whistled his favorite football team's anthem, and my warning radars pinged. He'd always whistled that blasted tune right before he hit me. "You're not listening to me, Monty," Cam said. "I asked you where Frank's files are. I know all about his dirty scheme. I don't just want in. I want to take over."

I watched Monty's reaction, but his shutters were down and not budging. Whatever he and Frank had been up to had to be worth a lot of something to make Cam willing to risk everything to take over the operation. My mind whirred with ideas, overheard snippets of conversation at the pub, and the events of the last two days. Monty Carlyle, one of the most powerful men in the London criminal underworld, had come to France in person to find me…

I snapped to attention. "Monty can't give you those files, Cam. He doesn't have them. He came to France to track me down because he believed I knew where they were. Same reason you wanted to talk to me."

Cam whirled around, aiming one revolver at Monty and pointing the other at me. "You just said you didn't know anything about Frank's operation."

"I lied. I wasn't convinced you really had a clue. I wanted to string you along until I was sure."

Cam's nostrils flared, and his index finger quivered over the trigger.

At that moment, Sidney made his move. He hurled the fake spear at Cam, forcing the man to duck sideways. Then Sidney gave the largest of the clothing racks a massive shove, toppling it onto Cam. Cam went down hard, hitting his head on the edge of another stand. I leaped to my feet and stomped on his wrist, making him lose his grip on one of the revolvers. Monty performed the same routine on the other wrist. Before either of us could pick up the weapons, Cam disentangled himself from the rack, whipped out a blade, and stabbed Sidney in the leg and Monty in the buttock.

I didn't care a jot about Monty getting stabbed, but

I cried out when Sidney collapsed, clutching his leg and moaning. This was the second time he'd been hurt during this hot mess I'd set in motion.

Having incapacitated the other men, at least temporarily, Cam hurled himself at me. His hands came around my throat, squeezing, squeezing, squeezing. Panic seized me, costing me vital seconds before the adrenaline kicked in. I tried to fight him off, but my body was weakened from the drugs Elektra and her pals had given me.

Sidney limped over to us and hit Cam over the head with a prop. It made no difference. Cam increased the pressure.

I fought him with the last of my strength, but it wasn't enough. My lungs were on fire and so swollen I thought they'd burst through my ribs. Black dots swam before my eyes, and reality started to recede. This wasn't how I wanted my life to end…

A shot zipped through the room. Cam's grip on my neck slackened. A look of total surprise spread across his face. And then I noticed the trickle of blood running down his cheek and open space where part of his skull used to be.

Cam's body slumped to the side, deader than dead.

I sucked air into my lungs, too dizzy to process what had just happened. The next moment, Monty and Sidney helped me to my feet, and I came face to face with our unlikely savior. "Francine?" I croaked. "What are you doing here?"

She stood in the doorway, her pistol dangling from her fingers, her expression dazed. "Is my aim improving?"

I wheezed a laugh. "Definitely. With a bit of practice, you'll be dangerous."

he days following the dramatic take-down at the costumier passed in a whirlwind of activity. In the immediate aftermath of Cam's death, Francine drove Monty and Sidney to the hospital, leaving me to contact Luc. For once, I wasn't resentful of his take-charge attitude. While I slept off the events of the day in Jerry's guest bed, Luc and Mirko made the bodies disappear.

My corpse collection, as Cam had so eloquently put it, was later discovered in a disused warehouse in Marseille. The cops concluded that they'd killed each other during a falling out among thieves. All the dead were well known to the police, and no one seemed inclined to probe the discrepancies in the case.

Thanks to Monty's intervention, the police in the UK arrested Becky for being an accomplice in Frank's murder. Monty claimed he'd accidentally shot Frank in the leg, but denied killing him. He was confident his oily legal team would get him off with a slap on the wrist.

In the company of Luc's lawyer grandfather, I spoke to the police on a video call and outlined what I'd seen. No one asked me how I'd gotten to France, and I wasn't inclined to enlighten them. No charges were made against me, and I was free to go.

On Monday afternoon, I took the bus to the hospital to visit Sidney. He was at a private clinic on the outskirts of Nice, complete with a room with a view over the Mediterranean. Clearly, Sidney's health insurance policy was a lot better than mine.

I knocked on his door and went inside. He was propped up in bed, chatting to a man in a wheelchair. "Sidney? And Monty?"

Monty Carlyle saluted me from his wheelchair. I tried not to notice that he was sitting on a rubber ring. The stab wound had got him in the buttock that was already inflamed after the allergic reaction. All things considered, the dude looked better than he had the last time I'd seen him.

"Antibiotics?" I asked.

"I don't know what they're giving me, but it's fine stuff." Monty gestured to Sidney. "I've been catching up with your friend here. He's been telling me all about your new venture with the Omega Group."

I shot Sidney a quelling look. "That's not yet for public knowledge."

And probably never would be. Since the chaos on Saturday night, I hadn't seen my mother. After she'd left us at the port, she'd gone in search of Elektra. When Luc informed her that Elektra was dead, my mother had headed straight to Monte Carlo on another mysterious assignment. We hadn't had a chance to discuss my bold claims of Sidney and me being her new employees. I still didn't know what, exactly, she and Jerry did, nor the legality of their set-up.

Monty gave me a coolly assessing look. "If you're interested, I have a proposal for you."

"Sorry, Monty. You're not my type."

He ignored my quip. "I want to hire you two to help me track down Frank's missing files."

"That sounds like a job for private investigators," I said. "Professional private investigators."

Monty chuckled. "Nice dodge, but I've done my homework. Your mother and Jerry Gallo run an exclusive P.I. agency. The sort of agency governments hire to do jobs they can't officially be associated with. If you're working for them, you'll have the skillset to find those files."

Bingo. At least one of my guesses about what the Omega Group turned out to be accurate. I avoided making eye contact with Sidney, knowing he'd be just as excited as I was. "We're new hires," I said. "Not yet licensed."

"I told Monty that already," Sidney supplied. "And he doesn't care."

Why didn't that surprise me? "What are you prepared to pay us if we make good?" I demanded.

Monty named a sum that was more than my lifetime earnings to date.

"Whoa. That's—"

"Not high enough," Sidney said firmly, and then proceeded to haggle over the price of our nonexistent services.

"This is all very well," I said, interrupting their good-natured argument, "but we don't even know what files you're talking about. What was Frank up to?"

Monty winced and readjusted his rubber ring before responding. "About eighteen months ago, one of Frank's black-market jobs brought him into contact with a piece of valuable information about an influential person. The details are irrelevant, but the upshot was that Frank got a taste for power. He began recording data about all his criminal contacts, and his net was pretty wide. That led to him bartering for information in quarters he shouldn't have strayed into."

"He tried to get information out of you?" Sidney asked. "Is that what you mean?"

Monty snorted. "Not *from* me but *about* me. If Frank had only left it at that, it would've been okay. Only, he had to go and hire an acquaintance of that fool Carruthers to hack into various databases on his behalf, thus leading us to our present situation. Carruthers found out about the scheme and foresaw a get-rich-quick scheme through blackmail on a grand scale."

"Hmm..." I folded my arms across my chest. "I wasn't best buddies with Frank but I have a pretty good handle on people. For him to take that kind of risk, there had to be higher stakes than power."

"Power is high stakes for many people," Monty pointed out. "And they're prepared to pay to keep it. Plus, Frank's mother is in an expensive care facility. The fees were draining all the money he was making on his black-market side hustles."

Most of his story had a ring of veracity, but he was telling his tale to someone who'd made a career out of being economical with the truth. Monty was holding bits back—bits I suspected were vital. "Can I have time to think this over? I'd like to discuss it with Sidney."

Monty took the hint that we wanted to talk about him behind his back. A grin spread over his pug-like features. "Sure. Take your time. I'll be in the hospital for at least another two days. Let me know what you decide."

I held the door for him, and he wheeled himself out. After he'd left, I sat on the visitor's chair next to Sidney's bed. "You sure know how to make friends and influence people. Do you seriously want to work for that creep?"

He looked horrified at the suggestion. "Oh, no. I just wanted to practice my negotiation skills. Plus, it's not every day that I get to converse with a real-life career criminal. I can use this experience in my acting."

"You can use the entirety of the last few days in your acting. Ugh. I can't decide who scares me more—Monty or Mr. Christianopoulos."

"They leave a similarly slimy trail."

I checked my watch. "It's four in the afternoon. You definitely didn't make it to your eight o'clock start for your first day at your new job. Bad Sidney."

"I never thought I'd be grateful for a stab wound." His grin faded. "Seriously, though, the last couple of days have shown me just how much I don't want to follow in my father's footsteps. Even if I can't make acting work as a career, I'm determined to live on my own terms. That means breaking free from parental purse strings. Actually, I'm considering taking your mother up on her offer."

"My mother made you an offer? What offer?" And why hadn't she made me one? Hurt and anger surged through me. What had I ever done to make my mother so disinterested in me?

Sidney blinked. "Didn't you check your phone? She sent us emails."

Yesterday, Luc had supplied us with yet more backup phones. I suspected they belonged to the Omega Group. I slipped mine out of my pocket and checked my inbox. "There's nothing here. Maybe it landed in my junk folder."

Sure enough, an email from sxydesi666 had been

marked as spam. I'd have to have a word with my mother about email monikers and spam filters. I took a deep breath and started reading.

> *Dear Angélique,*
>
> *I trust you're well after your ordeal on Saturday. Francine and Luc say you acted splendidly.*
>
> *I understand you and Sidney are currently at a loose end and between jobs. If you're interested in staying in Nice for a while, I need help running the businesses. Not, I hasten to add, as the Omega Group's new dream team. Much as I appreciate the offer, reckless though it was, neither of you is licensed to do what we do.*
>
> *Jerry's health is improving, but his recovery will be slow. What I need is staff to help Francine in the costumier and Maurice run the yarn shop. Do you think you can do that? We can discuss the exact terms when I get back from Monte Carlo on Friday. Accommodation would be included. At present, both my apartments in Nice have tenants. However, Luc has agreed to share the beach house with you until we can find an alternative.*
>
> *Let me know what you decide.*
>
> *Your loving mother,*

Desirée

What a letter to write to one's only child. I shook my head in bemusement. Truth be told, I was kind of moved. My mother had never shown any inclination to keep me around. And here she was, offering me a job and a place to stay. Yes, she'd made the offer because it suited her, but it was the closest she'd ever come to making me a peace offering.

My thoughts turned to Luc. How had he reacted to the news that he might have Sidney and me as roommates? And how did I feel about sharing a house with him?

"What do you think?" Sidney asked, cutting through my thoughts.

Funny, it'd never once occurred to me that sharing a house with Sidney might be problematic. Over the last couple of days, we'd formed a connection. Not romantic. Not deep friendship—it was too soon for that. But there was a mutual understanding, a bond between two lost souls trying to find their place in a world that didn't understand them.

"What I'm thinking is I don't trust my mother an inch." I slipped the phone back into my pocket. "But I'll accept the job."

"Awesome." He beamed at me. "My parents will freak."

I arched an eyebrow. "Is that your motivation for accepting?"

"No, but it's an added bonus. If we do a good job helping out, I feel sure your mother will promote us."

"Promote us? As in, let us do jobs we're currently not licensed to take?" I examined his face. "Would you want that?"

"Definitely." He said it without hesitation. "I want to learn more about what they do. The idea of an international P.I. agency intrigues me."

I had to admit I was curious. However, I'd be a lot more enthusiastic if working for the Omega Group didn't involve working for my mother. "I hope my next shift at the yarn shop is less dramatic," I said. "Being kidnapped on the first day of the job was no fun."

Sidney slapped his forehead. "The yarn shop. Of course. I forgot to give you your stuff back."

"Stuff?" I creased my forehead. "What stuff?"

"The notebook and pen you left at the yarn shop on Saturday. I had them with me when we boarded the Greek's yacht, but subsequent events made me forget." He reached into one of his nightstand's drawers and pulled out the notebook and pen. As he handed them to me, the pen slipped and smashed on the ground. "I'm sorry, Angel. It's the pain meds. They make me groggy."

"Don't worry about it," I said, bending down to clean up the mess. "It was just a cheap novelty pen."

And then I saw it, a dark object with a glint of metal. An item that had no place in a pen. My pulse pounded and my breath quickened. I picked up the flash drive with trembling fingers and showed it to Sidney. "I think we just found Frank's missing files."

We stared at the flash drive for several long seconds.

"What do we do with it?" Sidney asked. "Do you want to check what's on there?"

"It's likely to be a simple RTF file with a link to wherever the files are stored. That's what I'd do. He wouldn't store state secrets, or whatever dirt he'd dug up, on a cheap flash drive."

"You're assuming Frank had the technical know-how," he pointed out. "He may have been stupid enough to store whatever he had on that little flash drive. We won't know unless we look."

"I'm not sure I want to know. If we open those files —or that link—we can't unsee the contents."

"Do you want to accept Monty's job offer, and then sell the flash drive to him? It sounds like whatever's on those files is worth a lot to a lot of people."

I closed my fingers over the flash drive. "Do you have a private bathroom in your fancy private room?"

He pointed to a closed door beside a chest of drawers. I strode into the bathroom, located a tweezer, and took apart the flash drive, piece by piece. When I was done, I dropped the remnants of Frank's dirty little business where they belonged and pressed the flush button.

I returned to the room. "Does that answer your question?"

"I knew you'd do the right thing." Sidney gave me a thumbs up. "See? We are a dream team, after all."

~

Thanks so much for reading **_Knifed in Nice_**. I hope you enjoyed Angel and Sidney's first international adventure!

They're back and on the track of stolen treasure in **_Ambushed in the Alps_**, the second book in the Travel P.I. series. **Grab your copy today!**

Join my VIP mailing list to get notified when the next book launches (and I'll send you a **FREE** story). **Sign up at zarakeane.com/travelpinewsletter**

Happy Reading!
Zara x

**Join my mailing list and get news,
giveaways, and free stories!**

**Sign up on
zarakeane.com/travelpinewsletter**

Angel Doyle, semi-reformed thief and accidental P.I., is back for another adrenaline-fueled adventure in *Ambushed in the Alps*, out now.

Angel and her friend and sidekick, Sidney, are thrilled to get their first official assignment for the Omega Group, a super-secret international P.I. agency co-run by Angel's mother, former adult movie actress Desirée Chablis. The agency's mission: to recover a cache of stolen Egyptian artifacts for a prestigious auction house before an international gang of art thieves can sell them at a black-market auction.

With just seventy-two hours to locate the cache, Angel and Sidney are eager to be in the thick of the action. Finally, Angel will get to prove to Luc, the annoyingly hot ex-military P.I., that she's just as skilled an investigator as he is. Instead, Desirée sidelines Angel and Sidney, making them bodyguards-babysitters for the auction house CEO's bratty teenage daughter. The only upside to the job is the gorgeous setting. Who can say no to a free stay at a luxurious chalet in the Swiss Alps?

Anticipating a weekend of chocolate, cheese, and breathtaking views, the last thing Angel expects is to find a corpse in her bath. The duo soon faces an ambush, a snowmobile chase, and a literal ticking bomb. By the time Luc rolls up at the chalet, injured and expecting a peaceful recuperation, Angel and Sidney are knee-deep in snowdrifts and dead bodies. Can they escape the mountain before the bomb triggers an avalanche?

***Ambushed in the Alps* is available at all major book stores.**

EXCERPT FROM *AMBUSHED IN THE ALPS*

In the four months since I'd moved to the French Riviera, I'd helped unmask a catnapper, apprehend a killer, and stop a blackmailing scheme dead in its tracks. Sound exciting? It was—for the three whole days it lasted.

After my action-packed first weekend in Nice, my life stalled to soul-crushing tedium. I started work as a yarn shop sales assistant and moved into an awkward houseshare. My new roommates included Luc, a hunky French private investigator; Sidney, an English drama school graduate; and Mélisandre, Luc's prissy Persian cat. Of the three, the easiest to live with was the cat.

On this rainy Wednesday evening in early November, I was at the café-bistro Luc ran as an extra revenue stream. My presence at the café was no novelty. I stopped by most days to grab a takeout coffee or a bite to eat. But my reason for being here tonight was different. I was doing something I never thought I'd be doing—knitting.

Can you picture me, Angel Doyle—a semi-reformed thief and accidental P.I.—as a knitter? No? Neither can Maurice, the manager of the yarn shop and my new boss. For spacing reasons, Maurice hosted the Yarniacs meetings at the café. For keep-the-grumpy-boss-happy reasons, I'd agreed to attend. I regretted that decision.

"*Non, non, non,*" Maurice exclaimed in French, regarding my ragged stitches as one might a boa constrictor on the loose. His bald head, elaborate mustache, and fussy clothes reminded me of Agatha Christie's eccentric sleuth, Hercule Poirot. "This is terrible. You must improve your tension. Some of your stitches are loose enough to drive a steamroller through. Others are so tight I'd need a microscope to see them. You must relax your hands, find your rhythm, and have fun."

"In my world, the words 'fun' and 'knitting' don't belong in the same universe." I blew out my cheeks and glowered at my work in progress. "This looks more like a headband than a hat."

"It'll look like a hat once you've completed the crown." Sidney sat beside me, the rhythmic clicking of his needles producing row after row of perfect stitches. Like me, he'd been roped into joining the Yarniacs, Maurice's monthly knitting club. Unlike me, Sidney could actually knit.

"Easy for you to say. Your scarf looks like something a person might willingly wear." I stared mournfully at the tangled mess on my lap. "Remind me why I'm here, Maurice? As a living, breathing blooper reel of *How Not to Knit?*"

Maurice made a tut-tutting sound. "While you're working at La Belle Laine, it's important for you to learn more about yarn. Otherwise, how can you advise the customers?"

"I do advise them. I advise them to ask you."

Maurice's entire head turned Pink Pizazz, this season's must-have yarn shade. "I don't know why Desirée insisted you work at the yarn shop. You know nothing about yarn."

Heat stole over my cheeks. He knew exactly why my mother had foisted me on him. When I'd arrived in Nice, I'd discovered my ex-porn-star parent helped run a super-secret international P. I. agency called the Omega Group. Was I itching to join her team? Definitely. Did she want me? Sure—out of sight and out of trouble. Getting me a job at the yarn shop was her reaction to me wanting to train as a P.I.

"You have to admit I'm good at accounting," I said to Maurice. "Your books were a mess before I showed up."

The man gave a Gallic half-shrug. "My role is to order stock and serve the customers. I leave the bookkeeping to Jerry."

"Jerry's not exactly in a position to deal with the shop's accounts." This was an understatement. Two months ago, Jerry Gallo—my former stepfather and the brains behind the Omega Group—had been the victim of a vicious assault. He was still off work, recovering from his injuries.

Maurice sniffed. "That's no reason to let you loose in the shop. Desirée should've known better than to hire someone with no retail experience."

I doubted my retail experience, or lack thereof, had played a role in my mother's decision to put me to work in La Belle Laine. "I might not dazzle the customers with extensive knowledge of yarn and knitting accessories, but I can keep us afloat until Jerry's back in action. Wouldn't it be easier for both of us if we at least tried to get along?"

The man's pout conveyed his skepticism, disdain, and sense of superiority with one nonverbal gesture. His rejection of my olive branch stung. I'd done nothing to warrant his rudeness. Okay, I hadn't a clue about yarns and knitting accessories, but Maurice hadn't exactly helped me learn on the job. And as I'd pointed out to him, I was a whiz at keeping the accounts.

Maurice compounded my sense of ill-usage by turning his back on me and picking up Sidney's knitting. "Exquisite work. Perfect stitch definition." Giving a moan of ecstasy, he ran his fingers over the intricate cables and color changes, practically caressing the blasted scarf.

I fanned myself with a menu. "Easy there, boss. The atmosphere in here is becoming X-rated."

Ignoring my quip, Maurice continued rhapsodizing about Sidney's scarf. "You have a natural aptitude for knitting. It's a pity Desirée didn't assign *you* to La Belle Laine."

I didn't bother to defend myself. Sidney would've rocked the yarn shop job, just as he was proving to be a hit at the costume shop, one of the other businesses that acted as a front for the Omega Group. I didn't fit in at either establishment, and it was grinding me down.

Sidney cast me a look of sympathy. "I'm sure Angel does her best."

Maurice didn't dignify this statement with a response. He returned the scarf to Sidney. "Keep up the good work. I look forward to seeing the finished product."

"Thank you." A note of bashful pride crept into Sidney's voice. "I honed my knitting skills during my years backstage, waiting for my cue to go on."

"Dude," I whispered in English, "just think of the number of scarves you could've knit by now if you'd stuck with acting instead of sewing costumes."

"Tut-tut. If you're not careful, I'll knit you a scarf for Christmas. I'm thinking hot pink glitter with sewn-on sequins to match your sparkling personality."

This made me laugh. "Knit me one with a skull and crossbones, and I'll gladly wear it."

Sidney turned to Maurice and switched back to French with impressive ease for someone who hadn't grown up bilingual as I had. "Love the new bow tie. Lavender is your color."

My manager preened at the compliment. "Thank you. I try to look my best."

He looked like a dog's dinner to me, but what did I know about high fashion? Maybe Maurice's lavender three-piece suit with navy pinstripes represented the pinnacle of this season's trends.

Sidney aspired to similar sartorial elegance, but his

colors were louder than Maurice's. This evening, Sidney had opted for a bright orange waistcoat and pants, paired with black high-topped Converse and a skintight white T-shirt. He'd brushed his fair hair forward and had blasted it with enough hairspray to make my lungs burn.

Maurice moved to another table to critique his next victim, an elderly lady knitting a lime-green toilet paper cover, complete with a crocheted gnome on top.

I leaned into Sidney. "Watch out, mate. If you keep sucking up to him, he'll force you to join his jigsaw club."

He looked suitably aghast. "Maurice is into jigsaws?"

"Not only is he into them, but he's also the president of the local dissectologist society. That's a hardcore fandom."

"Dissectologist is a new word for me. Jigsaw puzzle lover?"

"In Maurice's case, it's more like a jigsaw puzzle obsessive. He has so many jigsaws that he's started storing them in the yarn shop's stock room. I had the misfortune to knock over a pile and got the pieces jumbled. When Maurice found out, he lost what's left of his hair."

Koffi, my fellow yarn shop assistant, detached himself from the chatty woman he was helping and reclaimed the seat to my left. He gave my arm a reassuring squeeze. "I'm sorry Maurice is giving you a hard time."

"You overheard?"

Koffi's warm smile brought out the deep crinkles around his dark eyes. "Your facial expressions when he critiqued your knitting told me all I needed to know. For what it's worth, it isn't personal. Maurice is rude to you because you're an easier target than your mother."

Even though he'd lived in France for almost thirty years, Koffi's deep rumble still held traces of a childhood spent on the Ivory Coast. I'd warmed to the older man the instant we'd met on my first day at the yarn shop. I still knew very little about his life before he'd started at La Belle Laine five years ago. From what I'd gathered, Koffi was a former stockbroker who'd opted for a radical career change after a bad burnout. If it hadn't been for Koffi's calming presence at the yarn shop, I'd have lost my cool with Maurice weeks ago.

"What's Maurice's deal with Desirée?" Sidney asked, dropping his voice to a murmur. "Do they not get along?"

Koffi counted the stitches of his knitting project before answering. "It's complicated. Maurice used to work for Jerry and Desirée in a…different capacity."

"*Maurice* used to be a—?" I stopped myself in the nick of time and mouthed the words, *private investigator*.

Koffi inclined his bald head. Apart from being roughly the same age—mid-fifties, give or take— baldness was the only thing the men had in common.

Maurice was a small ball of anger. Koffi was his tall, rangy, eternally calm counterpart.

Sidney leaned closer. "What happened? How did Maurice wind up managing the yarn shop?"

"An assignment went awry. Someone got hurt." He spread his palms wide. "I don't know the specifics, but that's the gist. After that, Jerry decided Maurice needed a break and put him to work at the yarn shop. The break became permanent."

I felt a reluctant pang of sympathy for the angry little man. "If he'd rather take a more active role, I imagine he's frustrated. Still doesn't excuse his behavior toward me."

"No, it doesn't. Hang in there. Unlike Maurice, your situation is temporary." Koffi patted my hand and rose from his seat. "Carine is having issues with her hat. I'll go and help." He ambled over to a dark-haired woman with a tight, 80s-style perm.

I turned to Sidney. "I hope Koffi's right about the yarn shop being temporary. It's not like my mother made any promises about our P.I. training."

Like me, Sidney dreamed of training as a private investigator for the Omega Group. I'd first met him on the Eurostar from London to Paris. He'd been on his way to start a sensible career at the British Embassy. I'd been on the run from a London gangster. A series of crazy circumstances had forced us to work together to catch the criminals and avoid the morgue. After that first wild weekend, Sidney and I had been well and truly bitten by the crime-solving bug. We'd accepted my mother's offer of jobs and accommodation as a stopgap solution, but I'd run out of patience by the time summer had turned to autumn.

Fortunately for him, Sidney was of a more easygoing disposition. "Have faith, Angel. Your mother said she'd discuss our training when she gets back from her latest assignment."

"Her latest assignment had dragged on for months," I replied gloomily. "Don't get me wrong. I'm grateful for the home and the job and the chance of a fresh start."

"You just feel like that fresh start is in permanent waiting mode," Sidney finished for me with a wry smile. "I get it. I feel the same. My family hasn't spoken to me since I ditched my embassy job. I need to prove to them I made the right decision."

"At least your family cares in their own strange way. My father hasn't spoken to me in over two years, not since I helped get his boss's son sent to prison. As for my brothers..." I trailed off, brooding over my fractured family. I was my mother's only child, but I had four half brothers on my father's side—three older, one younger. All had gone into the "family business," Dad's tongue-in-cheek reference to his career as a London gangster's longtime lackey.

"Have you decided what to do about Del's birthday?" Sidney's tone was soft and understanding. "It'll do no harm to send him a message."

I pulled a face. My twin from another mother, my brother Del, had been born three months before me. We'd been tight as kids, and that connection had stayed strong throughout our teenage years. Once we'd hit our twenties—and especially after my falling out with Dad —we'd had less contact.

Yet Del had been the only member of my immediate family who'd kept in touch after I'd helped the police convict Dad's boss's son. Del's failure to respond to my messages after my brush with death in July hurt, and I was still smarting over the rejection. I was now torn about sending him a message for his birthday, thus sharing my new phone number with him and, potentially, the rest of the clan.

"I'm trying not to think about Del. His birthday isn't until Friday. I'll decide what to do then."

Picking up on my reluctance to pursue this topic, Sidney switched back to our job situation. "Our current gigs aren't ideal. But, hey, at least Nice is a lovely place to hang out while we wait for your mother to decide about our future."

He was right. I was in a gorgeous city with sun and sea galore, money in my pocket, and a roof over my head. Even in November, the temperature rarely dipped below ten degrees Celsius, plenty warm to get away with a light jacket rather than the heavy winter coat I'd worn last year in London.

I regarded my knitting and sighed. "Right. Time to woman up and deal with this tangle."

For the next half hour, I attempted to fix my hot mess handiwork, ripping back rounds of knitting and starting over. Lather, rinse, repeat. I kept at it until Luc materialized in front of us with a tray. Luc left the café's day-to-day management in his assistant's capable hands while he was away on investigations. Last night, he'd returned from an assignment in Italy.

Yeah, I was jealous. And not just because of his assignment. Luc confined his role at this meeting to serving food and drink. While he looked mad, bad, and tattooed behind a tray, I struggled to knit my first hat.

Luc served our neighboring table their drinks. Then he handed Sidney a brandy Alexander and slid a strawberry margarita in front of me.

I blinked at the red drink. "I didn't order anything."

He stood close enough for me to smell his trademark spicy aftershave. A smile played over his annoyingly kiss-me-now lips. "Considering that tangle of yarn in your hands, you look like you could down ten."

I hated guys who assumed they knew what I wanted. And ordering for me? A cardinal sin. But the worst part? Luc nailed what I liked. Every. Single. Time. I glared at him but reached for the drink. I took a sip. It tasted good. Seriously good. And it took me every piece of my willpower not to show it.

And it wasn't as if Luc had shown the slightest interest in me. Maybe that was part of the problem. But why did I care? The last thing I needed in my life was a know-it-all boyfriend. Actually, any boyfriend. After my previous relationship had crash-landed, I'd promised myself I'd stay single until I found a man who was the polar opposite of my usual type. I had an unfortunate tendency to fall for bad boys, and Luc's broad shoulders and wicked smile ticked all my happy boxes.

Luc picked up my wannabe hat, and his lips twitched. "What's this supposed to be? A tea cozy?"

"It's a hat," I said with dignity and snatched it back. "Did you come over to insult me, or do you have an ulterior motive?"

He fixed me with his electric blue stare. "Why do you always suspect me of being up to no good? You don't even know me. How often have we even been under the same roof since you moved in?"

Twenty-three nights. Not that I was counting. Luc was my mother's semipermanent house-sitter for her beachside villa. When she'd invited Sidney and me to stay in Nice and work for her, she'd made Luc accept us as his new roommates. I'd expected him to be grumpy about sharing the place with two strangers. However, transpired that he spent most of his time away on investigations for the Omega Group. He considered us to be convenient cat-sitters.

I jabbed the air with a knitting needle. "I may not know you well, Luc, but I can always tell when someone messes with me. What's up?"

"Not messing, I swear. Do you two still want to become private investigators?"

Sidney and I exchanged wary looks, then nodded in unison.

An impish grin spread across Luc's overly handsome face. "In that case, I have a job for you."

Ambushed in the Alps is available at all major book stores.

ABOUT THE AUTHOR

USA Today bestselling author Zara Keane grew up in Dublin, Ireland, but spent her summers in a small town very similar to the fictitious Whisper Island and Ballybeg.

She currently lives in Switzerland with her family. When she's not writing, Zara loves knitting, running, unplugged gaming, and adding to her insanely large lipstick collection.

Zara has an active Facebook reader group, **Zara Keane's Mystery Mavens**, where she chats, shares snippets of upcoming stories, and hosts members-only giveaways. She hopes to join you for a virtual pint very soon!

zarakeane.com